A Cowboy in the Streets

ELIZABETH BRIGHT

A Cowboy in the Streets

Cover Design by Yummy Book Covers

Interior Formatting by Weaver Way Author Services

Digital ISBN: 978-1-7370702-8-3

Paperback ISBN: 978-1-7370702-9-0

For anyone who thought they had found their happily-ever-after only to watch it explode in their face...
Good news, my love. You're not done yet.

James

MAYBE THE PINK cowboy boots were a mistake. Dad had strong feelings about those boots. But then, so did I. They were such a part of me that if I looked down and saw something else on my feet, I wouldn't know who I was.

Dad bought me my first pair before I could walk, so I would look cute in the family photos. As my feet grew, he kept right on buying new pairs to fit. One of my earliest memories was Dad dancing with me in the kitchen while Mom cooked dinner, the pink cowboy boots on my feet.

"Pretty like your momma," he told me.

A bald-faced lie because I looked nothing like Mom. She was tall and blonde, whereas I was short with dark hair and freckles. The only thing I got from my mom was her curves, which was less of an asset for a horse trainer like me than a rodeo queen like her. I kept those suckers locked down so tight I might as well have been an A-cup. Or a man.

Dad always beamed when he saw me wear my pink cowboy boots with a skirt for a school dance or a date. But those boots were made for riding, and riding was what I did. He never failed to side-eye my pink cowboy boots when I stepped foot in the barn or the training ring. Like they didn't belong there.

Or maybe that was me who didn't belong.

I looked down at my feet critically, taking note that the bright pink was a bit dulled from the grime and dust of the stables. Nothing a little saddle soap couldn't take care of. They were riding boots, same as any black or brown pair. It would be a shame to waste them as pure decoration when they had a job to do. Anyway, I liked the dichotomy. Why couldn't something be pretty and useful at the same time?

"Hey, sunshine!"

I pulled my gaze from my boots and smiled at the lead trainer of Blue Skies Farm, the training facility for ranch and rodeo horses owned by my dad, Carl Campos. "Hi, Walter. Chocolate chip cookies are in the breakroom."

"That's the way to my heart. Tell Savanah thank you."

Walter winked, because he knew damn well that if

my mom had made them, she had done so with my help. But he also knew that my dad frowned upon me, as assistant trainer, bringing sweets and baked goods to the mostly male ranch employees. *They won't respect you*, Dad warned me over and over again. *They'll see you as nothing but a girl.*

The thing was, though, I *was* a girl. A girl who happened to like cookies. Once I started bringing in treats, the others followed. Some stable hands and trainers baked the treats themselves, and some brought store-bought treats. Either way, everyone was happy.

"You going in there?" Walter jerked his thumb in the direction of Dad's office.

"Yeah. We have a meeting in five minutes." Impulsively, I reached out, giving his arm an affectionate squeeze. "It's not too late to change your mind, you know. Put retirement off a couple more years and stay with us."

He gave a rueful chuckle. "It's been a good twenty years, hasn't it? I remember when you were barely this tall"—he held his hand waist-height—"bound and determined to ride horses men twice your size wouldn't have touched. I still have a few good years left in me, but I want to spend them with my grandkids. It's time for the next generation of trainers to take up the reins."

It was bittersweet, Walter retiring after two decades

with us at Blue Skies Farm. I would miss him for sure, but I couldn't deny the frisson of excitement that shivered down my spine at the thought of making his position my own. I had so many ideas.

"Listen, James." Walter grimaced, a furrow forming between his thick gray brows. "Carl wanted my thoughts on who should replace me. You were at the top of my list. I want you to know—"

"James!" Dad's head poked out of his office. His gaze landed on my boots and he shook his head. "Enough gabbing. Get in here."

"Good luck," Walter muttered. "We're all rooting for you."

"Thank you," I whispered, before high tailing it into Dad's office. "Good morning, Carl," I said, because he was never Dad at work, as I took my seat.

He sat across from me in the wood-paneled office, his immaculate oak desk between us. I took it as a good sign that he had called me in here for a chat rather than simply knock on my bedroom door or catch me over supper, which is what he had done six years ago, the first time he had passed me over for promotion—that time it had been from groom to trainer.

But here, this office, was his place of business. If he called me in here, it must mean that he was finally taking me seriously.

I had a good feeling about this.

Horses were in my blood. I was a colicky baby, and Mom swore the only way to soothe me was to strap me to her chest, saddle Redford, the gentlest, calmest horse at the stable, and go for a ride. Growing up, as Dad worked to expand the training facility into the large operation it was today, I spent every spare minute in the stables, shadowing my dad and the other trainers. No one knew this farm or the horses better than me.

But six years ago, being only twenty-two, Dad hadn't thought that experience was enough to earn a promotion. It had hurt to hear him say that at the time, but he was right. So I left Blue Skies for quarter horse facilities in Texas and Oklahoma. I learned new techniques and gained exposure to new ideas, working my way up without the benefit—or detriment—of being the boss's daughter.

A year ago, Dad called me home again, to take the position of assistant trainer. Of course I came straight away. I never said no to Dad.

Then last month, Walter announced he meant to retire to spend more time with his wife and grandchildren. I loved Walter—he had never shooed me away as a child, unlike so many other employees—but I knew an opportunity when I saw it. And this time, I was ready for it. More than ready. I was *right* for it.

"I have good news, James." Dad settled back in his burgundy leather wingback chair and clasped his hands over his stomach. "I think you're going to be very happy."

Relief whooshed through me. Even though I knew I deserved this promotion, that I had earned it, a small part of me doubted he would actually give it to me. In the back of my mind was the niggling warning that he had never hired a woman before, for *any* position, other than his own daughter.

"Let's hear it," I encouraged, trying to walk the line between confident and smug.

"Remember when you said women's rodeo events were on the rise, and Blue Skies should take advantage of that?"

I nodded. I had suggested Blue Skies hire a trainer specializing in women's rodeo events. Dad hadn't been interested.

"I've had some time to think it over and reconsidered. It could be a great opportunity for growth."

"Really?" My thoughts galloped ahead, already making plans. As head trainer, I would be responsible for bringing the new trainer on board and ensuring the program's success. My first challenge as head trainer for Blue Skies. I was practically giddy with excitement, but I swallowed my gleeful squeal. Dad didn't approve of squealing, gleeful or otherwise. At least, not in the stables.

"It will take some time to get it off the ground, slow and steady. What do you think?"

I nodded slowly. "I think that's great. Off the top of my head, I'd consider Allison Fields, Jessica Valdez, or Christy Sullivan as contenders for the position. Should I start making calls? Gauge their interest?"

Dad's lips twitched. "That won't be necessary. I already have someone in mind."

"Oh." I tamped down my disappointment. Dad was a control freak. I knew that. Convincing him to loosen the reins wasn't going to be easy or quick. Still, I had thought he would at least want my opinion. "Who were you thinking?"

"You." He grinned at me, as though he expected me to shout with joy. When I stared at him blankly, his brow furrowed. "I want you to oversee the new program focusing on women's events."

"Me?"

He nodded.

"Carl, I—" I looked around the room, my gaze moving across the various photographs of champion horses and rodeo events without really seeing anything at all. My brain whirled. "I don't think I can do that."

"Sure, you can. Who better? You were the junior world championship barrel racer in your day."

I smiled wryly. True, I had competed and won during my high school years. But my heart was in training, not competing, so I had given it up when I graduated rather than go pro, much to the disappointment of both my parents. "What I mean is that—"

"And you have some experience as a trainer, too. I have full confidence that you will make this program a success."

Some experience. Twenty-eight years of working with horses, six of them as a trainer. "Thanks," I said dryly.

Honestly, he wasn't wrong. I would be *great* at the new position. But I had my ambitions set higher than that, and there was no way I could do both at the same time.

"I'm flattered, but realistically, I can't oversee the startup of a new program while fully committing to my duties as head trainer. It's just not possible. There aren't enough hours in the day."

"James." He cleared his throat. "We've decided to go in a different direction. Eli Stanford will be taking Walter's place as lead trainer."

I must have heard wrong. The room was so quiet all I could hear was the distant sounds of horses neighing. I wasn't breathing, I realized, and inhaled sharply to rectify that. "What?"

"Eli Stanford. He starts Monday. You've met him before, remember? At that rodeo in Oklahoma."

"I remember."

"He's got experience under his belt. Knows what it takes to compete. To win. He's been working under Harrison at Silver Stables in Idaho, so he knows his stuff. Good guy."

All true. But—

"Eli is great, but he's not more experienced than me. He's what? Two years older? He didn't even start at the rodeo until he was fourteen, if I recall. And I know for sure he didn't grow up on a horse farm like I did. He told me so."

My hands were shaking. I clasped them together, pinching myself in the muscle between my index finger and thumb, a trick I learned a long time ago to keep tears at bay. An important skill, because the moment water leaked from my eyes was the moment Dad would stop listening. *You can't be reasonable and emotional at the same time*, he was fond of saying. I saw his point, but I wondered if maybe sometimes it was reasonable to be emotional. Like now.

"My record as a trainer these past six years is top notch. Three of the top ten reining horses in the country? I trained them. Lucky Thirteen, the world reserve champion? That was me. I'm not just good at what I do, Carl. I'm great. And there is no one, except maybe you, who loves Blue Skies more than me. I would dedicate my life to this farm if you would let me."

Dad's brows pushed together in a dark line across his forehead. "To be honest, James, I thought you'd be pleased. Of course I knew you wanted to be head trainer. The new position, suited to your particular skillset, seemed like the perfect solution."

Solution. The word slid into my heart like a hot knife through butter. "I didn't realize I was a problem," I said softly.

"Now, James, listen to me. This isn't personal. Make no mistake, I've seen how hard you work, and I'm impressed. Never think that I'm not. But head trainer is more than just training horses. It's leading other trainers. It's having a vision. It's making tough choices."

"I can do that," I said. "I know I can. Eli Stanford hasn't trained a single reining horse to make it in the top ten. He will, someday. He's good. But not as good as me."

"You don't have what it takes," Dad said flatly.

"You mean I don't have a penis." The words were out, dripping with disgust and disappointment, before I could bite my tongue.

Dad frowned. "Don't be crass, James. It's not ladylike."

I forced myself to hold his gaze, letting him know without a word that his dodge of my accusation had not gone unnoticed. We stayed that way for a long moment, anger crackling between us like a live wire.

He blinked first. "Take the weekend to think it over. Cool off. Be ready to get to work on Monday."

I shook my head. I didn't need the weekend. "Thank you for your offer, but I decline."

"James, for god's sake." Dad rolled his eyes, exasperated. "This is exactly what I'm talking about. You're too hotheaded to take the reins of our entire program. You're making a decision in the heat of anger when you're all emotional. Be reasonable. Blue Skies is your home. Where are you going to go?"

Hotheaded. Emotional. It wasn't the first time he had called me that. And maybe he was right, in a way. I definitely felt things, and I acted on those feelings. But just because I let emotions guide me didn't make my decisions wrong.

"I don't know." Like that was going to stop me. "But there's no doubt in my mind that someone will be thrilled to have me."

If I wasn't appreciated here, then it was time to go where I was.

2

Adam

"Sell the bitch." Blaine, a junior trainer here at Lodestar Ranch, smacked the dust from his ass, which he had been tossed on by Belle of the Ball. Not unceremoniously. There had been, in fact, a hell of a ceremony. Bucking and spins galore.

Blaine joined me at the fence. "I'm serious, Adam. She's got the attitude of a stallion." His eyes narrowed on the palomino, minding her own business on the other side of the pen. "If she were a stallion, at least we could lop her balls off." He sounded downright bloodthirsty. "She's unrideable."

I grunted noncommittedly. "By you, maybe."

"I don't recall seeing anyone else stay on."

"I have," I said, earning a dubious side-eye from Blaine. "I've seen someone stay on," I amended, because I sure as shit hadn't even tried. I had an eleven-year-old son, not a death wish.

My mom, though. She stayed on. I thought back to that day two years ago, her body frail from cancer, Mom bound and determined to have one ride on the filly she had hand raised herself. Belle had barely started her training at that point, but she didn't kick up a fuss at all when my dad gently placed Mom on her back. Mom died a week later, and precious few people had managed to ride Belle since. Sometimes I thought she was heartbroken, like the rest of us.

Then I remembered she was a fucking horse.

"Couldn't sell her even if I wanted to," I said. "Not without a loss."

Belle's bloodlines were impeccable. Winners on both her sire's side and her dam. That quality of sperm didn't come cheap. Not to mention the thousands of dollars we had already spent on Belle's care, feeding, and training. Dollars we no longer had to invest elsewhere. Dad had let a lot of things slide when Mom got sick, including the business. Belle was our best hope for putting Lodestar Ranch back in the game.

Hell, she was our only hope.

"So take the loss," Blaine said. "Someone will buy her. I mean, look at her."

I didn't disagree. Belle had come by her name

honestly. Golden coat the color of a summer hayfield, cream-colored mane and tail, four white stockings and even a white star on her forehead. But there was no denying the truth—the beauty was a bitch.

Blaine shook his head. "You're never gonna sell."

"You got a problem with that?" I twitched an eyebrow. A dare.

One that Blaine wasn't stupid enough to take me up on. He was young, barely out of high school, but he had been here long enough to know better. "Nope."

"Good."

I pushed away from the fence and squinted at the sky. It was one of those gorgeous, late-spring Colorado mornings, all blue skies and sharp sunlight. But I wasn't fooled by the beauty of it all. We had maybe an hour before the storms rolled in over the Rockies that rose, jagged and lethal, in the distance beyond our green fields. Rain and thunder were imminent. Possibly hail, too.

"I'm going to check on Ben," I said. It was a Saturday, so he wasn't at school. My son was old enough that he didn't need constant supervision, but young enough that he still got into dumb shit if I looked away too long. Anyway, he'd want lunch right about now. "You know how to find me if you need me."

I made my way past the stables, pausing to check in on

the grooms and horses and make sure all was well, and up the driveway to the main house. Ben and I had shared a small two-bedroom cottage on the property for most of his life, but we had moved into the main house with Dad when Mom passed away two years ago. Dad had claimed it was so he could be available to help out with Ben, but in truth I thought he was lonely in that big house all by himself.

"Ben?" I called as I stepped into the foyer. "Where are you?"

"He's on the deck out back," Dad answered. He poked his head out from the kitchen off the living room. "Come in here a minute. I'm making sandwiches."

Of course he was. None of us were adept at cooking, so we ate a lot of spaghetti, burgers, and mac and cheese. None of that was great but at least it was edible. My dad, though, was a genius at creating sandwiches. No PB and J for us.

Unless Ben requested it specifically, that is. Dad didn't have the heart to say no to that kid. There was a kinship between them because they had the worst possible thing in common: cancer had claimed the most important woman from each of them. The difference being that Dad had lost the love of his life, his wife of thirty-five years, and Ben had lost his mom when he was only a year old.

I entered the kitchen to find the counter completely covered with slices of bread, cheese, meat, and condiments. Dad had a whole assembly line thing happening.

"What do we have here?" I asked.

"My best invention yet. Turkey, ham, provolone, pickles, shredded lettuce, onion, garlic mayo, and potato chips for crunch." He pointed at each ingredient in turn with his knife. "I'm calling it the Good News Sub, because we got some today." Dad always named his sandwich creations.

"Oh, yeah?" The last time Dad had good news it was that the new barista at the coffee shop was cute. Frankly, I was more interested in the sandwiches. My stomach rumbled.

"Yeah. I found us a new head trainer. Can't say it was easy, either." Dad gave me a pointed look, which I ignored. "Seems word has spread that you're not the easiest man to work for. Got a reputation for firing trainers before they fully unpack their bags."

I snorted. "Pretty sure if those trainers had done their damn job, they would have found much more pleasant of a boss."

"You gave them an impossible task, Adam. And we've been short-staffed for three months now. I need you to promise me you're going to give this one a fair shot. Six months, not a day less."

"Hm." I made no promises. "Who's the new hire?"

"James Campos. We got damn lucky."

"James Campos, huh?" I rubbed my chin, noting the way the scruff scratched against my fingers. I had forgotten to shave...again. "I've seen his name around. Good reputation. I'm surprised he'd be willing to come on board such a small operation." *A flailing operation*, I add silently.

"As I said, we got lucky." Dad tilted his head, studying me. "Adam, you do know James is—"

"Hey." I held up my hands to stop him. "You're the HR department, not me. Not one person I've interviewed accepted the job. Whatever James is or isn't, I trust you." I reconsidered. "Mostly, anyway. Hell, we can't do worse. We *have* done worse. He's hired."

"Right. But James is—"

"Dad, I know who James is." I was exasperated now. I'd already agreed to the hire. Why were we still talking about this? "I might not live and breathe quarter horse statistics and trainer biographies like you do, but I pay attention. I know he's trained some good winners and he's on his way up."

Dad smirked at the sandwich he was currently

layering with mayo. "Well. I guess you know everything, then," he murmured.

"I know enough."

"Okay, then." Dad made a sound like he was swallowing a laugh. "But mind what I said. I have a good feeling about this one. Don't ruin it. Six months. That's all I'm asking."

I wasn't in the habit of making promises I couldn't keep, so I shrugged and changed the subject. "Let's eat outside."

We loaded up three plates with subs and a side of baby carrots—the only vegetable Ben would eat. He wouldn't even eat regular carrots, no matter how much we promised him that they were literally the same thing, just bigger.

"We've got lunch, kiddo," Dad said, leading the way onto the deck that looks out over the pastures. Horses grazed contentedly, swatting flies with their long tails. Beyond the pastures, the Rockies rose up, majestic and brutal.

I had to admit, Dad couldn't have chosen a more idyllic spot to build a ranch.

Ben was in one of the chairs, staring out at the horizon. No screen, no book, no distraction. He did this a lot. I had no idea if this was something to worry about, but of course I worried anyway.

"I think I want to grow something," Ben said as we gathered round the table.

"Oh, yeah? What's that?" I asked after I swallowed a bite of sandwich, which to my dad's credit, was damn good with just the right amount of salt and crunch.

"Watermelon," Ben said. "That would be nice. I could plant it right there, in Grandma's garden." He pointed to the side of the house, where weeds had overrun the flowers, peppers, and cucumbers she used to grow there.

I looked at Dad, eyebrows raised in question.

He shrugged. "I like watermelon."

Ben beamed. "Great." He took a huge bite of sandwich, chewed, and swallowed it down. "This is your best one yet, Gramps. What did you name it?"

"Good News. Because we got some today." Dad's eyes glinted with amusement. "And I can't wait to see how it turns out."

ONE WEEK LATER, clouds gathered overhead as I hustled through my list of errands, pushing out the morning sunlight. Bank, groceries, feed store for watermelon seeds, gas. I ended the afternoon at Jo's, the local coffee shop. Probably a bad idea. It was late enough and I was old enough that a shot of caffeine would keep me up past midnight. But we were expecting the new hire, James Campos, this evening. I needed to be sharp for that, and like always, I was drained from the day's work.

The new barista was there. Chloe. She was cute, like my dad said. She was also frowning at me as I approached the counter.

"Coffee. Black," I said, pulling out my wallet.

She nodded, grabbed a to-go cup, and stepped to the coffee pot, leaving me face-to-face with my reflection in the long mirror behind the counter. And shit, I was frowning, too. In fact, it was entirely possible I was frowning first, and her frown was only a response to my own. I wiggled my jaw, trying to relax, but my face felt stiff and frozen.

I was stressed. All I did was worry, it seemed. I worried about Ben. That whole thing with the watermelons was weird, right? Or maybe not. How the hell would I know? It wasn't like I had a posse of eleven-year-old boys running around that I could ask.

And I worried about Lodestar Ranch. This place had always been important to me, but for most of my life I was a secondary player while my dad ran things. He stepped aside when Mom got sick, and while I didn't blame him for his grief, all that responsibility was a heavier weight than I was prepared for. I felt like I was constantly failing. There was too much to do and not enough hours to do it in. And, fuck, I was tired.

And now I had James Campos to worry about, too. Whether he'd get along with the other staff at Lodestar. Whether he'd be man enough to train Belle the Bitch. Whether he had what it took to turn this business around.

Chloe passed me my coffee and I paid up, slipping a dollar in the tip jar, aware that I was still frowning while I did it. Fucking hell.

And then the bell jangled as the door opened, boots tapping lightly against the old wood floor beams, and I could swear my back felt warm, like I had walked into a sunbeam. Chloe smiled past me. An honest smile, not the fake kind.

I stepped aside, letting the woman take my place at the counter. She beamed at me like I had done her a favor, when all I did was get out of the way. She smelled like hay and vanilla, and suddenly I was hit with a memory. Sitting between my mom and dad when I wasn't more than six years old, watching the horses in the fields, the warm summer sun on my back. All of us licking vanilla ice cream cones. It was a good memory. Happy.

I frowned harder, lowering my gaze so she wouldn't

think it was directed at her. My eyes fell on her pink cowboy boots. Like something a little girl would wear. Or a rodeo queen. But she was definitely not a little girl, although there was something youthful about her face. The freckles maybe, or her big cow eyes. I wouldn't peg her as a rodeo queen, either. If she was wearing makeup, it was minimal, and her clothes were distinctly lacking in rhinestones.

She raised an eyebrow at me. "Sorry, were you done?"

It dawned on me that I'd just been standing here, staring at her like a creep. "Yeah. Go ahead."

"Great." She lit up like I'd just told her she won a fifty-dollar scratch off ticket. "Thank you."

I moved to the bar cart across the room, where I could add cream or sugar to my coffee, if that appealed. It did not. There was literally no reason for me to linger there when I already had everything I needed.

But I lingered anyway.

I didn't recognize her. I knew everyone in Aspen Springs, and most of their cows, too. Which was harder, actually, because there were more cows than people here. But she was definitely a stranger.

The woman said something and Chloe laughed. I'd never seen Chloe look anything but aggravated, and now here she was, laughing. Then the woman laughed too. Loudly. Head tossed back, her thick brown hair reaching almost down to her exceptionally nice ass. She laughed like she enjoyed it. Not just the joke, but the actual *feel* of laughing. She laughed like she wasn't holding anything back.

I haven't had sex in three years.

The thought popped into my head unbidden. Probably having something to do with the way her ass looked in those jeans. Though if I was honest, it had more to do with her laugh. I didn't know what that said about me, that I was more turned on by her laugh than her ass. That I was pathetic, probably. Because watching her smile at Chloe, hearing that booming laugh, I couldn't think of anything more attractive than someone who actually enjoyed my company. Not a single thing.

And *that* probably had something to do with Ben's mom, my ex-wife, Emily. But I wasn't going to give that thought another second of my time.

I'd lingered enough for one day.

Chloe grabbed a card, wrote something on it, and passed it to Ms. Pink Boots along with the iced coffee she ordered. I knew in my gut it was her phone number. *Damn.* I felt more disappointed than I should, considering I had zero interest in a relationship with either woman. Relationships were for people with time and good mental health and I was seriously lacking in both.

Ms. Pink Boots flashed one last grin and then practically skipped over to the bar cart, where I was still standing for no apparent reason other than I'd decided to take up stalking as a hobby.

She waved the card at me. "I made a friend!" she said, like that was a totally normal conversation to have with a complete stranger. But *friend*. Not potential date. I took note of that, for no good reason at all. "That's a good omen, don't you think?"

I grunted. Dad would be so disappointed. *Use your words, son.*

She clamped the card in her teeth while she added a hefty amount of cream to her coffee.

"You new around here?" My voice came out rough. I wasn't used to making small talk with women. Mostly I scowled at them, would be my guess.

"Oh!"

She must have been surprised that I could speak actual words, after grunting at her like a caveman. Fair enough. Her mouth popped open and the card fell out, fluttering to the floor in a pinwheel. Without even thinking about it, I crouched and swiped the card off the floor. Because Mom raised a gentleman.

She did the same, except I got there first.

We looked at each other, surprised, both squatting

low, balanced on our toes, and our knees knocked together.

And then we both fell forward and smashed into each other.

Nose to nose.

Lips to lips.

Arms flailing, reaching for support, finding it in each other's bodies and catching our balance. We froze like that, holding each other's shoulders in a death grip, as though tumbling three inches to the ground was the same thing as plunging into the Grand Canyon.

Fucking hell.

She made a strangled noise. Against my fucking *mouth*.

She pushed away from me, jerking her head back. Her cheeks were beet red. My face felt...entirely normal. Which probably meant I was frowning again. Shit.

She stood. I remained squatting at her feet, stunned into my best deer in headlights impression.

"Well," she said. "Bye!"

She shot out of there like the building was on fire, leaving me still holding the card with Chloe's phone number. My gaze cut to the barista, who bugged her eyes out at me, her jaw flapping open.

"Dude," she said. "What the heck just happened?"

My sentiments exactly.

3

James

Coming from California, I should have been less impressed with the Rocky Mountains of Colorado than I was. In my defense, Blue Skies Farm was located in central California, where the ocean and the Seirra foothills were both an hour away in different directions, so mostly the view consisted of flat fields. I had visited Yosemite and all that with my parents, but somehow the Rockies were just a little bit *more*. A little wilder, a little more intense.

Every five minutes I shrieked "Holy shit!" to my empty car and pulled over to snap a picture with my phone. It made the drive from the coffee shop to Lodestar Ranch a lot longer, but—

A stranger's lips pressed to mine, the scent of horses and pine, teetering on my toes—

Gah! No! The memory popped into my brain like a jump scare. Instinctively, I squeezed my eyes shut, remembered that I was driving, and forced them open again. Fortunately, the dirt road leading to the ranch was straight and flat, lined by fields the fluorescent green of late spring.

"It's fine," I said out loud. "I never have to see him again. It's fine, it's fine, it's fine." I chanted the words like a mantra.

That didn't stop the hot flush from spreading across my cheeks, but who cared? No one was here to witness my embarrassment. Anyway, these things happened. Not to me, usually. I wasn't the sort of person things happened to, the kind of person who always had a story where *hilarity ensued* like in a romantic comedy. Hilarity literally never ensued.

Until today.

A laugh bubbled out of me, ending on a drawn-out groan. It was hard to say who had been more startled, me or the grumpy cowboy who had been minding his own business before I went and accosted him with my mouth. Safe to say, *hilarity ensued* had not been on either of our agendas for the day.

I drove underneath a metal sign that proclaimed the property to be Lodestar Ranch. The main house—a picturesque white with green trim—was straight ahead, and behind that I could see the green-tiled roofs of the stables. There was a mess of rose bushes front and center of the circular driveway. The whole scene was so dang pretty that I let out an excited little squeal as I put the SUV in park and stepped out.

Good lord, it was *gorgeous* here. I felt like Dorothy waking up in Oz. A black-and-white existence ending in screaming color.

I stretched out my arms, easing the cramped muscles of my back, taking it all in with a wide smile.

The green door banged open. "James Campos?"

The man who greeted me was tall and trim, despite being well on his way to seventy, if he hadn't hit the milestone yet. I recognized him instantly from our video interview. "That's me. Ted Hale?"

He nodded. "Thought it was you, but my eyes aren't what they used to be."

Ted came down the steps, offering his hand. I took it firmly. His eyes glimmered with surprised approval as we shook, and I bit back a smirk. My strong handshake caught everyone by surprise. Strong, but not aggressive. A handshake should be a statement, not an assault.

"Nice boots," he said.

"Thanks."

Cowboy boots weren't my first choice for road trip footwear. I had spent the first two days of driving in comfortable sneakers, only switching to my pink cowboy boots when I reached Aspen Springs and pulled into Jo's for coffee. Maybe it was silly of me, but these boots were my good luck charm. I wanted everything to be perfect.

"How about I take you to your cabin to settle in, and then give you a tour of the property? As I told you in the interview, my oldest son, Adam, runs the show around here, but he's out doing chores and picking my grandson up from school. We have some time to kill before he gets back."

"Sure, that would be great." I did wonder why, if Adam was the real boss, Ted had been the one to hire me. Adam was the one I'd be taking orders from, and I still hadn't met him. That made me nervous. "I don't have much. Just two suitcases. Are we walking or driving?"

"Driving, but not far. We'll take your car, if you don't mind."

I drove with Ted riding shotgun. He took the opportunity to point out the various buildings as we went. "The training barn is to your left. That's where you'll spend most of your time. Your cottage is in walking distance, but don't let anyone tell you that means you're on call twenty-four hour a day, seven days a week. You get weekends and vacation days. I expect you to use them."

"Good to know." I appreciated that, but I had the

feeling I was going to ignore those expectations for the next few months, at least. I liked to play hard as much as the next person, but my idea of play was really just more work.

"The cabins aren't spread out, but they're situated in such a way as to afford everyone a little privacy. A few are empty. Braxton, my middle son, hasn't stayed here since his mom passed. He does the books for us, but he lives in town. You'll meet him for Sunday dinner. My youngest son, Zack, mostly spends his summer with the rodeo. He might be here for a couple weekends now and then, but it's possible you won't see him until winter."

We swung around behind the barn. I took note of some fencing that needed repairs, but the horses out to pasture looked healthy and content. That mattered a lot more to me.

"That's the foaling barn over there. Empty right now. We had to let a few things slide when my wife got sick, and the breeding side of things was one of them. We're hoping to get it up and running again in the next year."

I nodded, making a sympathetic noise. He had told me that his wife died of cancer and what the repercussions of that were on the ranch. Ted had been very blunt about the fact that Lodestar wasn't where he wanted it to be, financially or otherwise. My job was to help restore the ranch to its former glory. It wouldn't be easy, but I was up for the challenge.

And I couldn't wait to rub Dad's face it in when I succeeded.

TED GAVE me some time by myself to settle in and take a breath, telling me to meet him at the training barn in thirty minutes. I didn't bother to unpack, instead using the time to take stock of what was here and what I'd need to find for myself.

The cabin was a good size for one person, with a sitting area, a bare-bones kitchen, a bedroom, and a bathroom. The couch looked new and I definitely recognized the design from Ikea. No television, but I didn't mind. My laptop would suffice for streaming shows and movies. There was a small table, built for two but could fit four if they squished. The bathroom didn't have a tub, much to my disappointment because I loved a good soak, but I could make do with a shower.

The kitchen had been stocked with the basics, Ted had told me, but I would need to go into town for groceries tomorrow. There were bananas, a loaf of bread, peanut butter, and a jar of strawberry jelly were laid out on the counter.

And the view. Holy shit, the *view*. Horses to the front. Mountains to the back.

I had died and gone to heaven.

I looked around, smiling. The cabin had clearly been tidied in anticipation of my arrival. No cobwebs in sight, and the bed linens were fresh. I had such a good feeling about this place. Sure, I had done my research on this place before accepting the position of head trainer. The high turnover rate did give me pause. But how bad could Adam really be, when Ted was his dad?

I was about to find out.

I hustled over to the training ring with two minutes to spare. Ted was already there, along with a boy I assumed to be his grandkid. Another man leaned on the fence, his back to me, watching another man work a palomino on a longe line.

"Right on time," Ted greeted me. Something about the way his eyes sparkled reminded me of a kid in a candy store. Mischief was written all over his face. "This is my grandson, Ben. Adam, meet your new head trainer."

The man at the fence pushed back, straightening to his full height, and turned around.

The smile I had been aiming at Ben evaporated from

my face, my earlier feelings of well-being replaced with dawning horror.

Oh, no.

It was *him*. The guy from the coffee shop. The one I unintentionally assaulted with my mouth.

He was a mountain of a man, from his broad shoulders to his scruffy jaw, sharp as the jagged peaks that surrounded us. Dark hair grown a little long, like maybe he had forgotten to get a haircut. Gray eyes under furrowed brows. Scowling. Of course he was scowling.

Fuckity fuck fuck fuck.

"Adam, this is James Campos," Ted said, making the introductions. His voice sounded odd, like he was holding back a laugh. "James, this is my son, Adam. You'll be reporting to him. In the ring there is Blaine Weatherspoon, your second in command."

I nodded to the Black man, who lifted a hand in greeting.

"No," Adam said. Angrily, but with a hint of desperation, like he was trying to wake himself out of a nightmare.

Same, buddy. Same.

Ted burst out laughing. I blinked at him, confused. "He thought you were a man," he explained. "Wouldn't let me tell him otherwise, in fact. Lordy, the look on his face right now." Ted clutched his stomach as he doubled over, chuckling.

I suspected that the look on Adam's face had more to do with the coffee shop incident than my gender, but who was I to ruin the man's fun? I arched a brow at Adam. "Did you, now?"

"That's not—I don't—" He pinched the bridge of his nose. "Dammit, Dad."

"Language, son. There's a lady present." Ted could barely get the words out before he was laughing again.

His laughter was contagious, so I joined in. Adam did not join in. He continued to scowl. That, I decided, was his problem.

"Tell me about the horse," I said.

He looked at me like he wanted to refuse, but he nodded. "Belle. She's four years old. Impeccable bloodlines. We're hoping she will be the foundation of our breeding program here."

Blaine brought her over. I pulled a carrot out of my windbreaker and offered it to her on my palm. She lipped it up, her velvety muzzle tickling my skin.

"She's gorgeous." Even though I knew the coat didn't make the horse, I had a soft spot for palominos. Kinda like the way men preferred blondes.

"Yeah, well, she needs to be more than gorgeous to be a good dam," Adam said, like he was telling me something I didn't know. "She needs to be a winner. And so far, that hasn't happened."

"She's unrideable," Blaine cut in. "If she can't be ridden, she can't win. I'll get her tacked up so you can see for yourself." The glint in his eyes told me he wouldn't be unopposed to seeing me hit the dirt. I didn't take it personally. A little hazing was normal in tight-knit communities.

"Gee, thanks," I said drily. "But that won't be necessary."

"Is it because you don't want to get your boots dirty?" Ben asked, earning a frown from his dad and a smirk from Blaine.

I turned to look at him, sizing him up before I responded. He was tall for his age and I was short for mine, which put us not quite eye-to-eye. I had a few inches on him. Thanks to my height, kids often saw me as one of them, and they often talked to me as such. What might sound disrespectful was often just sincerity. On the other hand, some kids were just assholes. But I had the feeling Ben wasn't one of them.

"Nope. These boots were made for riding, same as yours." I pointed to his boots, noting the emblem on the ankle. "Ariats?"

"Yeah." His eyes were wide as he looked from my

boots to his and back again, recognizing the similarities underneath the color differences.

"Mine, too." I beamed at him. "I'm not going to ride Belle today, but when I do, I'll probably be wearing these boots. The thing is, though, Blaine just told me she's unridable and I believe him."

"You should." Ben looked very serious. "She'd dust you pretty quick. You're not very big."

Adam twitched, grimacing, his gaze darting between Ben and me. He nudged his son's shoulder. "You can't say things like that, Ben," he said quietly. "You don't want to hurt her feelings, right?"

Ben shot me a worried look and I smiled. "It's okay. I don't mind it when you tell me the truth."

"Uncle Zack says the truth is like jalapenos. It's all right, in small doses, but there's no need to go throwing handfuls around where it isn't wanted."

I choked on a laugh. Uncle Zack seemed like an interesting character.

"Belle's not unridable," Adam said, his voice riding the line between patient and exasperated. "We just haven't figured her out yet."

I liked that. He hadn't given up on her. She was a puzzle that needed to be solved.

"The last trainer called her a man-eater," Ben said.

I laughed and gave him a conspiratorial wink. "Then it's a good thing I'm a woman." I turned back to Blaine, who was scratching Belle behind the ear. "She doesn't bite or kick?"

"Nah, she likes people. Just doesn't like them on her back."

"Huh." That was interesting. With horses, a bad attitude wasn't usually constrained to riding. Still, I could see for myself that Blaine spoke the truth. She was high spirited and curious, and not at all vicious, at least with us all on the ground. "What do you make of that?"

Blaine straightened. "You want my opinion?"

I nodded. "Yeah, you must have some theories, having worked with her. Let's hear them."

"It's who she is." He fingered the nylon longe line thoughtfully. "We've gotten her a full health inspection. The vet can't find anything wrong with her. No sore spots, nothin.' It's her nature. Some dogs don't like to get wet, and even if you train them to swim, they're never going to enjoy it. I figure it's the same with Belle. Even if by some miracle you do get her to take a rider, she's never going to love it. Not the way she needs to. Winners have spirit. They love their work. Belle?" He shook his head. "She just doesn't have it."

I took that in, not missing the worried looks Adam and Ted exchanged. They thought Blaine might be right.

Maybe he was. Maybe Belle would never be a winner. Maybe I was about to fall flat on my face.

But I wasn't about to let that stop me from trying.

I took hold of Belle's halter, bringing her face closer to mine, letting her get a good whiff of my scent. "What do you say, girl? You want to find out?"

Her nostrils flared and she snuffled my neck, making me laugh.

I would take that as a yes.

4

Adam

"Six months. That was our deal." Dad didn't look up from the pot of water he was bringing to a boil—which meant spaghetti for dinner, again—didn't even wait for me to get a word in when I entered the kitchen before he spoke.

Although, to be fair, he wasn't wrong. I was here to renege.

"I don't recall making that deal," I said. "In fact, I specifically recall not saying anything."

"Silence is acceptance, legally speaking. They said so on one of those legal dramas so it must be true. Anyway, as it so happens, her contract says she gets six months pay, whether we terminate her tomorrow or she stays on until Christmas. I figure we might as well get the work out of her if she's getting the money out of us."

I stared at him. "That's not the usual contract we offer."

"No, it's not. But James is special. If you can't see that, you're an idiot."

I grimaced. I wasn't an idiot. Of course I could see that James was special. She was like the sun. Anyone fortunate enough to stand next to her felt a little bit warmer, a little bit brighter. Dad, Ben—they both liked her. Even Chloe from the coffee shop had been smitten.

I saw the way Blaine reacted to her, too. In that quick half-hour meeting, she had managed to make him feel valued and respected. *I believe him*, she had said, and he had stood taller. That went a long way with Blaine. I would have said she'd played him exactly right, except I didn't think she had been playing. She actually meant it.

Goddammit.

"Now, I know you were surprised that she showed up looking like she did when you were expecting a man"— Dad fought his grin mightily, lost, and allowed himself a chuckle before getting serious again— "but you know that has nothing to do with how well she can do the job. Your mother was the best horseperson around. She could ride circles around any one of us, except maybe Zack. So I know you're not going to stand here in your mother's kitchen and tell me that James isn't man enough for the job."

No, I wasn't going to say that. Mom would rise up from her grave to spit in my face if I said that. I had no problem with James being a woman. James being *that* woman? Yeah, I had a huge problem with that.

Dad heated a glug of olive oil in a pot, then tossed in a palmful of fresh minced garlic. Then he popped open a jar of store-bought pasta sauce and dumped it in, followed by a splash of red wine. That was Dad through and through: store bought but fancied up a bit.

"See, here's the thing. We'd met before."

Dad looked up sharply. "What do you mean?"

"I mean this evening at the barn wasn't the first time we met."

"Then how come you didn't know James was a woman? The name is too uncommon to be a coincidence. But I saw your face. You were shocked."

I scratched my unshaven jaw. "It wasn't the kind of situation where names were exchanged."

"I don't like the sound of that." Dad pointed the wooden spoon at me. "Do not tell me you met her at some shady, rent-by-the-hour—"

"Dad, for heaven's sake," I said, exasperated. "Aspen Springs doesn't have motels that rent rooms by the hour."

Dad eyeballed me speculatively. "That's the sort of thing a man wouldn't know unless he tried."

I pinched the bridge of my nose. Heaven grant me patience. "Dad."

He grinned, unrepentant. "I'm just saying."

"Well, I didn't meet her at some shady motel. I met her at Jo's, getting coffee."

And then I told him all of it. Mostly. I left out the part where James walked in looking like sunshine and smelling like a memory, and the combination had been far too interesting to my dick. But the part about us smashing our faces together, yeah. I told him that.

A normal man might have understood that this was no laughing matter. Not my dad. No, he laughed himself sick. Tears rolled down his cheeks as he howled, gasping for breath, bracing his arms on the counter for support.

"I'm glad you find it funny," I said. "Because I sure don't."

Dad pulled himself together, though it took effort. "Son, it's hilarious. Quite frankly, the fact that you don't think so makes me worry about you. You never laugh anymore. You never smile. Life is gonna knock us down time and again, that's a fact. Nothing you can do except laugh about it. Why take everything so seriously?"

I ground my molars together. If I didn't take things seriously, who would? Not Dad, clearly.

"But you understand why James isn't going to work out, right? We can't work together after that."

"No, I don't understand, as a matter of fact. She must have been every bit as embarrassed as you, but she still acted professional. If there's a problem here, it's your problem. And I know you're not going to make your problem the ranch's problem. Lodestar is struggling and you know that. We're not going to pay James six months to not work just so you can save face."

"I'm thirty-five, Dad. I don't need a lecture about responsibility and duty." Especially not when I had been the one to step up when he needed me the most.

"Good. Then you won't have any problem with James coming to dinner tomorrow."

I did have a problem with that. It was hard to put my finger on exactly what my problem was. Not embarrassment. It took a hell of a lot more than an accidental collision—even a collision involving our mouths—to make me blush. James was...an aggravation. Something about her seeped into my skin and made me itch. Like a sunburn.

Obviously, I couldn't say that.

Dad turned his back to me to grab a beer from the fridge. I took the opportunity to flip him off. Because he was right and that was galling.

"I saw that," he said, making me wonder if it was a lucky guess or he really did have eyes in the back of his head.

I made myself useful setting the table for dinner. Three plates, three glasses of tap water, three sets of utensils. It didn't take long, but it gave me a second to get my thoughts in order.

Six months. Longer, if she succeeded. And if she didn't...well, then James would be the least of my problems. If James failed, so did the ranch. I didn't have it in me to hope for that, not even a little bit. We needed James to succeed. Everyone was depending on me to make this happen. And dammit, I would. I would do whatever I could to help her succeed.

But that didn't mean I had to like it.

5

James

MOM
Call your dad.

JAMES
Why? Did he forget how phones work?

MOM
What do you mean?

JAMES
He doesn't have to wait for me to call him. He can literally call me whenever he wants. My number is programed into his phone.

MOM
He wants you to call him. He misses you so much, honey.

JAMES
Then he can call me.

MOM

You know he won't do that.

JAMES

Because he's too stubborn.

MOM

Well, I guess that makes two of you.

I SHOWED up at the main house Sunday evening promptly at 5:30, bearing cobbler, nervous as heck about seeing Adam again. Our first encounter had been a disaster. Our second went better, but I couldn't shake the feeling that my new boss was less than pleased about the arrangement. He hadn't said much, letting Blaine do most of the talking while he stood there, arms crossed, terse and unsmiling.

Third time's the charm, I told myself as I rang the doorbell, hoping it was true.

Was it too much to ask that I charmed the pants off him? Figuratively, not literally, despite my mind choosing this exact second to relive the feeling of his mouth smashed against mine, the hard muscles of his shoulders under my hands.

I squeezed my eyes shut. "It's fine, it's fine, it's fine," I muttered.

Was it, though? Was it *really*.

Well, fake it 'til you make it, as Mom always said. Of course, Mom never had to fake anything except her hair color. So.

The door flung open and I beamed a smile without knowing who the recipient would be. It landed on Ben.

"Hi," he said. Then tilted his head, considering me, before slowly smiling back. I liked that. I got the feeling this kid didn't say or do anything he didn't mean.

"Hi," I said back.

His eyes fell on the covered dish in my hands. "What's that?"

"Cobbler. I stopped by the farmer's market in town, so it's got a mix of fresh local berries. Do you like cobbler?" I asked hopefully.

He lifted a shoulder. "Never had it. But I'll eat it. Gramps says the only person who gets to complain about the food is the cook."

I laughed. "That's a good rule. But you'll tell me if you like something better, right? So I'll know what to bring next t—"

Adam appeared, looming over Ben like the Rockies over the plains. Glowering, of course. "You coming in or what?"

I blinked, my smile wavering ever so slightly. What was it about this man that always made me feel like I had been caught doing something naughty?

Worse, made me *want* to do something naughty. Just to see what he would do about it. He was all roped forearms and broad shoulders. Furrowed brow. Scowling mouth. This man had buttons I wanted to push. *Hard.*

I stepped inside. Ben disappeared, leaving us alone in the foyer, staring at each other. I lifted the dish higher, like a peace offering. Not that we were at war. It was just...tense. "I brought cobbler."

He frowned. Literally frowned. As though my cobbler were a personal affront. He had that mean teacher vibe. Like he was on the brink of issuing detention to a precocious student.

Unfortunately for him, I had always been precocious. So, really, it was his fault that when he reached for the cobbler, I said, "Careful. You wouldn't want to accidentally kiss me again."

A muscle in his cheek popped as he stared at me. Then his gaze trailed from my face down my body to the cobbler in my hands, all the way down to my pink boots and back up again. His voice was perfectly flat when he said, "That's not going to happen."

Clearly he found me lacking.

It would have been unnerving if I hadn't had a

lifetime of experience disappointing men. Maybe I should give him my dad's phone number. Let them commiserate.

I maintained eye contact, smiling the whole time, as he relieved me of the cobbler. He didn't smile back. Maybe that was a good thing. Scowling, he was already the most beautiful man I'd ever clapped eyes on. Smiling? That might be too much. He was my boss. We needed to keep this relationship strictly professional, which would be hard to do if his smile melted the panties off my body.

The scowl was dangerous enough as it was.

"Thank you," he forced out, like the words were physically painful in his mouth. The tips of his ears were red beneath the glints of silver in his dark hair. Was he blushing? Or merely annoyed?

"You're welcome," I said.

Once again, we were staring at each other. Awkwardly.

Okay, no. We could not go on like this. This job was too important to me to allow something as stupid as an accidental kiss to mess it all up. I had won over psychopath stallions with murder on their minds. Could one grumpy cowboy really be that hard?

Other than his very hard shoulders, obviously.

"Do we have a problem?" I asked. "I mean, I realize the way we first met was…" I waved a hand in the air, lacking words to adequately describe what that was. "But we're both adults, right? We can move past it. We *have* to move past it if we're going to work well together."

His brows pushed together. "We don't have a problem."

"Oh," I said. "Great. Your scowl sure had me fooled there for a second." I offered him a cheeky grin.

His scowl deepened, if that was possible. "I'm not—" He lifted his hand to his forehead and mouth to verify. He blinked, his expression changing to baffled exasperation. "Well, shit."

I burst out laughing and he blinked again, like it had caught him by surprise. "That's okay, boss. Now that I know you have Resting Grump Face, I won't take it personally."

"Hey, there you both are. We're all in the kitchen." A man who matched Adam in height, but was slightly slimmer through the shoulders, appeared in the hallway. He took the pan from Adam, gave it an appreciative sniff, then turned to me. With the cobbler balanced on one palm, he extended his other hand out to me. "I'm Braxton Hale. Brax. You must be James Campos."

"That's me." His large hand engulfed mine, but I held firm.

His eyebrows went up. "Nice grip."

"All the better to hold on for the ride."

Adam's eyes narrowed into slits as he looked between us, but Brax laughed, his blue eyes glinting. "Spoken like a true horsewoman. Mom would have loved you. Welcome to Lodestar Ranch, James."

Well. That was a nice change from his older brother. "Thank you," I said. "I'm happy to be here."

"Good. Because we're happy to have you."

The scowl on Adam's face suggested otherwise, but at least this time it wasn't directed at me. It was aimed squarely at his brother. Maybe his Resting Grump Face really wasn't about me, at all.

I was happy about that. Truly I was. I didn't want my new boss to hate me. But maybe there was a tiny, stupid part of me that felt a sharp jab of jealousy, like I wanted to keep all his scowls to myself.

A totally normal, acceptable reaction to one's boss.

Keep telling yourself that, babe.

TWO HOURS LATER, stuffed to the ribs with chili, cornbread, and cobbler, the dishes done—I insisted on washing, despite Ted's protests—I took my beer onto the back patio to enjoy the view at golden hour.

If I had known my grumpy cowboy boss was already out there, I might have made a different choice, but it was too late now. I wasn't the type to turn tail and run.

He sort of grunted at me, which I took to mean hello, so I smiled and tipped my beer to the mountains. "This place is incredible."

He grunted again. I took that to mean, *I agree. Please keep talking.*

"My cabin is really nice, too. Thank you for that." I paused to give him time to reply. He jerked a nod, which was at least a step up from grunting, and took a pull of his beer. Words were clearly not this guy's forte. I switched tactics. "Tell me about the ranch."

He squinted at me. "We train quarter horses. Sometimes we breed them." Said drily, with a smidge of irony lacing the words.

I laughed. He ducked his head and the corner of his mouth twitched up. It wasn't a smile, but it wasn't a scowl, either. "No, I mean tell me about the history. I want to know everything."

"Everything?" He rubbed his stubbled jaw. My fingertips tingled, like I could feel the scratch of his unshaven beard against my skin. "This land has been in the Hale family for generations, ever since the gold rush days of the eighteen hundreds. Thomas Hale came over from England without a penny to his name. Figured he would strike gold."

"Did he?" I asked, fascinated.

"No. But he did open a whorehouse and proceeded to make a tidy little fortune selling women and booze." Adam smirked when I let out a shocked laugh. "He bought acres of property. The next generation started a cattle ranch. The generation after that discovered the land was worth more than the cattle and sold a good chunk of it. By the time my dad inherited, we were down to ninety acres."

I gazed out at the green pastures that stretched to the mountains. "It's a good ninety acres, though."

"That's what the developers say, too."

My head turned sharply in his direction. Coming from California, I knew all about developers. Open land was at a premium these days. Everyone wanted this view, even if there wasn't enough water to go with it. "Would Ted ever sell?"

Adam shook his head. "Nah. Not unless there was no other choice. Lodestar Ranch means too much to him. Horses were always his dream, but he didn't know what form that would take until he met my mom. Jenny. She was the brains behind it all. They built this place together. Made his dream a reality."

I was quiet for a moment while I took that in. Ted had

told me he had lost his wife to cancer a couple years ago. He had been up front with the toll that loss had taken on him—and the ranch. I saw that loss a little more clearly now. No wonder it had been hard for him to show up every day at the stables, when everything was a reminder of how much he had lost.

"He must have loved her very much," I said softly.

"That I did," Ted said, startling me as he stepped through the doorway to join us on the terrace. "I still do. That's what grief is, isn't it? Missing someone you love. I miss her every day. I named this place for her, you know. Lodestar. That's what she was to me. My lodestar, guiding me through the dark. She never steered me wrong."

Shit, my eyes were wet. I blinked rapidly. "That's beautiful."

"We met in high school. Three months later, I put a promise ring on her finger. Gave her the real thing the second we were both eighteen. Both our families went nuts, of course, because we were so young, but we knew what we were doing. Love like that, it only hits once, and when it hits, you know."

Only once.

I tried to wrap my mind around that. The *confidence* of it. It was hard to fathom. In my twenty-eight years, I'd had a handful of boyfriends, none of whom lasted longer than a year. Horses were my focus, not boys. But they had all been good guys—great, some of them. Twice I had even been in love, and those breakups had hit hard.

Yet looking back...*phew*. I couldn't imagine being married to any of them. Not happily, anyway. But if someone had asked me three months in, if this was forever? With my last boyfriend, Todd, I would have said yes. Now, a year past the breakup, all I could say was thank god it wasn't.

"I'm going to see what Ben is up to. I'll leave you two to the sunset," Ted said, slipping back into the house.

I peeked curiously at Adam behind my beer, wondering what he thought of his dad's love story. Ben's mom wasn't around, I knew that much. There wasn't a ring on Adam's finger and no one ever mentioned her. Were they divorced? Had they ever been married at all? Where was she now? I scrunched my nose.

Adam took a pull of beer. "What?" he asked.

"Just thinking about what your dad said. How love like that only happens once." I shook my head. "I can't decide if that's romantic or terrifying. What do you think?"

He stared silently out at the mountains so long I figured he wasn't going to answer. And then, finally—

"A relief," he said.

He disappeared inside before I could ask why.

6

Adam

ZACK

Adam and James, sitting in a tree, k-i-s-s-i-n-g

ADAM

<eyeroll emoji> I see you've been talking to Dad.

BRAX

Please tell me James is a dude and not our new head trainer.

ZACK

Why? You want her for yourself? Dad says she's a looker.

BRAX

No, ass wipe. Dad's not wrong, but Adam is her boss. Banging his employee would be a shitty thing to do. That's the rule.

ZACK

Even if she's hot? Let's make a rule that rules don't apply if she's hot.

ADAM

Fuck off, both of you. And for the record, I didn't kiss her.

ZACK

That's not what Dad said. He could barely get the story out, he was laughing so hard.

BRAX

What the hell happened? Goddammit, I hate it when you gossip without me.

ADAM

It wasn't a kiss. It was a collision.

BRAX

With your truck?

ZACK

With their mouths <cry laughing emoji>

ADAM

Shut up, asshole.

ZACK

I'm thinking it's time for a visit. Maybe a long weekend. She's not MY employee. < grin emoji>

ADAM

You like being able to breathe air? Then don't even fucking think about it.

BRAX

Ohhhh you made Adam MAD

I wished I could say that the buzzing in my veins was from the second cup of coffee I'd gulped down that morning, but I knew that wasn't true.

It was 7:30 a.m. Any second now, James was going to appear and the real work would begin.

I wouldn't go so far as to say I was optimistic, but I was cautiously hopeful. We had cycled through four trainers—not counting Blaine—each one more determined than the last, and each just as cocksure that he had the solution. And each trainer ended the same way.

In the dirt.

But James was different. She didn't seem to hold a lot of preconceived notions about Belle's training, just eager curiosity. More interested in asking questions than in laying down the law. Of Blaine, of me, even of Belle. *What do you say, girl? Want to find out?* She had posed that question to the horse—the fucking *horse*—but something in me perked up and answered.

Hell, yeah, I wanted to find out.

For the first time, I felt hope. Faint and cautious, but there.

That's what this crackling feeling was. The hope that maybe this time would be different. That maybe James really could be the one that tamed Belle the Bitch and turned Lodestar around. It wasn't caffeine. More important, it wasn't anticipation of seeing her again. I was her boss, she was my employee, this was a professional relationship and—despite the inauspicious beginning—we were going to keep it that way.

"Morning, boss. You waiting for me?"

I jerked my head up as Blaine sauntered into the ring. "Looking for James, actually. Figured she might have a few questions this morning."

"She's already here. Out in the paddock with Belle. I drove past her on my way in."

Damn. That was unexpected. Other than the grooms, I was usually the first to arrive.

"I'll head that way, then." I pushed away from the rail.

"Sure thing. Hey, what do you think of her? Is it going to work out?"

I looked at the cloudless sky, aware that his gaze was on me. "Too soon to tell."

Lodestar Ranch had more than one paddock, but

since Blaine had seen her on the drive in, I knew which one he meant. It was farther than I wanted to walk, so I figured I'd kill two birds with one stone and get some chores done while I was at it. I saddled up Devil, a retired black gelding who was as gentle as a lamb, and headed towards James on horseback.

As I approached, I saw James on one side and Belle wandering several feet away, grabbing mouthfuls of grass. The paddock was our smallest one, meant for gentle isolation. We used it for injured horses needing peaceful recovery, or mamas and their newborn foals. I wondered if she had chosen it for that reason.

James leaned against the fence, her arms spread wide against the top rung, a bucket of grooming brushes and combs at her feet. She had her sunglasses on and her face tipped up toward the sun like it was the mothership calling her home, a small smile hovering on her lips.

I shook my head. Did this woman ever *not* smile? It was like she hadn't yet discovered how fucking *exhausting* the world was. Where did she find the energy? Looking at her standing there, fresh as a damn daisy, bright as one of the buttercups dappling the grass like spilled sunshine, I felt every single one of my thirty-five years and then some. Ancient. Like my weary bones might crumble to dust at any moment.

Hearing the soft clomp of hoofbeats on the damp

earth, her head turned. When she caught sight of me her smile widened. My bones decided it might be worthwhile to hold together a little longer.

"Hey, there," she greeted me.

"Hey." I eyeballed her from beneath the brim of my baseball hat. She wasn't wearing her pink boots today. Instead, she was wearing cutoff denim shorts and beat-up sneakers. Clearly, she wasn't intending to ride today, either. I loosened the reins, giving Devil permission to stretch his neck. "What are you doing?"

Maybe my tone left something to be desired or my face was scowling again, because she quirked an eyebrow at me. "Waiting."

She crossed one leg over the other. Short legs, like the rest of her, but nicely curved by lean muscle. I jerked my gaze determinedly to her face.

"For?" I asked gruffly.

"For Belle to decide she wants to start our grooming session." She waved the rubber curry comb she was holding in one hand. "She got distracted by clover."

"It might have been easier to put her in crossties in the barn. Why here?"

It was curiosity, not an accusation. I noted the lead rope dangling from the fence. If James had wanted to keep Belle in place, she could have made do with the rope clipped to her halter. James was a hell of a trainer, according to her references. I figured she must have her reasons for being out here, and I wanted to know what they were.

She smiled, because of course she did. "Disruption. Her groom—Jesse?" I nodded and she continued, "Jesse told me he puts her in crossties to groom her every morning before Blaine works with her. Blaine works with her on the longe line, gets her exercise in, and then if he's feeling brave, he'll saddle her after that."

I nodded again.

"Jesse says she hates being groomed. Fusses up a storm when he puts her in crossties before Blaine works her."

"You think something's hurting her? Or he's being too rough?" It was hard to imagine. He'd only been with us for a year, but he seemed like a nice kid.

She shook her head, her dark hair gleaming like polished mahogany in the morning sun. Why the hell was I noticing that? "Nah. We chatted while he worked. He's good. Loves the animals. Takes time to give them a good scratch where they like it, and he knows all their ticklish spots. He said with Belle, it's hard to tell if something is hurting her. She starts getting ornery the second she sees him."

I mulled that over. "Maybe she hates him." Animals were like people in that respect. Took a shine to one person, would kick another in the teeth just for spite. No rhyme or reason to it at all.

"That's the question, isn't it? Does Belle hate Jesse, or does she hate being brushed?" She cocked her head. "Maybe it's neither of those things. She knows she's going to get worked after Jesse grooms her, but she doesn't know if someone's going to ride her. So I figured, let's find out."

My gaze flicked to Belle, who was now watching us curiously, her ears forward as though to catch our conversation. "Disruption," I mused.

"Exactly. Belle and I are starting from scratch. We're going to spend the week getting to know each other. No longing. No riding. Then we'll see where we're at."

I rubbed my thumb along the braided leather reins resting idly in my fist. There it was again, that egoless curiosity. James wasn't the first trainer to disrupt Belle's routine. One after another, they watched Blaine work her, decided they knew better, and smugly implemented their own way, which ended in resounding failure, and pissed Blaine off in the process. One suggested Belle didn't like Black people, though he used a different word. He hadn't lasted thirty minutes and never made it to Belle's back, since I kicked him right the hell off our property.

Plenty of those trainers asked questions, but then

they went ahead and provided their own answers. James was the first to ask questions without feeling some kind of way about the answers. She was the first one to roll Belle's training all the way back to the beginning so Belle could answer those questions for herself.

"Do you mind if I get some chores done while you're out here? Is that too much of a distraction for Belle?"

James lifted her shoulders in a lazy shrug before once again offering her face to the sun, her dark hair spilling over her shoulders and back. "Do what you gotta do. We're in no rush."

I dismounted, loosened Devil's girth, then removed his bridle and replaced it with a halter and lead rope, tying it loosely to the fence rail. This might take a while, and I didn't want him to be uncomfortable while I worked. Grabbing my bag of tools, I headed for the water trough along the short side of the rectangular paddock, pausing to give Belle's forelock a scratch along the way.

The trough was self-watering—in theory, anyway. Troughs could get nasty pretty quick if they weren't looked after regularly. Slimy with algae, toxic with mosquitoes. Especially now with the last frost long behind us. We were short staffed, so I had added this responsibility to my growing list. What was one more chore, anyway?

I had noticed the trough was dry last Friday during

my weekly trough scrub, but with our breeding program at a standstill, the paddock was rarely used, so fixing it wasn't high on my list of priorities. If James was going to make use of it, however, she'd want clean, fresh water available for Belle.

All of our troughs were self-watering, powered by a solar pump. The system was generally low maintenance and had the further benefit of sparing me from lugging huge canteens to all the troughs. Last week I'd only had time for a cursory glance at it, but I was pretty sure the problem was the float valve. At least, I hoped so. We couldn't afford a costly fix.

I tested the pump manually, relieved when water spurted out. That was a good sign that the issue was localized to the float valve. I just needed to shut off the pump, replace the float valve, and—

James stretched her arms overhead, reaching for the sun. Her tee shirt rose with the motion, revealing a mouth-watering expanse of toned, tanned belly. Her waist would fit easily in my hands. It would be no trouble at all to hoist her onto the top rung of the fence. Put my mouth right there and—

"Dad."

I jerked to attention, rising so fast I felt light headed. Fucking hell, what was wrong with me?

"Hey, Ben." I ruffled his hair and tried not to take it

personally when he ducked away from my touch. He wasn't a little kid anymore. It was normal for him to pull away, right? "What are you doing out here?" It was the first day of summer break. I had figured he'd sleep in.

"I wanted to see how Belle was doing." His eyes were glued to James. Not the same way I had been looking at her. At least, I sincerely hoped not, because I wasn't ready for that stage of parenting yet. More like he was curious. "What are you doing?"

I blinked at the trough. Shit, what *was* I doing? "The float valve is broken, so the pump thinks the trough is full even though it's empty. Gotta fix that. Can you hand me the wrench?"

It was a quick fix. The new float valve did its job. Water immediately gushed from the pump, splattering into the empty metal trough, soaking my face and arms with cool water—because, like a dumbass teenager, I had been too busy salivating over James to focus on turning off the pump before replacing the float valve.

Judging from the peal of laughter that floated across the paddock, James saw the whole thing.

Fuck my life.

7

James

Sweet merciful heavens.

Laughter died in my throat. Adam was dripping wet. Rivulets of water ran down his face and forearms. He tossed his baseball cap aside and his mouth flattened to a grim line as he peeled his black tee shirt over his head. My jaw flapped open as I took in the sight of his tautly muscled torso, stripped bare and glistening. He pressed the shirt to his face—

Belle chose that exact moment to decide she was ready for me. She stepped between us, snuffling the brush in my hand, blocking my view of the most beautiful abdomen on this floating green rock. I bent over and peered at Adam from beneath her belly just in time to see him pull the shirt on over his head. Sighing, I straightened.

"Rude," I muttered. "You couldn't wait thirty more seconds?"

She blinked her big brown eyes at me expectantly.

I shook my head. "It's a good thing you're so pretty."

I started at her neck with small, vigorous circles. Clouds of dust and loose hair formed in the wake. Belle was well cared for and groomed regularly, so I focused more on her reactions than worrying about cleanliness. She had a ticklish spot on her belly but loved when I dug in hard on her flank.

"Hey."

I glanced up and found that Ben had joined us by the fence. "Hey," I said.

He stuffed his hands in his pockets. "Can I help?"

I hesitated. It was a sweet offer, but I really wanted this time to learn Belle. Still, something in his face made me change my mind. He looked like he expected me to say no. Like he was bracing for it. I knew the feeling. Growing up at Blue Skies as a child, I had always been underfoot. Some of the staff let me know it but some, like Walter, had shown me kindness. I wanted to be like Walter.

"Here's what we're doing. Belle is brand new to me. I don't know her yet. So I need you to pay attention. Tell me where she's ticklish, if she has any sore spots, what she likes. You think you can do that?"

He straightened. "I can do that."

I beamed. "Great. I'll do her left side, you do her right. Grab a curry comb."

We got to work. I started from her neck again. There was much less dust and hair this time around, but I figured a second round wouldn't hurt her. More likely, she'd enjoy all the attention.

My gaze strayed to Adam as I lifted Belle's cream-colored mane and rubbed her neck. He walked the fence perimeter slowly, checking for damage, occasionally stopping to tie a red ribbon where repairs were needed. I checked a sigh as he spun his ballcap backwards and bent at the waist to examine the middle rail, looking like a goddamn Levi's ad the way his ass filled out those jeans.

Ben's movements mirrored mine as we moved from Belle's neck to her withers and then along her shoulder to her belly. When Ben remarked, "She's ticklish here," at the exact point I had found on this side of her belly, I knew I had made the right decision. The kid was observant and careful.

Another peek at Adam. He was closer now. I never saw him look directly at us, but I had the feeling he was paying attention.

We reached her flank at the same time, both of us

stretching on our toes to reach, and grinned at each other as Belle let out a deep sigh of contentment.

"She likes it!" Ben exclaimed, sounding as delighted as if someone had just handed him a gigantic bowl of chocolate ice cream.

"I think you're right," I agreed.

I was aware of Adam approaching us with slow, deliberate movements, coming from an angle where Belle had a clear view of him, so as not to startle her. He dropped his work bag near Devil, who gave it a nonchalant sniff before returning his attention to the tasty clover.

"Everything okay here?" he asked. He dusted his hands against his thighs, his brow furrowed as he split a glance between us.

Ben looked up at his dad with bright, wide blue eyes, giving me a glimpse of what Adam might look like without the scowl. "I think Belle likes me, Dad."

Adam didn't smile, but his entire demeanor softened when he looked at his son. The deep creases in his forehead smoothed, his lips reversed their downward tilt, and the rigid line of his shoulders relaxed.

"Of course she does," he said. "She's a smart girl."

It was obvious that beneath the gruff exterior, the man had a Ben-shaped soft spot.

"I'm heading back to the barn," Adam said. "You want to ride with me?"

"I want to stay with Belle," Ben said. "And James," he added, but it was clear I was an afterthought. Horses came first. I grinned. Oh, I liked this kid.

Adam looked at me. It was the same expression Ben had worn when he had asked if he could help. Eyebrows raised in question, the clench of his jaw bracing for disappointment. I had the feeling he would take the rejection harder than his kid.

"I could use the help. You want to introduce me to the other horses when we're done here?" I asked Ben.

His eyes lit up. "Yes!"

"Great."

Adam stepped closer, pretending he was focused on untangling a knot in Belle's mane, but using the opportunity to lean in and ask quietly, "You sure you don't mind babysitting?"

Babysitting? I glanced at Ben. Did eleven-year-olds need a babysitter? An alarm clanged in my brain. *Don't let them treat you like a girl*, my dad always warned me. *They won't respect you.* To my dad, watching a kid—like baking cookies—was definitely a girl job. I had feelings about "girl" jobs being a thing at all, and even stronger feelings about "girl" jobs being less valuable, but I also wanted Adam to take me seriously. I was a horse trainer, not a babysitter. Nothing wrong with being a babysitter, but that wasn't what they were paying me for.

"Does Ben need a babysitter at the barn?" I asked carefully.

Adam blinked, like the question had caught him off guard. His brow furrowed.

"I don't need a babysitter," Ben piped up, because of course he heard the whole thing. "Dad said last summer that I'm old enough to be responsible. The rule is I can't go past the ranch sign alone and I have to text him every two hours so he knows I'm alive, and I have to be at the big house for lunch at one."

"What happens if you don't text?" I asked, curious. Ben didn't strike me as a rule-breaker.

Ben's blue eyes widened. "I don't know," he said, confirming my suspicions.

"I come find you," Adam growled.

Heat scalded my cheeks. Even though the words weren't for me, they sent wholly inappropriate shivers down my spine. If this man ever came looking for me all grumpy and growly like that, I'm not sure I would mind being caught.

I turned away so he wouldn't see me blush, hiding behind my hair and sunglasses. "Well, there you go. I'm not babysitting. Ben is helping out."

Ben beamed.

"All right," Adam said after a pause. He pulled his phone out of his pocket, glanced at it, and lifted his chin to Ben. "It's 9:47 now. Set your alarm so you text on time."

"Okay, Dad."

I watched him do it, half tempted to set my own alarm, just in case, but thought better of it. I wasn't his unpaid babysitter, and I damn sure wasn't going to let anyone think it was okay to treat me like one.

Adam looked at me. "Essie Price has a two-year-old she's looking to start. She's bringing him by around two-thirty today. If she likes us, she'll leave him here for the next month. You want this one, or should I pass it to Blaine?"

Essie Price was a star on the rodeo circuit, nearly unbeatable at the barrel race. No way was I going to pass up this opportunity. A grin split my face ear to ear. "Hell yes, I want it."

I had always been told my enthusiasm was contagious, but Adam didn't seem in any danger of catching it. He nodded without even a hint of excitement. "Meet me at the ring at two, then."

He swung a leg over Devil and settled into the saddle with effortless grace. I had spent my life around cowboys. A man on a horse was nothing new to me. But hot damn, there was something about the way Adam sat so tall and easy, his brow furrowed as he stared down at me, that made my belly quiver.

"Don't be late," he said and I blinked.

Excuse me? I had never been late for anything in my life. Hadn't I gotten to work an hour before him this morning? He had no reason to think I'd be anything but punctual. He just wanted to put me in my place.

I scowled at his retreating back as he trotted back toward the barn. No doubt about it, the hot cowboy was also kind of a jerk.

BEN KEPT HIS WORD, texting his dad on time without any prodding from me. At lunchtime, he headed back to the big house and I took the opportunity to run back to my cabin, grab some lunch of my own, and change my clothes. At precisely 1:58, I was back at the training ring in jeans and my pink riding boots.

Adam was already there, along with Blaine and Jesse. A third man who looked vaguely familiar joined them at the rail. When Adam saw me approach, he waved me over and made the introductions.

"Steven came on six months ago. Spent the last seven years bronc riding on the rodeo circuit."

Ah. That's where I'd seen his face.

He grinned. "Thought it might be a nice change of pace to ride horses that didn't aim to kill me."

I laughed. "And how's that working out for you?"

"I think I found my true calling." He braced his forearms on the rail, tipped his hat back with his thumb and let his gaze linger on me in a way I didn't appreciate. "I like the feisty ones. The ones that put up a good fight before I break them. It makes the ride that much sweeter."

I nearly rolled my eyes straight out the back of my head at his innuendo. *Subtle, dude. Real subtle.* "You must have had a good time with Belle, then." My eyes were wide and innocent, because if he'd been even a little successful with her, I wouldn't be standing here now.

Blaine let out a hoot of laughter, earning an elbow to the ribs from Steven.

"Well...she didn't buck him off." Adam looked as scowly as ever, but there was a glimmer in his eyes that on another man I might have called amusement. "She stood rigid as a mountain, no matter how hard he dug his heels into her side. And then she dropped and rolled. He had to bail so she wouldn't break his leg."

That's my girl.

The crunch of tires on gravel made us all jerk to attention. A moment later, a cherry red SUV towing a horse trailer pulled into the driveway. Essie Price jumped out, followed by a slightly older woman who I figured was her sister. She looked enough like Essie to be related, minus the pierced nose, a sapphire blue streak in her hair, and bright red lipstick that matched her truck.

"Hey, y'all," Essie greeted us.

While Essie unloaded the horse from the trailer, the other woman introduced herself. "I'm Kat Price, Essie's mom. Real pretty place you have here."

Whoops. Either Kat knew the secret to eternal youth, or she'd had Essie when she was only a kid herself.

Essie clucked her tongue, leading a gorgeous bay Arabian. "This is Magpie."

"He's beautiful." I rubbed his intelligent, dishy face.

"Fast, too. I think he'll make a hell of a racer, with the proper training."

"I'm James, by the way."

Essie grinned, white teeth flashing against her cherry red lipstick. "I know who you are, babe. I broke your record."

Jesse, Steven, and Blaine made noises like they expected us to square off and put up our fists. Adam shot them an irritated look and shook his head, but I felt tension rolling off those boulder shoulders of his.

I only had one record, so I didn't need her to clarify. At seventeen, my ride that clinched the World Championship Junior Rodeo title also broke the record for fastest youth time around the barrels. Essie had beaten my time three years later by a mere tenth of a second. Her record still stood, a fact I was aware of because even though I focused on training horses for reining events now, I still had a lot of love for the sport.

Anyway, despite the hoots and whistles from the men, I didn't hear any bitchiness in Essie's words. Pride, competitiveness, sure. But it was all good-humored teasing.

"Hell yeah, you did," I said emphatically. "It was a brilliant ride. I wasn't there, but I caught the replay."

Essie's smile broadened. "I couldn't believe it when Adam told me you were the new head trainer at Lodestar. We thought we were going to have to haul Magpie all the way to Texas for training. I'm so glad I can keep him local."

"You live here in Aspen Springs?" I asked.

Essie nodded. "Mom and I have a house in town."

She brought me up to speed on Magpie's training so far. He was used to the feel of the saddle and bit but hadn't had his first ride yet. I nodded, looking him over as she talked. He seemed alert and energetic, but not at all skittish after the drive here.

"Let's get him settled in." I glanced at Adam, my brows raised in question. "Where——"

"Last stall on the left. It's ready for him."

A thrill of anticipation shot through me as we led Magpie to his temporary home. He would a different kind of challenge from Belle. Not necessarily an easier one, though. With Belle, the only person who seemed to truly expect me to succeed was Adam. With Magpie, everyone expected him to be a winner, and if he came up short, then the blame would rest solely on my shoulders.

At Blue Skies, Dad would have been looking over my shoulder the whole time. Second-guessing me. Making me second-guess myself. As head trainer at Lodestar, I called all the shots, made all the decisions. Some of those decisions would be bad. I knew that. But I also knew I could do this and do this well.

I was ready.

8

Adam

Blaine shoved a cookie into his mouth. His eyes rolled back into his head and his face went slack with bliss. "Oh, fuck *me*."

Pretty sure that was his O face, right there. Great. I could have happily lived my whole life never witnessing it with my own two eyeballs if James Campos hadn't waltzed in here with fresh-from-the-oven chocolate chip cookies, served up in a plastic container that Blaine now nestled lovingly against his chest.

"Hand them over," Jesse demanded, reaching for the container.

Blaine swatted his hand and pivoted, curving his body protectively around the cookies like a running back cradling a football.

Steven and Jesse exchanged a glance, silent communication passing between them. It did not bode well for Blaine, although he was too busy devouring another cookie to notice. A second later, it was all over. Blaine rubbed his ribs where Steven got him with an elbow and Jesse held the container over his head. He pranced in a circle, holding the container high like a trophy, in a stupid little victory dance.

"Will you shitheads cut it out?" I snapped. "You're going to spook the horse."

The four of us were at the ring, watching James work Magpie. Only three days into his training with James and he was coming along nicely. Essie planned to swing by next week and I had a feeling she was going to be pleased with his progress. That was a relief. Working with Essie was great for our business, and it never would have happened without James.

"If Magpie is going to be a rodeo horse, he needs to get used to chaos," Blaine pointed out. "Anyway, James has him in hand."

That was true. I watched as Magpie fidgeted, hopping and tossing his head like a fool, but James kept her hands calm and steady, refusing to fight. Then she opened one rein wide, giving him freedom to turn into it, and urged him forward in a tight circle.

"You got this, James!" Jesse called encouragingly.

I side-eyed him narrowly. The ranch hands weren't exactly a touchy-feely group. We showed up, we did our jobs, and we got along, for the most part. What we did *not* do was holler on the sidelines like fucking cheerleaders.

She'd been here less than a week, and already she was making my men as soft and gooey on the inside as her chocolate chip cookies. I saw the way they fell all over themselves to open doors for her or arrange their chores so they happened to be in her vicinity. Dumbasses.

James widened the circle progressively as Magpie settled down, until finally they were loping around the full perimeter of the ring. James had a huge grin on her face and, swear to god, Magpie looked like he was having the time of his life. Damn, there was something gorgeous about the way that woman rode a horse. The deceptive ease of her seat. The strong grip of her thighs wrapped around his belly.

Lucky horse.

She gave him his head and let him pick up more speed before gently bringing him back down again. When she brought him to a halt, she leaned forward and gave him a firm pat on the neck. "Such a good boy!" she cooed.

Apparently my dick was just as dumb as these

assholes, because it twitched like her words were meant for me. *Jesus*.

"Damn fine job." Blaine grinned. "Guess those pretty pink boots of yours were made for riding, after all."

"So's that pretty little ass," Steven muttered as James swung her leg over Magpie's back and dismounted.

My hand shot out and smacked the back of his head. "The fuck's wrong with you?" I growled.

"Damn, boss." Steven rubbed the back of his head. "I'm just saying what we're all thinking."

The fact that it was true made it not one whit better. I still wanted to personally remove his eyeballs from his head to keep him from looking at her the exact same way I had. She was just doing her job, and we were all staring at her like goddamn perverts. It was hard to say who I hated more in that moment: him or me.

Oh, who the hell was I kidding? It was me. It was definitely me.

I was her *boss*. I could hear Brax's lecture in my head every bit as loudly as if he were standing next to me, shouting in my ear. The fine folks of Aspen Springs liked to claim that we were two peas in a pod, Brax and me, both of us living life with a stick shoved right up the ass. But I knew the nature of that stick was different for each of us.

I had never cared much for rules. Duty was what got

my ass out of bed every morning, working my dad's ranch, keeping the family together as best I could, making sure Ben wanted for nothing. Brax, on the other hand, liked to say a man had to live his own way. He cared not one bit about duty, but good lord, how that man loved rules. He especially loved enforcing them.

And the way I was looking at James was wrong on both counts. Shirking duty and breaking rules.

"I'm not here to police your thoughts, but you need to keep that shit to yourself. Have some goddamn respect."

"Yes, sir."

Disgusted with myself, I pushed away from the rail. "I've got work to do. And so do the rest of you. I don't pay you to stand around eating cookies all day."

That got their attention. Steven disappeared into the stable. Jesse ducked between the rails to take Magpie's reins from James. They headed off to the cool-down station out behind the barn, chatting away like old friends.

Blaine gave me a long look.

"What?" I grunted.

"Nothing," he said, in a way that clearly meant *something*.

"You think I was too hard on him?"

"Nah. Steven needs to learn some manners." He

shook his head. "He can't go running his mouth with every fool thing that pops into his head."

"Then what's the problem?"

"I don't have a problem. Do you have a problem?"

"I don't have a problem," I ground out. "Except for this stupid conversation."

He held out the container of cookies and gave it an inviting shake. "Have a cookie."

I glowered at the container. Fuck, they looked good. Smelled good, too. "I don't want a cookie."

Blaine's lips twitched. "See, I think maybe that's your problem, right there. You *do* want a cookie. You just don't want to admit it."

My mood did not improve as the morning went on. I couldn't get my mind off those cookies. Around noon I finally caved, but of course they were long gone by then. I hadn't seen Ben since breakfast. He had texted an hour ago, so I knew he was alive, but there was no sign of him anywhere—or James, for that matter. That meant they were probably together.

Like everyone else, Ben had taken a shine to James. I wasn't sure what to make of that. He had always been a barn rat, but mostly he stuck to the horses, not the people. When he wasn't hanging around the stables, he was in his room, reading—also alone. He had two close friends at school, but both of them lived far enough away that he didn't see much of them when school was out. I felt guilty about that. I worried that he was lonely, that I wasn't doing enough to give him the kind of childhood a kid should have.

His quick attachment to James was just one more thing to worry about. Was it weird? Did he miss his mom? His grandma? Or maybe he—

The sound of laughter jerked me out of my thoughts. It was the same laugh I first heard at Jo's. Full and robust, like she pulled it deep from her soul. Something in me shifted at the sound. I headed toward it, exiting the barn, blinking in the sunlight.

There she was. On horseback, Ben riding next to her on Ginger, coming down the dirt path back to the barn. Her head was thrown back as she laughed at something Ben said, and Ben? Ben looked at her like she hung the damn moon.

Irritation rolled through me in a wave. Of course he did. She was fun. She didn't have to worry about things like rules and duty and responsibility.

"What the hell is this?" I demanded.

James's pink lips popped open in surprise at my tone. "A trail ride? I wanted—"

"I don't care what you wanted," I cut her off. "You took my kid for a ride without telling me. I had no idea where he was."

Ben blanched. "Dad—"

I held up my hand. "Ben, you know the rule."

James's head whipped in his direction. Her eyebrows went up in a question. "We didn't leave the property."

"He knows he's supposed to tell me before he goes for a ride. If he's on horseback, I need to know where he is, even if it's only in the training ring. You had no business taking him anywhere on horseback without telling me."

Two red splotches appeared on her cheeks. Her eyes narrowed. "Do I need to remind you that I'm not the babysitter?"

The anger in her dark eyes caught me by surprise. It might have been the first time I had seen her anything but smiling. And why? What the hell did she have to be mad about? "Damn right, you're not. I would expect anyone I paid to watch my kid to know what is and isn't acceptable behavior. Untack the horses. When you're done, I want to see you in my office."

The heat of her glare scorched my back as I strode

back into the barn. Figuring I would get some paperwork done while I waited for James, I threw myself into the rolling chair behind my desk. A wheel popped off and it wilted on one side. Great. Fucking *great*.

Fine. I wasn't in the mood for paperwork anyway. Actually, I was never in the mood for paperwork, but I could usually force myself to focus long enough to get it done. Right now there was no chance of that happening. I pushed to my feet, resisting the urge to kick the chair on my way out. Because I was an adult.

Needing something to take the edge off, I grabbed a pitchfork and headed for a stall. Nothing like shoveling shit to work out a shitty attitude, Dad always said. And my attitude *was* shit, I couldn't deny that. There was no reason for me to lay into James like that. She was right; she wasn't the babysitter. It was on Ben to tell me he was going riding, not her. He knew the rule.

Goddamn it.

I didn't want to do this right now. He had just spent the last hour having a fantastic time with James and now I had to come in and dole out the punishment. It was always me. I didn't have a wife I could share the crappy parenting jobs with. Lord knew my dad wasn't up to the task—and I didn't want him to be. Grandparents were for love and sugar, not lectures and punishments. Keeping Ben safe was my responsibility.

Good times came from literally anyone else. Bad times always came from me. Sometimes I worried about what that meant for our relationship. Maybe the second he turned eighteen he would shake off the ranch dust and get as far from me as he possibly could. I hated the thought of that.

My shoulders felt tight, like a heavy weight had been set there. Whether by someone else or my own stupid self, who was to say.

I leaned the pitchfork against the wall and rested my forehead there, too. Stalling.

"Are you mad?" Ben's voice was quiet. Anxious.

I raised my head wearily, prepared to give him the whole, *I'm not mad, just disappointed* speech when I realized he wasn't talking to me. He was talking to someone outside the stall.

"Yeah, Ben, I'm mad," James said.

Immediately my hackles went up, whatever the hell hackles were. My instinct was to jump in and defend Ben. But from what? The truth of the matter was, she had a right to be mad. And she wasn't raising her voice at him. She was just stating a fact.

"The thing is, you knew the rule and I didn't. I didn't know that you had to tell your dad before you got on a horse. You put me in a bad spot with him and now he's mad at me. Why didn't you tell him what we were doing?"

I could hear the sound of Ben shuffling his feet against the straw-covered dirt. "I don't know," he muttered.

There was a pause. "Yes, you do."

"Yeah." More shuffling. "I left my phone in the breakroom when I went to get some water. You were mostly tacked up already. I figured you wouldn't want to wait for me to text my dad and tack up Ginger."

My ribcage squeezed tight.

"I didn't think you'd get in trouble," Ben went on. "I thought as long as we were back before lunch, he wouldn't find out I went without telling him. Dad never says no to riding, as long as I'm with someone. He would have said yes if I had told him. That's almost the same thing as actually saying yes, right?"

I pinched the bridge of my nose, choking back a laugh and a sigh. Goddamn, this kid.

"Compelling logic, but no." There was a hint of a smile in James's voice. "I would have waited for you."

"Yeah?" His voice was full of hope.

"Of course. I could have managed on my own. I like exploring. But it's better having someone along who can show you where all the cool stuff is. You're a great trail guide." Her voice turned serious when she said, "But you broke my trust, Ben. That can't happen again."

"It won't," he said hastily. "I don't break rules."

That was true. He and his uncle had that in common. I shook my head. Funny how I found it a lot more endearing in my kid than in my brother.

"Why not?" she asked, that same curiosity she had about Belle now directed at my kid.

"Never had a reason to, I guess. Dad doesn't make a lot of rules and they're not all that hard to stick to, usually."

"Huh." She sounded surprised by that. "Good for you, I guess, but that's not always going to be the way of it. There are going to be rules you want to break, sometimes for a good reason and sometimes for no reason at all. And when that happens, I want you to ask yourself: Who is it going to hurt if I break this rule? If the answer is no one but yourself, have at it, understanding the consequences might not be all that fun. Learn your lessons."

I frowned. I didn't want Ben hurt. Ever.

That wasn't exactly a reasonable request of the universe. Of course he was going to do dumb shit. Of course he was going to get hurt.

"But if the answer is anyone else at all, I want you to stop and think twice. That's what friends do for each other. Okay?"

"Okay," he said softly.

"Good," she said. "Then I'll see you tomorrow."

He let out a big breath and so did I. Like that weight on my shoulders had lifted somewhat. It didn't disappear entirely, but it got a little lighter. I was just so used to doing this alone.

Imparting life lessons to my son wasn't her job, but here she was anyway, nudging him gently in the direction of being a decent human being. Not in the same way I would have done it, but maybe that was a good thing. Maybe he would actually *hear* it, coming from her. And it was such a goddamn relief not to be the mean guy for once.

I heard them move off—Ben heading toward the big house, where Dad had a sandwich for him, and James turning in the direction of my office—and counted to ten before slipping out of the stall and following her.

I caught up with her right when she slapped open the door and found my office empty.

Her hands went to her hips. "That mother fucker," she muttered.

The placement of her hands drew my attention to the way her hips and ass curved from her small waist. I allowed myself a single second to eye-fuck her as I leaned against the doorframe behind her. What Brax didn't know, he couldn't lecture me on.

"Now, that's not fair. Haven't fucked a mother even once, to my knowledge," I drawled.

She let out a startled yip and spun on her toes, clutching her throat. She recovered quickly and narrowed her eyes at me. "Was that a joke?"

Well, shit. I guessed it was. The words had rolled off my tongue all natural and easy without me thinking much about it. I cocked my head, studying her. It had been a long time since I had joked around with anyone, but I was pretty sure the point of it was to make someone laugh.

James wasn't laughing.

She was scowling.

Might have something to do with the way I lectured her in front of my kid and then summoned her to my office for more of the same. She probably expected me to yell at her again. Although, come to think of it, she didn't look meek or apologetic, the way I would expect an employee to look when they were about to get reprimanded by their boss.

No, she looked like she was squaring off for a fight.

"Well?" she demanded, crossing her arms over her chest.

It suddenly occurred to me that, compared to her lower body, her upper region was oddly...shapeless. Almost androgynous. She could have an A-cup or Dolly Parton tits under her tee shirt for all I knew.

"Do you have something you want to say or not?" James pressed. "Because I have somewhere to be."

I jerked my gaze to her face. The size and shape of her breasts wasn't a mystery I was going to unravel today...or ever. "Where are you going?"

"Jo's. I'm meeting a friend for coffee." She glanced at her watchless wrist, like she could tell the time by her freckles. "And now it's my lunch break, so..."

James had been in Aspen Springs for less than a week. As far as I knew, she didn't have any friends. Unless she had hit it off with one of the ranch hands. She and Jesse had seemed pretty friendly this morning. That didn't give me a good feeling.

"I'll drive," I said. "No use in wasting gas when we're both heading in the same direction anyway."

She eyed me with deep suspicion. "You're going to Jo's?"

"Thereabouts."

Her lips pursed. My gaze snagged there, on that plush pink mouth. Hard to believe my mouth had ever touched hers. Brutally unfair that it would never happen again.

"Fine," she said. "But this is my break. Not an excuse to trap me in a car so you can yell at me some more. In fact, no work talk at all. Got it?"

I grunted noncommittedly. Not that I had any

intention of yelling at her, but what the hell were we supposed to talk about, if not work?

"I mean it," she insisted. "The second we're off Lodestar Ranch, you're not my boss."

Ah, hell. There were lots of reasons to keep my mouth off Ms. Pink Boots, but that right there was the best of them. And she had just stripped it away.

9

James

FIFTEEN MINUTES INTO OUR DRIVE, I regretted my embargo on work talk. This being Colorado, we got the weather out of the way first. After that, we fell into silence—and not a comfortable silence, either. Adam wasn't much of a talker, but I was, and right now I sure as shit had a lot to say. The problem was, my self-imposed work embargo meant I couldn't say any of it. Instead, I stared out the window.

It would be fair to say I was pouting.

Pouting was a new experience for me. I didn't keep things bottled up. I preferred to say my piece and move forward. Let it out and let it breathe, as my mom liked to say. Otherwise all those thoughts and feelings would turn toxic and poison you from the inside out. It was one of the things my dad appreciated most about my mom.

She never made him guess what she was thinking. He never had to ask what was wrong.

Of course, when it was me, he called it a temper tantrum.

I wondered if Adam would say the same thing. Probably. An hour ago he was accusing me of dropping the ball on a job that wasn't mine to begin with and now look at him. Completely at ease, one arm resting on the console between us, his other hand on the steering wheel, his fingers tapping whatever melody was playing in his head. Hot and unbothered.

Infuriating.

"What?" he asked, glancing at me out of the corner of his eye.

You owe me an apology.

"Nothing," I bit out.

He shrugged. "Okay, then."

We snagged a parking spot half a block from Jo's. I could see Chloe waiting for me out front of the café. I barely waited for Adam to put the truck in park before I unbuckled and sprang out. I started for Chloe but Adam was quick. With a gentle hand on my hip, he guided me to the inside of the sidewalk and fell into step beside me.

"You're coming to Jo's?" I asked. When he had said "thereabouts," I had figured he meant the feed store.

"For a minute. Could use some caffeine. Not all of us OD'd on sugar this morning."

"You didn't have a cookie?"

"Nope."

I shook my head. "Figures. It'd be hard to keep that whole grumpy cowboy thing going while eating a cookie. You might have lost your scowl."

"I'm not scowling now, am I?"

He wasn't, but I wasn't ready to let go of my attitude yet. "Well, you're not smiling, either."

He smirked a little at that. It did something to me, the way one corner of his mouth tucked in. What would it take to turn that little smirk into a real smile? I wanted to tickle him, share a dirty joke, anything to make it bloom.

"James!" Chloe lifted a hand. "I figured we could sit outside since it's nice. If people see me inside, they assume I'm working and ask me for stuff." She glanced at Adam and then back to me. "Do we need three chairs?"

"He's not staying," I said firmly.

Adam arched an eyebrow. "Why don't you both sit down and I'll get the food? What are you having?"

"A black iced coffee and a turkey sandwich," I said, fishing a twenty out of my bag to pay for it.

He ignored it. "Chloe?"

"Sparkling water and a BLT, please. Give them my

name. I get a discount." She reached for her wallet but he shook his head.

"I've got it."

I frowned. "I'm not comfortable with you buying my lunch. You're my boss. It feels weird."

"I'm not your boss off Lodestar property, remember?" The glint in his eyes made the words mean things they shouldn't. I stared back at him wordlessly, my stomach fluttering. "I've got it."

He disappeared inside before I could protest again.

"Huh," Chloe said.

"What?" I asked as we grabbed a table for two in the sunshine.

She shrugged. "He's come in at least once a week for as long as I've worked here, but he looks different today. Swear to god, I thought he was his brother, Brax, for a minute there. I don't think I've ever seen Adam when he wasn't frowning."

I laughed. "Sounds about right. I told him he has Resting Grump Face."

"My point is that he's not frowning today. With *you*."

"Maybe he got it all out of his system yelling at me this morning," I muttered.

Her eyes widened. "He yelled at you? What happened?"

I chewed my lip. If Chloe had been one of my

girlfriends back home, I would have poured out the whole story. But we didn't know each other yet. Not really. Realizing I had left her phone number behind, what with all the accidental lip-mashing, I had swung by the café last weekend and we had agreed to meet up today.

I didn't want to kick off a fledgling friendship by talking shit about someone behind his back. I hadn't been in Aspen Springs long, but I had taken note of the "Made in Colorado" and "Don't California My Colorado" bumper stickers. I was an outsider here, unlike Adam. He might be a grump but at least he wasn't from California.

"It was nothing," I said finally. "Just a rough day."

"Hm." Her eyes darted to where he stood at the counter, waiting for our food and drinks to be ready. "Things not going so well with your new boss? You mean you didn't take one look at each other and fall right into each other's arms? Oh, wait." Overcome with her own joke, she laughed so hard she snorted.

"Stop that right now," I hissed. "He's coming back."

"Hate to break it to you, but he already knows how y'all met. He was there for it." She giggled. "Especially his mouth."

"Stop talking," I muttered frantically. Why did the one friend I had in this town have to be the same barista who had witnessed my humiliation? "Not another word."

I jumped to my feet to open the door for him, since his hands were full, took the cardboard tray of drinks, and set it down on our table. After he set the food on the table, I handed his cup of coffee back to him. "Here you go."

"Thanks." He took a sip. "I'll be back for you in thirty minutes." He touched the brim of his hat. "Ladies."

We watched him go because that ass wasn't something to look away from.

Disgruntled, I poked my straw into my iced coffee with a little more force than necessary. "Damn it. Why'd he have to be all nice and gentlemanly? Now I definitely can't bitch about him behind his back."

Chloe snickered as she popped open her can of sparkling water. "That's not a gentleman. That's a cowboy. Completely different breed of animal." She grinned at me. "You know what they say, a cowboy in the streets, a beast in the sheets."

I nearly choked on my drink. "That's not how the saying goes."

"Well, it should be. Look at that man and tell me he couldn't throw a woman around and make her enjoy it." She let out a dreamy sigh. "Those *thighs*. Like tree trunks."

I narrowed my eyes at her. "You cannot have a crush on my grumpy boss, Chloe. I will not allow it." I growled when she laughed. "Ugh, he makes me want to stab something."

"I like to stab things," a soft, sweet voice said from behind us, making us both nearly jump out of our skins in shock.

"Jesus Christ, woman. You about gave me a heart attack." Chloe pressed her hand to her chest, her eyes wide. "Who the hell are you?"

The woman frowned and pushed her glasses up on her nose. Her tidy bun of dark blonde hair and ankle-length prairie skirt gave her an old-fashioned vibe. She didn't look like someone who enjoyed stabbing.

"You know who I am, Chloe. I'm Hannah Bell. The librarian?" When Chloe still looked baffled, Hannah shook her head. "I've come here nearly every day for the past three years. Usually I sit in that corner right there." She had something sharp and shiny pinched between her thumb and forefinger, and she used it to jab the air in the direction of the cozy chair by the fireplace inside. It was a needle, I realized. A long blue thread dangled from it and disappeared into the heap of fabric in her lap.

"Oh," Chloe said, looking doubtful. "Right. Of course."

Hannah's rueful expression suggested she didn't

believe Chloe's epiphany for even a second. "It's all right. I have a way of fading into the background."

"I only moved here a week ago," I offered. "I haven't been to the library yet."

Hannah scooched her chair closer to us. "I'm starting a sewing circle at the library. Saturday mornings at ten." Her bright blue eyes were wide and hopeful behind her glasses. "Everyone is welcome. It's going to be a lot of fun."

Sewing wasn't exactly my idea of fun. It required sitting still and the only time I liked to sit still was on horseback—technically, the horse was moving for both of us. But I didn't want to hurt her feelings, either. Chloe and I shared a look.

"You get to stab things," Hannah pushed. "It's great for stress relief."

"I don't know how to sew," Chloe said.

"That's okay! I'm there to teach you. Look at this." She held up the fabric in her lap to show us the embroidery. Bright, cheerful flowers formed a message between their petals: *fuck the patriarchy*. "It's going to be a pillow."

We burst out laughing.

"We're in," I said.

"Hey!" Chloe protested.

"Why not?" I grinned wickedly. "Maybe I can embroider Adam's face. That might be fun to stab."

"Great." Hannah pushed to her feet with a swish of her skirt and started gathering her things. I had the feeling she was making a quick exit before we could change our minds. "I'll see you at the library Saturday at ten."

When she was gone, Chloe stared at me like I'd lost my mind. "Her first words to us were literally *I like to stab things.*"

"She seems nice!" I protested.

"She seems weird."

"Okay, maybe that's true. But it's hard making friends as an adult, and that pillow she was making was awesome. This could be fun."

"Okay," Chloe relented. "But if she's secretly a murderer, I'm tripping you and saving myself."

10

Adam

THE SECOND we passed under the sign welcoming us back to Lodestar Ranch, James tapped a dainty finger on my forearm that rested on the console between us.

"Pull over," she said.

I steered the truck into the narrow patch of overgrown grass that separated the dirt drive from the fenced pasture and shifted into park, then turned to face her. "What's up?"

"We're back on Lodestar property. You're my boss again."

The tone of her voice suggested this did not bode well for me.

"Okay," I said carefully.

"Which means we can talk about what happened today with Ben."

Oh, for shit's sake. Did we really have to do this? If she hadn't insisted on no work talk during her lunch break, we'd have laid it to rest by now.

"Look," I said, "it was a mistake. I get it. You didn't know any better. Let's move on, okay?"

The ensuing silence was long and deafening. A trickle of trepidation crawled down my neck. I shifted in my seat to face her and found her considering me thoughtfully with those big doe eyes of hers.

"We are going to talk about what happened with Ben today," she said, as though I hadn't said a damn word. "The way I see it, you already had your say. Now it's my turn."

"Fair," I grunted.

She blinked. I had surprised her. Apparently she didn't expect me to be reasonable.

Also fair.

"I feel like there's been a misunderstanding," she said. "If we're going to work together, we need to be on the same page."

I nodded briskly, hoping to hurry this up so I could get back to work.

"I am not Ben's babysitter or nanny. I was very clear on that. But that doesn't mean I don't have a duty to keep him safe when he's with me. I owe him the same care I would owe anyone else. More, really, because he's a kid. I know that. And I *did* that. I kept him safe. But it's not my job to make sure he follows your rules. That's on Ben. That's on you."

My brows furrowed deeper with every word. She wasn't wrong. I had come to pretty much the same conclusion five minutes after I had reamed into her. Maybe I was a little miffed that she had no problem articulating her feelings on the matter. I put a burden on her shoulders that didn't belong there, and she simply shrugged it right off again, easy as you please. People could do that?

"Yeah," I said.

"Yeah?" she prodded.

She stared at me, waiting. I stared back at her, dense.

"You know, apologizing doesn't mean you're weak," she said. "It means you're smart. It means you can take in new information and use that information to course correct. To become better."

Her words brought to mind the way she rode Magpie for the first time, opening the rein and giving him space to make the right choice. And, like Magpie, I did the same. Because I might be dense, but I was at least as smart as a fucking horse.

"I'm sorry." The words came out gruff, but at least they came out at all. "I shouldn't have yelled at you, especially in front of Ben. It won't happen again."

"Thank you." She tilted her head, studying me. "For what it's worth, I think Ben's a good kid. One infraction doesn't mean he needs to be watched twenty-four seven. But I'm not his parent, so if you think he does need watching, then hire a real babysitter. You can't shove that duty on me just because I'm the only female on the premises and happen to bake cookies."

"James, it happened because Ben glommed onto you. If he had been with Jesse or Blaine instead, I would have gone off just the same. Baking cookies had fuck all to do with it." I looked at her from beneath my drawn eyebrows. "Why would you think it did?"

She turned away, looking out the passenger side window at the empty pasture. "Oh, you know. It was something my dad used to tell me. You can't expect men to respect you if you're baking them cookies and acting like a girl."

"Acting like a girl." It took me a beat to fully comprehend that. "But you *are* a girl." Or woman. Female? Shit.

She smirked at me over her shoulder. "Noticed that, did you?"

A little too much for my comfort, to be honest. And then I remembered Steven's crack about her ass and straightened so fast I nearly bumped my head on the cab roof. "Have any of my guys been less than respectful?" *To your face*, I added silently. "Said something or touched you or—"

"No. That's not—" She shook her head and I exhaled sharply through my nose. I didn't have to fire anyone today. "The guys have been great. I'm saying I want to be valued for my skill at training horses. That's all."

I was silent for a moment. She studied her nails. Short, unpainted, with a tiny bit of stable dirt around the edges. Her mouth twisted in a grimace, like maybe she was regretting this conversation. I couldn't blame her. I wasn't exactly the sort of man people felt naturally inclined to unburden themselves to. Normally that was fine by me.

But this time, it wasn't fine. I wanted to say the right thing. Do right by her the way she had for my boy.

Unfortunately, I had no idea how to accomplish that. But I was going to try anyway, even if I made a mess of it.

"Let's go," she said. Eager to be done with my company, I was sure.

I settled my hand on the gear shift and put it in drive. "We checked your references, you know."

"Yeah?"

I could feel her eyes on me, but I kept my gaze peeled to the dirt road in front of us. "Yeah. Heard a lot about how you had a special touch with problem horses. How you could get a little something extra out of any horse in your care. Even the ones that were performing well already, you took them to the next level. But not a single one of them said anything about cookies."

She hummed a little, sounding pleased.

"I'm not saying your cookies are *bad*..." My voice trailed off, suggesting exactly that.

She smacked my arm. "Hey!"

"Prove me wrong," I dared.

"You can't be serious. There's no such thing as bad cookies. You're just messing with me so you can have a batch all to yourself."

"Peanut butter is my favorite."

She crossed her arms over her bewildering chest. "Dream on," she scoffed. "I'm not baking you cookies."

"You keep talking, buttercup. But all I hear is you lying to yourself."

11

James

JAMES

Cookies on your desk. I swear they're not poisoned.

ADAM

Cool. Ben can have the first one.

JAMES

Father of the Year

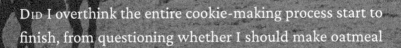

DID I overthink the entire cookie-making process start to finish, from questioning whether I should make oatmeal raisin out of shear spite to wondering if Adam preferred chewy to crispy? Absolutely I did.

Buttercup.

What the hell was that about?

And why did it make me feel...warm? As warm and soft as the inside of the cookies I had baked him, hoping he liked it that way.

Like that was an appropriate way to feel about my boss.

I wasn't here to catch gooey feelings for a grumpy cowboy. I was here to train an unrideable horse.

I was here to prove my dad wrong.

With that in mind, I headed for Belle's stall.

"Morning, Ted," I said as I passed him in the aisle.

"Hey, there, James." Ted greeted me with a smile.

He seemed a little aimless. Not lost, exactly. But unsure. I paused. "Do you need something?"

"Nah. Just missed the horses, that's all. Figured I'd say hello to my old friends. I haven't spent as much time here as I used to."

Before his wife died. That's what he meant. I nodded in understanding. "I keep a bag of carrots in the breakroom. You're welcome to them."

"Thanks." He rubbed the back of his neck. "Maybe I'll do a deep clean of the saddles, too. Might as well, since I'm here."

It almost sounded like he was asking for permission. "That would be great."

"Good." He grinned. "I'll do that, then."

For the rest of the week, I focused my attention on Belle. I spent the next week slowly and carefully rebuilding her foundation. The more time I spent with her, the curiouser I became. It was clear that she loved people and was eager to please. She also had a sly sense of humor, often knocking over the bucket of grooming brushes at the end of a session to show she wanted more scratches. What was it she hated about riding?

Some horses hated work, but Belle was far from lazy. Another possibility was that she simply hated being told what to do. That would pose a bigger obstacle to overcome if she was ever going to be a reining champion. Reining was all about communication, discipline, and eagerness to do the work asked for by the rider.

Something told me that obstinacy wasn't Belle's issue. I hoped I was right. Otherwise, she was going to need a new career and I very much doubted Adam would be thrilled about that.

The lore surrounding Belle was almost legend at this point. She had only been ridden once, no tack. No saddle. No bridle. Just the weight of a rider she loved. Maybe I was a sentimental fool—my dad would certainly say so —but the story of Belle's first and only ride stuck with me. I couldn't shake the feeling that it was the key to everything.

So that's where I started.

On Thursday, while giving her a thorough brushing, I kicked over the bucket, used it as a stool, and leaned over her back to continue brushing her other side. Under the guise of grooming, I gave her most of my weight. She didn't seem to notice, much less care.

On Friday, I didn't even pretend. There in her stall, I sprawled over her back, giving her my full weight, letting my legs dangle a bit. She grabbed a mouthful of hay and chewed contentedly.

When Sunday rolled around, I figured Belle had earned her break. Our first week had ended on a high note, and that was something to feel proud about. Tomorrow the real work would start.

I bit my lip. Maybe I should text Chloe and cancel the whole sewing circle thing. Ted had made it clear he took weekends seriously, but still. There was so much work to be done. Belle and Magpie were scheduled for a day of turnout, but that didn't mean I couldn't work with another horse.

On the other hand, I was new in town, and while I didn't mind spending time alone, I knew it wouldn't be long before I was lonely. For me, good girlfriends were crucial to good mental health. Hannah's sewing circle was an opportunity to make some friends.

Anyway, I had a whole list of chores to do, too. Thanks to the seventeen-hour drive from California to Colorado, my SUV needed an oil change and a wash. I had a larger-than-normal pile of laundry to do, groceries to pick up, and it wouldn't hurt to take a quick peek at the shops on Main Street and maybe find something to cozy up my cabin a bit.

On the long dirt lane that ran from the big house to county road, I saw Adam out in the cow pasture on horseback and I couldn't help it, I eased my foot off the gas so I could watch as my SUV rolled by at two miles per hour. The chestnut gelding must be a young one, because it was clear he didn't quite have the hang of his job yet.

But Adam sure did.

My god, the man was magnificent on a horse. Calm and steady, all the power of his muscled form never veering into brutality. This was a man who loved his work and did it damned well.

And then—a breakthrough. The chestnut headed off a cow that broke from the herd. A grin flashed across Adam's face, there and gone again like the sun peeking through a storm cloud. Even from a distance it hit me like a lightning strike.

Jesus.

I clamped my thighs together and hit the gas. One thing I would *not* be doing this weekend was wasting time lusting after my boss.

"You came." There was a note of eager surprise in Hannah's voice that made me think I wasn't the only one who needed girlfriends.

Chloe followed in my shadow as best she could, considering she had a solid five inches in height on me. She wasn't completely sold on either the sewing circle or Hannah and regarded anything that happened before noon on a weekend with deep suspicion. But she was here anyway because I wanted to come. That boded well for our friendship.

My bribe of brunch and mimosas after probably didn't hurt, either.

"I know I called it a sewing circle, but it's really more of a sewing *line*," Hannah said, indicating the row of brilliantly patterned Turkish floor pillows lined neatly against the wall opposite the door. "We use this room for yoga, too, so it doesn't have any tables. I thought it would be better to have some back support."

"Is it just us?" Chloe asked, eyeing the five pillows suspiciously.

"A few others could show up," Hannah hedged. She grabbed each of us by an elbow and steered us across the room. "But let's go ahead and get started. I created a sampler for each of you so you can learn the more common stitches. French knots, chain stitch, satin stitch, stem stitch. The best way to learn is by making something pretty, so I incorporated the different types of stitches into a flower garden."

We settled onto the cushions and Hannah walked us through getting started. She showed us how to place the fabric in the bamboo hoop so it was tight as a drum, how to separate the thread into multiple strands, and how to thread the needle with a bit of scotch tape.

"We'll start with the satin stitch because you're going to use it a lot. It's also super easy, but if you don't pay attention it can look like a hot mess in no time."

Chloe and I didn't say much as we concentrated on learning the stitches. Hannah was right. It was easy to catch on, but also easy to screw up.

"Where did you learn how to do this?" I asked. I didn't know anyone who could sew.

"Oh, all the girls on the compound learned pretty young. It was part of our schooling. Sewing, cooking, and homemaking." Hannah leaned in to get a better look at my stitches. "Make sure you place them right next to each other. Don't be afraid to take it out and try again if it gets crooked."

Chloe and I looked at each other. *The compound?* I mouthed.

"What did the boys learn?" Chloe asked.

"Math and Bible study."

"Ew," Chloe said. "Tell me more about that."

I nudged her with my elbow. "Rude," I hissed.

Hannah's lips quirked up. "It is pretty ew. Some day I'll tell you more about it, okay? A little bit at a time. I don't like to focus on it. If I think on it too much, I get..." She jabbed her needle through the fabric hard enough that I could swear I heard the *ping*.

"Stabby?" I suggested.

Her lips tilted in amusement. "I was going to say annoyed."

Chloe nodded and turned her attention back to her own hoop of fabric. "Do you know what annoys James?" she asked conversationally, like the mousy town librarian hadn't just confessed she had been raised in a religious cult. "Her smoking hot boss."

I gasped. "Chloe!"

"It's called a segue, James."

"It's called throwing me under the bus, Chloe."

She looked at me, her green eyes wide and far too

knowing. "Are you saying you don't want to talk about him, James?"

I narrowed my own eyes back at her despite the words threatening to burble out of my stupid mouth. Because maybe I *did* want to talk about my smoking hot boss.

Hannah's gaze ping-ponged between us, her face scrunched up like she was trying not to laugh. "Did you know, women have been meeting like this for centuries. Communities would form sewing circles for charitable causes, or sometimes less formally, just to make a quilt or something for a new mother or a family in need. That was the main point of a sewing circle. But the other important part was to give them a reason to sit and talk to friends."

It was the way she said *friends*, with that same eager hopefulness I had noted earlier, that made me say, "Okay, let me tell you about my boss, because you will not *believe* what he called me."

And when Hannah and Chloe leaned closer, I felt a little shimmy of giddiness in my chest. Aspen Springs wasn't home. Not yet. Half my heart and a good portion of my soul was still yearning for Blue Skies.

But I was feeling more settled in my choice to be here every day.

12

Adam

EVEN WITHOUT THE pink cowboy boots, I recognized the legs sticking out from under the SUV as James's. For one, the SUV was hers. For another, those legs had managed to imprint so brightly on my brain that I could trace every curve of muscle and sinew with my eyes closed.

I parked the four wheeler behind her SUV and approached, noting the lone decal in the rear window. *I hope something good happens to you today*, spelled out in cheerful bubbly letters. I shook my head. Of course she did.

"I am calm." Her voice floated out from under the car, enunciating every syllable with measured precision. But one leg lifted and then lowered with force, her sneakered heel bouncing against the dirt. A foot stomp if I ever saw one.

I grinned.

"I don't..." She heaved a sigh. Her hips wiggled as she wiggled her torso out from under the car. I leaned my hip against the front bumper and waited. "I don't—"

Her eyes met mine. Shiny and wet. Like she was on the verge of tears.

No.

Absolutely fucking not.

With a low growl, I swiped the phone from her hand, ignoring her gasp of surprise. I kept my gaze narrowed on her face as I snapped, "This is Adam Hale. James can't talk right now. She needs both hands for the oil change she's working on."

There was a pause. And then a smooth voice said, "Well, Adam Hale, this is Carl Campos of Blue Skies Farm."

Her dad. Oh, shit.

James didn't look like she wanted to cry anymore. She had that look of someone watching a person fall flat on their ass. Like she wanted to laugh but was waiting to make sure there weren't any broken bones first.

I stared at her. She stared back, eyebrows winged up as if to say, *now what?* Clearly she wasn't going to save me. I should never have grabbed the phone from her. I should've minded my own business and walked away.

But seeing that almost smile shimmering in her eyes? I didn't regret it.

I cleared my throat. "What can I do for you, sir?"

He chuckled. "I'm glad you asked. We have an important event coming up. I was just telling James that Lodestar did just fine without her before she joined your team and surely you can spare her for a week."

I ground my teeth so hard I could feel the tension in my jaw. He couldn't be serious. He couldn't honestly be telling her that she was unimportant while in the same breath asking her for a favor.

But the way James's gaze faltered told me that was exactly what he was doing.

And again, absolutely fucking not. She might be short but no way was I going to let this turnip of a man make her feel small. I didn't care who he was.

It took me a good second or two to wrangle my rage enough to unclench my jaw and speak. "Unfortunately, you're wrong on both counts. We weren't doing fine without her and no, we can't spare her a week. James isn't available to help with your event. Good luck figuring out how to do fine without her, I think you'll need it. She'll call you back after when she has a minute."

"Probably not," James muttered as I hung up the phone and handed it back to her. She stared at it a moment and then pushed to her feet, tucking the phone into the pocket of her denim cutoffs. "I can't believe you did that."

"I can't believe he's asking you to come back. You've only been here a week."

"It's a show Blue Skies hosts every year. I usually take care of all the details." She toed the dirt with her sneaker. "Maybe I could figure something out."

I crossed my arms. "No, you won't. I meant what I said, James. You have a job to do here and we need you to do it."

Her eyes searched my face. "Okay," she said softly. And then grinned.

Something ached inside my chest. I'd have that conversation with her dad every damn day if it meant her looking at me like that.

The warmth of that smile soaked into me, making my voice deepen when I said, "Need any help with that oil change, buttercup?"

"Nah, I've got it." She scooped the bottle of synthetic oil by her feet and leaned over the engine, giving me an excellent view that made me bite my fist. "What are you doing here, anyway?"

"I—" It was hard to remember anything with that perky ass issuing an invitation I knew damn well not to accept. I looked around, reminding myself of the task at hand. "I've got a list of things that need to be fixed.

Figured I'd swing by and see if you had anything to add for your cabin now that you've lived in it for a week."

"You're working?"

"Yeah, buttercup." I tilted the brim of my hat with my thumb. "This isn't a social call."

"It's Sunday."

"I'm aware."

"You worked yesterday, too. I saw you training with the cows." There was a gentle accusation in her voice.

I grunted. She'd get to her point eventually. Sooner rather than later, I hoped.

She straightened and wiped her hands on the rag dangling from her back pocket. "Your dad said Lodestar Ranch takes weekends seriously."

I guffawed. "He would say that."

She cocked her head. "He doesn't mean it?"

"Oh, he means it. But unfortunately some of us have to be grown-ups. Horses don't care if it's the weekend. They want their grain fed to them and their shit shoveled every day of the week. Can't say that I blame them for that, either. The stable hands work five days a week. That's their contract. But I'm the owner's son. I don't get that same leeway."

Her brows furrowed. "Your dad makes you work seven days a week?"

"He doesn't make me. It's how things shake out, that's all. If I didn't do it, it wouldn't get done."

"Hm."

Amazing how much meaning she managed to pack into that one little syllable. "What?" I asked.

She shrugged. "Maybe some things don't need to get done. I mean, you don't *have* to be here now. Right? Don't get me wrong, it's so nice of you to make sure I have what I need, and I'm grateful, truly. But you could just assume everything is fine until I tell you it's not. That would take at least one task off your plate. I don't want to be the reason you're working on a Sunday."

"It's no trouble," I said. The truth was, it was the highlight of my day.

"Hm," she said again.

I leaned against the SUV, settling in for the conversation. Enjoying myself, though I wasn't going to tell her that. "What?" I prodded.

"Each little thing on its own might be no trouble, but when there's dozens of them, it becomes trouble real quick. When I saw you working Crackerjack yesterday, I thought to myself, *now there's a man who loves his job*. It was such a joy to watch."

A pretty wash of pink bloomed on her cheeks. Her eyes darted from mine and her tongue peeked out to wet her lower lip. My focus zeroed in, watching the movement with avid interest. Why was she blushing?

"I do love my job," I answered. Then took a beat to consider because she wasn't wrong about it all adding up to something heavy. "Mostly."

She smiled. "Right. *Mostly*. And I would hate to see that love slowly drained from you at the weight of all these self-appointed troubles. Even though you say they're no trouble, everyone deserves a break."

"I didn't say they're no trouble. I said *you're* no trouble. Some of these chores...well, it's not how I would necessarily choose to spend a Sunday morning."

The flush on her cheeks deepened. Damn, I liked it more than I should, knowing it was my words that had caused it. She was my employee. I had no business making her blush.

"But it *is* your choice. I—" She broke off with a shake of her head. "Sorry. I'm overstepping. It's none of my business."

"Let's hear it." I waved a hand at her to continue. James had been here all of one week. She thought she had the answers? I was more than willing to hear her out...and then tell her how wrong she was.

She peered at me sheepishly from beneath her dark fringe of eyelashes. "You don't think I'm a nosy asshole?"

"Oh, that's definitely what I think," I assured her.

She laughed and swatted my arm. Like we were friends or something. I liked it.

"I was thinking, your dad..." She worried her bottom lip with her teeth. "I know he hasn't done much of the day-to-day barn chores and responsibilities since your mom passed—"

"He hasn't done *any*," I interjected. Not to throw him under the bus, but because it was true.

She nodded. "Well, maybe he's ready for that to change. I saw him hanging around the barn the other day, looking for something to do. Have you talked to him about getting back to work?"

"No, I—" It hadn't occurred to me that Dad might be ready to come back. He'd sobered up months ago, and since then he'd spent his time taking care of Ben and running the house. "I don't want to pressure him. When he's ready, he'll tell me."

"Sure," she said doubtfully. I raised my eyebrows in question and she shrugged. "Maybe he's embarrassed. Maybe he doesn't want to step on your toes. Maybe he's worried you don't trust him anymore. There's lots of reasons men don't talk."

I frowned at my boots and rubbed my chest. Dad had been at the barn more than usual this past month. I hadn't thought much about it, but maybe I should have. Shit.

I thought about it now. I thought about it after I left James to what remained of her Sunday and I kept right on thinking about it as I joined Ben and Dad for dinner.

"I was thinking I might take Ben fishing tomorrow morning," I said casually as we tucked into spaghetti. "Think you could take the morning chores?"

There was a quiet pause during which I cursed James and her interference. Why was I taking advice from someone who had only been here a week, anyway? Dad wasn't—

"I could do that."

At his soft words, I looked up from my plate. He grinned.

"I thought you'd never ask."

13

James

"You really gonna do this?" Ben asked. Ever my constant companion, he had climbed up on the rail to watch me work. "You're gonna get on Belle?"

"Oh, I'm definitely going to get on. The question is how I get off." I laughed, but quickly stopped when I saw the look of genuine fear on Ben's face. "Hey, don't worry, bud. Falling off is part of my job as a trainer. You've seen people get thrown before, right? I'm going to be okay."

He nodded. I clipped a lead rope to Belle's halter and led her to the mounting block. With a steady breath, I swung my right leg over Belle's bare back and settled my weight behind her withers. Belle lifted her head. I breathed. Once. Twice. Then I dismounted and clucked my tongue as I tugged gently on the lead rope, walking her in another circle.

"You did it, James," Ben breathed. "You rode Belle."

The moment had left me almost giddy, but I knew we weren't there yet. "That wasn't riding. That was sitting on her back. It was a good start, though."

"I'm texting my dad. He needs to see this."

I nodded even though I had the feeling Adam wasn't going to be half as impressed as his son. This was progress—*huge* progress—but we still had a long way to go.

On our second loop around the ring, we once again stopped at the mounting block. I stayed on a beat or two longer before sliding off again and making a third loop around the ring.

Adam appeared for our third try, his arms crossed over his chest, brow furrowed as he watched us silently. A week ago, I would have taken that as disapproval, but now I understood him a little better. Resting Grump Face. He wasn't mean, he was thoughtful. Careful.

Unfortunately, he was also hot. I had to work extra hard not to fidget on Belle's back as he stared at us beneath his dark brows.

On our fourth try, Belle stopped at the block without me asking her to. This time, hoping I wasn't pushing my luck, I squeezed my calves against her belly and clucked my tongue, urging her forward. At first she didn't move. I squeezed again, clucked again, and she stepped forward.

"Good girl," I said, rewarding her with a pat on the neck.

She gave her head a shake and nickered. We ambled around the ring, following the fence like we had before. I didn't have anything to guide her except my legs and the lead rope, but my smart girl had figured out the routine by now. We came to the mounting block and I gave the rope a gentle tug, sinking my weight into my seat and leaning back. She got the message and stopped.

When I slid off, I wrapped my arms around her neck and scratched exactly where she liked it. "You're going to get so many carrots," I promised.

Ben whooped and I laughed. I chanced a peek at Adam, who shook his head slowly, like he couldn't believe what he had witnessed. At least, that was how I took it.

"I'm going to tell Gramps!" Ben said and took off for the big house.

I busied myself with Belle, pretending I didn't care that Adam hadn't said a single word. "I know we have a lot of work to do—"

"You did good," he cut me off gruffly. "You've made more progress in two weeks than we've made in two years."

I beamed. God, I was such a sucker for head pats. "I

think her problem has to do with the tack. It can be a long process, getting the right fit for everything."

"Could be so. We never got far enough in the process to isolate the issue. She never gave anyone a chance, once they were in the saddle. You're the first one stupid enough to try to ride her bareback with no bridle."

I might have taken offense to that if his whole face hadn't brightened. Lightened. Good lord, the man was smiling. Full on *smiling*. At *me*. And it was every bit as dangerous to my well-being as I had suspected it might be.

He was *gorgeous*.

"Where do we go from here?" he asked.

Straight to hell, I thought. *Where bad girls go for lusting after their boss.*

"I mean, what's your next step with Belle?" he clarified, when I stared at him like an idiot.

"Oh, right. Well, I think we need to keep moving forward slowly and really be thoughtful about it. If her issue isn't having someone on her back, we need to isolate the problem. Tomorrow I'll—"

My words cut off as an SUV pulled up and a man stepped out. Adam went rigid, his smile replaced by another frown. And this time it wasn't simply Resting Grump Face. He scowled like he meant it.

"Adam." The man touched the brim of his baseball hat.

Adam stood with his barrel thighs wide, arms crossed over his chest, scowl firmly in place. "Deacon," he grunted.

My eyes darted between the two men nervously. Even Belle felt the tension.

"Would have called first, but I didn't want to have this conversation twice," Deacon said. He rubbed the back of his neck and squinted at the sky. "It sucks."

"Yeah," Adam agreed, and I wondered how he knew that. Was this conversation a long time coming?

Whatever else it was or wasn't, this moment was private, that much was clear. I turned to lead Belle back through the barn to the paddock out back for some well-deserved turnout, but Adam's gaze cut to me and stopped me cold. I didn't know how he felt about having an audience for this conversation, but something in his face made me reluctant to leave him alone. If he wanted me gone, he was going to have to ask.

Deacon looked at me, clearly wondering why the hell I was still standing here.

"She stays," Adam gritted.

Well. That settled that.

"Emily left some things," Deacon said. He kept his face averted, never quite looking Adam in the eye. "Photos. Those watercolors she did. Journals. A letter—" His voice cracked.

Adam stared at him, waiting out the man's obvious pain without a single word.

Deacon's throat worked as he swallowed hard. "She wrote him a letter. Made me promise to give it to him when he's fifteen. She figured that was old enough."

"He's only eleven," Adam said roughly, and I realized that the *he* Deacon referred to was Ben.

"I won't be here when he's fifteen. I'm moving on. I got a job in Washington. It's time. This town is too—" He broke off again and shook his head. "I'm leaving it in your care. I don't know what it says. She sealed it shut. But she wanted him to have it. She's his mom, he has the right—"

"I'll give it to him," Adam bit out. "The journals?"

Deacon looked to the ground. "She said she didn't care who read them, but the only person who can destroy them is Ben. I read them. It's all...it's all there. The whole mess of it. It's probably too much for a kid to understand, but when he's older, if he wants to know his mom, her words and feelings are right there." He lifted his head, for the first time meeting Adam's gaze head on. "She wasn't unfaithful to you."

"She loved *you*." Adam's voice shook with helpless fury. I sucked in a sharp breath, wanting to go to him, comfort him somehow, knowing I shouldn't. Couldn't.

"Physically," Deacon amended. "She wasn't *physically* unfaithful to you. I don't know if that makes it better."

Adam tilted his head, looking like he was actually mulling that over. "No," he said. "It doesn't."

"Yeah." Deacon looked away. "How's her boy?"

Despite the fact that I was one hundred percent on Adam's side, even without knowing what the hell was going on, my heart cracked at the look on Deacon's face. Ben meant something to him.

Adam must have seen it too, because his eyes flickered with a hint of compassion. "He's good," he said gruffly. There was a pause while something battled inside him, and he sounded almost angry when he said, "You want to see him?"

Deacon jerked in surprise. "Yeah?"

Adam nodded. "He doesn't know about you. He knows his mom and I weren't together when she passed, but I didn't...I figured it didn't matter. All he needs to know is that his mom loved him."

Deacon nodded. "I—"

He was interrupted by Ben himself running out.

"Gramps can't believe you rode Belle! He says—" He came to a sudden halt as he caught sight of Deacon.

Adam pulled him against his side. "Ben, I want you to meet a friend of your mom's. This is Deacon."

Ben's eyes went wide. "You knew my mom?" he asked eagerly.

"Sure did." Deacon glanced at Adam and then back to Ben. "I knew you, too, when you were a baby. I've got some pictures of the two of you. You and your mom. Your dad will give them to you."

"Are you in the picture too?" Ben asked.

Deacon's lips tilted up, but he looked sad. He shook his head. "No. I was the one holding the camera."

Adam's grip must have tightened on Ben's shoulder, because Ben suddenly looked at his dad's hand and then up at his face. His expression turned far too assessing for an eleven year old.

"I gotta see about my watermelons. Nice to meet you!" He pulled free of Adam's hold and zoomed off.

Deacon stared after him. "He's got a lot of his mom in his face."

"Yeah," Adam acknowledged.

"Well." Deacon cleared his throat. "I've got a box in my truck."

When Emily's box was in Adam's possession, Deacon didn't waste time in getting the hell out.

For a moment Adam stood rooted to the spot, the box in his arms, staring into nothingness. I wondered what he saw. I doubted it was anything good.

"Adam?"

He blinked like he had forgotten I was there. He shook his head. "I need a drink."

14

Adam

THERE HAD to be alcohol in here somewhere.

I shoved open the door to my office, kicked it closed behind me, and looked around. The desk, probably. I set the box of Emily's stuff in the corner and went to investigate.

Before I had taken over Lodestar Ranch, this had been Dad's office. He had put on a good show the first couple weeks after Mom's death, showing up here every day to "work." By evening he would stumble home, smelling of liquor, and pass out on the couch. I was willing to bet there was still a bottle or two somewhere.

The bottom drawer was the obvious answer. It was locked and I had never opened it. I located the key from the middle drawer, turned the lock, and bingo. Whiskey. And a nice glass to go with it. Good ol' Dad.

I poured a finger's worth into the tumbler and tossed it back in one gulp right as the door opened and James slid inside. The whiskey burned, but its heat couldn't reach the coldest parts inside me. I needed more. Two fingers, this time.

"You here for a drink, buttercup?" I glanced at her as I poured.

She glanced at the clock on the wall, registering the fact that it was not yet noon. "No."

I shrugged. "Suit yourself. I don't mind drinking alone."

"You're not alone." She closed the door quietly behind her.

I leaned my hips against the edge of the desk, crossed one leg over the other, and eyed her over the rim of my whiskey glass as she came closer. "You offering to keep me company?"

There was an invitation in my tone that shouldn't have been there. Fucking whiskey.

For once she wasn't smiling. She took the chair in front of me, folded her knees up to her chest, and looked at me with those big brown eyes that saw far too much. "What was that all about? With Deacon?"

I grunted into my whiskey. I never talked about Emily. Never. Out of respect for Ben, I kept my mouth sealed tight. But fuck, I had a lot to say. And right now, I wanted to say it to *her*. I could probably blame that on the whiskey, too.

"We were high school sweethearts, Emily and me. She was...shit, she was the love of my life. From the moment I saw her, I knew I was going to marry her. That was when I was fourteen. Same age my dad met my mom, so that made sense to me. When we graduated high school, I stuck around here in Aspen Springs. She went to the University of Colorado in Boulder."

James propped her chin on her knees, listening, nothing but compassion in her eyes even as I took another sip.

"I had my whole life planned out and I was thrilled about it. Work the ranch with my dad. Take over the breeding program. Marry Emily when she graduated. Have a couple kids. Live happily ever after. Step by step, I did all that." I laughed. Not a happy sound, judging from her flinch. "Well, except the happily-ever-after part. I didn't do that."

I stared at the amber fluid, swirling it around the glass, seeing how it caught the light. "I used to visit her on weekends. She had a friend. Deacon."

James sucked in a breath.

"Yeah." I shook my head. God, how stupid was I? Thinking they were just friends. "We hung out a few times. I could tell he had a thing for her, but I was so sure she loved me. So sure our story would be just like my parents. I didn't doubt her for a second."

I fell silent, remembering what Deacon had told me only moments ago. She wasn't unfaithful to me, physically. She hadn't slept with Deacon while we were together. But still...she had loved him even then, hadn't she? Why hadn't she made a clean break back then, before marriage and a kid made everything messy? I glanced at the box in the corner. How badly did I want to know?

Not enough to find out, I decided. Why torture myself with reading how my wife fell in love with another man?

"She graduated. We got married. Deacon moved to town right when she got pregnant with Ben. It was a hard pregnancy. She was sick for most of it, but her doctors told us it was perfectly normal. It wasn't until after Ben was born and she kept right on feeling sick that we discovered the cause wasn't pregnancy at all. It was cancer."

"Oh, god, Adam. I'm so sorry."

James leaned forward and touched the outside of my leg, right at the knee. I stared down at her hand, so tiny against my leg. It was an oddly intimate gesture, but it felt right somehow. I could feel the heat of her palm through my jeans. It sank into my skin, burning as hot as the whiskey in my throat.

She squeezed and then released my knee, leaving me cold again. I frowned.

"Stage four. There was no question it would kill her. It was only a question of when. The doctors told us it could be weeks or months or, if she was really lucky, a year. I spent the next month dragging her to specialists all over the country, but they all told us the same thing. Finally she put a stop to it. She didn't want to spend what time she had left searching for a miracle. She wanted to spend it living. With the people she loved."

I could tell from the way James's entire body tensed that she suddenly understood where this was going.

"I came home one day to find her bags were packed and ready by the door. She told me..." I gripped the glass so tightly I could almost feel it start to give way beneath my fingers. "She told me she couldn't die as my wife. Her heart belonged to Deacon and it was time the rest of her did to."

Her plush mouth went slack. "What did you do?"

"I drove her to Deacon's, of course. I sure as fuck wasn't going to let that asshole step foot on my property. She lived another fifteen months. Long enough to get that divorce she wanted and die with his name. She wanted Ben with her full-time for as long as she could have him. I agreed to that, knowing what was coming."

I paused, remembering. That had damn near killed

me, parting from Ben. Deacon, being a decent human being despite his wife-stealing tendencies, had made it easier on me by bringing Ben to a park every day so I could spend an hour or so with my boy.

"That lasted only a couple months before her body wore down to the point she couldn't care for a baby. Ben came home with me, and I brought him to her every day for a visit. Sometimes only five minutes before she was in too much pain or fell asleep again."

"Oh, Adam," James said softly.

"A love like that only happens once in a lifetime. That's what my dad says. It was true for him. I figure it's true for me, too." My god, I had loved Emily. Even at the end. "Kinda sucks that my once-in-a-lifetime love was nothing more than an obstacle in theirs."

James pushed to her feet with so much force that the chair went rolling across the room behind her. "That's bullshit, Adam. *Bullshit*. Humans have an infinite capacity for love. And we're not static. We grow. We change. *Love* changes us. The person you were then? The person who loved Emily? He's not here. Loving her changed you. How could it not? My god, Adam. You went through hell. The person you were then, he had his once-in-a-lifetime love, and you're right. That sucked. But you're not him anymore. The man you are now still gets a shot."

She probably meant that to be encouraging. It wasn't. It was terrifying. Holy shit, I had barely survived love once. No way in hell was I looking to try that again.

I had no interest in love.

But the woman standing in front of me, smelling like hay and vanilla, had my attention. Maybe it was the way she looked at me. Like I was something worth looking at.

Or maybe I was kidding myself. She's had my attention since the moment I heard her laugh in the coffee shop. Warm and full. She was like the sun. The closer I got to her orbit, the warmer I felt. And I was so fucking cold. Cold and empty.

Which was why with one quick motion, I captured her arm at the elbow and pulled her into my space. When I parted my thighs to bring her closer, she fell forward against my body, catching herself with a hand against my chest.

Our hips lined up together, my cock against her belly. Her fingers curled into my shirt as she arched her head back to look at me. Those doe eyes searched my face. Thinking. Assessing.

I didn't want to think. I wanted to burn.

With one hand still holding her elbow, I slid my other hand behind her neck to cup the back of her head. Held her steady as I pressed my mouth to hers. Completely fell apart when she welcomed me in.

I slid my tongue against hers. She whimpered into my mouth and I greedily swallowed the sweet little sounds, letting them heat me up inside. Felt myself slowly thaw like a winter garden inching toward spring.

Her hands slid up over my chest, leaving trails of fire on my neck, coming to rest on my cheeks, her fingertips digging into my skull. Now we were both holding on like we were afraid the other one might let go.

I had no intention of letting go first.

I couldn't remember the last time I had kissed a woman like this. Felt a woman touch me like this. The intimacy of it jolted me awake, like I had been sleepwalking until she breathed her warmth into me. I soaked it up. Asked for more. Grabbed a handful of that sweet ass of hers and ground my hardening cock against her. She pushed back almost frantically.

And then I felt her smile against my mouth.

Like she was *happy*. Like she didn't know I was too fucking wounded to make anyone happy.

Fucking hell, what was I *doing*?

I wrenched my mouth away. Grabbed her by the biceps and pushed her off me. She stared at me as I slid away from her body. Her hair was mussed from my hands, her lips all puffy and wet, her eyes dreamy. I almost reached for her again, but she deserved better than that so I kept my hands to myself.

"I shouldn't have done that," I said, knowing it was the wrong thing to say even if it was true.

"I beg your pardon?"

"My mind was...in a bad place. The whiskey..." Like any of it excused my behavior.

"Oh." She blinked away the glassiness in her eyes. "Right. No, I get it. You were caught up in your feelings about your ex-wife, and you kissed me. A surrogate for what you couldn't have, I guess."

There was a bite to her words. *Hurt.* My brow furrowed. I had lost my fucking mind, no doubt about that, but one thing I was certain of was that I had not been thinking about Emily when I put my mouth on James.

"James—"

"Don't," she said. "You were vulnerable and I...I should have known better. I don't know what I was thinking. That wasn't what you needed."

I stared at her. What was James apologizing for? She hadn't done anything wrong.

I tried to find the words to tell her that. I wasn't fast enough. She slipped out the door, shutting it quietly behind her.

Leaving me cold again.

15

James

CHLOE

Your cowboy was the scowliest I've ever seen him this morning. What did you do to him?

JAMES

He's not my cowboy. He's my boss.

CHLOE

Maybe that's the problem. The cowboy in the streets needs a little time being a beast in your sheets.

JAMES

I'm not going to dignify that with a response.

CHLOE

Dignity, schmigity. I'm beneath that.

How could I have been so wrong?

The man had needed a hug, not a mouth mauling. But I hadn't been able to see that through my lust-fueled glasses. Worse, it hadn't been only lust. I had thought we were having a moment. A connection. When really he was having a moment with his dead ex-wife.

Humiliating.

So I did what I always did when life had the audacity to screw with me. I held my chin up and focused on the horses.

And I avoided Adam like the plague.

Which proved surprisingly easy for the first two days post kiss. He did his thing, I did mine. Hell, he probably thought *he* was the one avoiding *me*. For some reason, that annoyed me. What was he so afraid of? Did he think I was going to corner him in his office again and force him into round three of humiliating mouth encounters?

Now that I had determined Belle wasn't truly opposed to riding, per se, I narrowed my focus to her tack, starting with the saddle. Plenty of horses were less than thrilled with having the girth cinched tight around their belly. Unfortunately, that was a safety concern for the rider, so it was non-negotiable.

But that didn't mean we couldn't make it more comfortable for her.

I examined Belle's saddle carefully. It was in good shape, and I could tell the fit wasn't the issue—it had been sized appropriately for her back and shape.

"Heard you managed to stay on Belle."

I looked up from the saddle to see Steven leaning against the doorframe of the tack room, arms crossed. "You heard right."

"We should celebrate. You ever been to the Painted Cat?"

I shook my head.

"It's the good bar in town."

"As opposed to the bad bar?" I asked.

He grinned. "Now, honey, I don't think there's any such thing as a bad bar. So long as there's alcohol, I ain't picky. But it does have the benefit of being walking distance from my house."

If that was an invitation, I wasn't biting. I didn't like being called honey. I probably shouldn't like being called buttercup, either, but somehow that felt entirely different. I suspected it had to do with the man.

Steven was plenty good-looking. He had that whole tall, dark, and handsome thing nailed down. But he reminded me of a babbling brook. Lots of noise without a whole lot going on beneath the surface. He didn't pull me in deeper.

Unlike a certain grumpy rancher.

Maybe I was misreading the situation with Steven. It wouldn't be the first time this week I had thought a man was into me when his mind was somewhere else. Maybe he wasn't asking for a date. Maybe he was arranging a group outing. I wouldn't say no to that.

"What do you say? You and me? A date?" he said.

Well, that clarified things.

"That's not a good idea. We work together. If you ever want to get a group together and go out as friends, I'd be down." I hated rejecting anyone, but I had learned long ago that if you weren't blunt and quick about it, you could end up accidentally dating a meh guy for three solid months.

Steven cocked an eyebrow. "There's no rule against us dating, honey."

Apparently he wasn't good at taking hints. Shocking. "I'm not interested in dating a co-worker," I said firmly.

"Calm down. No need to go all *me too*." He laughed like he truly believed he was funny and held up his hands as if pacifying a filly having a tantrum. "If you want a group thing, I can make that happen. A friendly get-together."

I was already regretting leaving the door open for friendship. I stared at him, eyebrows raised.

"Tonight?" he prodded.

"Not tonight," came a voice I had been avoiding for two days now. It could not be denied that I was happier than I ought to be to hear that voice again.

Steven fell forward into the room with a little help from Adam. He caught himself and sent an annoyed look behind him. "My mama always taught me to say excuse me."

"And my mama taught me not to stand in doorways like a jackass."

His words were for Steven but his gaze was on me. Scowling, of course. It did things to me, that scowl. Unfeminist, horny things.

I tossed my ponytail and smiled like the tension in the room didn't have my insides quivering. "Steven and I were just talking about getting a group together for drinks at the Painted Cat. You want to come?"

"Brax wants us at Colorado Springs for the rodeo this weekend. We're leaving in an hour." He ripped his gaze from me and narrowed it on Steven. "Don't you have things to do?"

Steven slid out of the room, muttering something under his breath that I doubted was very friendly.

"I'll go pack." I moved toward the door, but Adam's hand shot out and lassoed my wrist.

"Wait." I looked up at him, but he kept his gaze on that connection—his hand, my wrist—like it was a lifeline. "Has Ben said anything to you? About...stuff?"

"Stuff?" I echoed. It didn't take me long to figure out what he meant. "Do you mean Emily?"

His fingers spasmed on my wrist at the sound of her name. I hated that. Hated that she still had this power over him, all these years later. Which was stupid. Why should I care if my boss was hung up on his deceased ex-wife? I had no business kissing him anyway. That was no way to earn the respect of my co-workers.

"Yeah. I figured he'd have questions after meeting Deacon, but he hasn't said a word. I know you're not his nanny, okay? I know that. It's just that—"

"I'm his friend," I cut in softly. Because it was true.

His gaze jerked to mine. He reflected for a beat and then everything softened. His lips, his forehead, his attitude. "Yeah. You're his friend. So I figured, he might have talked to you about it. He didn't talk to me." His voice dipped gruffly on the admission.

I had zero parenting experience, but I had enough experience as a human being to know it didn't feel great when the person you loved most in the world kept you at arm's length. I also knew that box was still sitting unopened in Adam's office. Men were such cowards when it came to feelings.

"Have you tried talking to him?" I asked. Gently, because men were also sensitive about their cowardice.

He rubbed his jaw. I took that as a no.

"He didn't say anything to me about Deacon or his mom," I said. "But he's thinking about it. He's seen the box in your office. It has her name on it. He's waiting for you."

"Dammit." He sighed. "I was afraid of that."

I hesitated, not wanting to overstep. "I'm not a parent—"

"Tell me what you think. I'll take all the advice I can get. All I care about is making things good for Ben."

God. The way this man loved his son would kick anyone's ovaries into baby-making mode.

"It doesn't have to be fraught, you know," I said. "Tell him you haven't had time to go through the pictures with him, but you'll do it when you get back from the rodeo. It will buy you some time to think about what you want to say—which doesn't have to be much, you know. A story or two about her from before he was born. Something sweet or silly." I fully realized I was avoiding saying *her* name again. I didn't want a repeat of the hand flinch. Men weren't the only cowards, apparently.

He nodded slowly. "That's good. I can do that."

"Of course you can."

"Okay. I'm going to find him and then pack." He nodded again, like he was trying to convince himself. "Meet me at the big house in an hour?"

I had a lot of questions about our rodeo trip, but what I led with was "Just you and me?" Like that was the important part.

"Just you and me. Brax wants us out there, showing people who matter that you're at Lodestar Ranch now. Networking." He spat the word like it tasted bad. "He had business cards made for you. We have to swing by his office in town on the way out. He booked us rooms at the Marriot."

"Okay." I couldn't stop the grin from spreading across my face. "I love rodeos. This will be great."

"Yeah. Great," he repeated flatly.

I cocked my head, taking him in. The purple halfmoons under his eyes. The heavy down-tilt of his mouth. The way his shoulders bunched up to his ears.

The man was tired. *Exhausted.*

It couldn't be easy, running a ranch, being a single dad, and taking care of his own dad on top of all that. And then Deacon showing up three days ago with a box full of ugly memories? That had to keep him up at night. Otherwise he wasn't human.

A weekend rodeo probably seemed like one more

thing he had to soldier through. I hated that for him. Sure, we were going there for work, but rodeos were fun! Only a week ago he had told me he missed the fun of ranch work, the kind he used to have before his mom died. This was a chance for us to get away from the regular grind of barn chores and have a good time. And maybe, for Adam, to get some much-needed rest.

"How long is the drive?" I asked.

"Three hours."

His lips were already forming the next words, but I got there first.

"I'll drive."

16

James

JAMES

We're swinging by Jo's on our way to Colorado Springs. Do me a favor. When we order coffee, make Adam's decaf.

CHLOE

Decaf?! That's a violation of the Barista's Oath, babe.

JAMES

Just do it.

CHLOE

Fine. But in return, I want you to do something for me.

JAMES

What's that?

CHLOE

Save a horse, James. Save so many horses.

"You've got to be kidding me," Adam said.

The apologetic look on the hotel receptionist's face indicated that he was not, in fact, kidding. "I'm sorry, sir. We're booked solid for the rodeo. As I explained on the phone when Mr. Hale made the reservation, this is the last room available. You are welcome to try your luck at other hotels, of course."

"This is fine," I said hastily. No way was I going to risk forfeiting the only bed left in Colorado Springs. Would it be easy sleeping next to the man I wanted to climb like a wisteria vine? No. But I would be a professional about it if it killed me. I needed to focus on why we were here, that's all.

"Fucking Brax," Adam muttered. "Nice of him to give us a head's up."

Brax was no idiot. "So you could yell at him for something outside his control?" I asked.

"Exactly."

He was rumpled from his two-and-a-half-hour nap. His hair stuck up at weird angles and there was a red crease along his right cheekbone from where his head had fallen against the seatbelt. I grinned.

He had fought it, but I had won. The decaf coffee Chloe had handed him with a bored expression that gave nothing away hadn't been up to the task of keeping him awake when I was determined to put him to sleep. With my Willie Nelson playlist crooning through the car speakers, the back windows rolled down to let in the warm, dry breeze, and me droning on about hoof oil, Adam was dead asleep in thirty minutes.

The poor man never stood a chance.

"Let's drop our bags in our room and go meet Zack for dinner," I suggested. Zack had texted Adam shortly before he passed out. We were meeting him for dinner tonight. Tomorrow he had the roping event and then the next day was his bareback bronc ride. He was a top contender for both.

We were on the twelfth floor with a great view overlooking the city. In the distance, enormous red rock formations jutted toward the sky.

"Wow," I breathed. I dropped my bag next to the bed and went straight to the window.

Adam peered out the window from behind me.

"Garden of the Gods. We can go Sunday before we head back home if we have time."

I couldn't get enough of the way the setting sun made the rocks glow like fresh lava. "We'll make time," I promised myself.

I turned away from the window to take in the rest of the room. One queen-size bed. A desk with a rolling chair. No couch.

Welp.

"I'll take the floor," Adam said.

"Okay," I said agreeably, even though I would never in a million years do that to him. The carpet felt thick enough under my feet, but under his back it might as well be a plank of wood. Anyway, all hotels were a little bit gross, even the nice ones. You could boil sheets. You couldn't boil a carpet.

But there was no point in having the same fight twice. We could save that conversation for after dinner.

"I'm going to change in the bathroom," I said. I had taken a quick shower before we hit the road, so I didn't smell like a horse, but I was wearing my standard road trip outfit of leggings and an old Maren Morris tee shirt that proclaimed me a "lunatic country music person."

I brought my bag into the bathroom. "Casual or fancy?" I hollered through the closed door.

"Casual," he called back.

"Good. I didn't bring a lot of fancy."

I settled for a sundress with a flirty hem that hit me just above the knees. It was meant to hit around mid-thigh, but given my height issues, things tended to run long on me. The elevation in Colorado Springs meant even summer nights could be chilly, so I paired that with a chunky cream-colored cardigan with big wood buttons. After a swipe of mascara and a slick of pink lipstick, I walked out of the bathroom barefoot.

His gaze raked over me, quick and greedy, before he wrenched his eyes away, his mouth flattening into a grim line. "Shoes on, buttercup," he growled. "Let's go."

"Okay," I said, like his hungry perusal of my body hadn't turned my insides into something hot and liquid. Totally chill and unaffected, that was me.

Lies. All lies.

I grabbed my socks and boots and shoved my feet into them. "I'm ready."

ZACK HALE WAS the polar opposite of his older brother. Where Adam was scowls and grunts, Zack was smiles and charm. Like his brothers, he had the Hale blue eyes and jawline that could rival the Rocky Mountains for rugged strength. But his hair was a lighter brown, shot through with warm honey, and he had a dimple that promised a good time.

And good lord, the man was a flirt.

"Heard you had some trouble at the hotel," Zack said as we all sat down at a corner booth. His blue eyes were the picture of faux concern. "You can shack up with me for the night."

"Thanks, but I'd rather take the floor than share a bed with you," Adam said drily. "I spent enough nights sleeping in a tent with you to know you kick like a donkey."

"I wasn't talking to you," Zack said. "The offer was for James."

Adam's face darkened like a storm moving over the mountains. Zack leaned back and flashed me a wink, clearly delighted at having gotten under his brother's skin.

"Thanks," I said. "But I'm happy where I am."

Zack's eyebrows shot up. My cheeks heated as I realized he took my words to mean I was happy to sleep with *Adam*. "Is that so?" he smirked.

"For fuck's sake, Zack," Adam said, exasperated. "I'm taking the floor."

"I didn't even have to rock, paper, scissors him for the bed," I chimed in. "He was a perfect gentleman about it."

A cowboy in the streets, a beast in the sheets.

Maybe Chloe had it right. Too bad I was never going to find out. I hid my blush behind a sip of my vodka soda. Damn Chloe and her agenda to get me laid. When I had opened the white paper bag she had given us with our coffee, I had found a handful of condoms in there with the muffins. Fortunately, I had managed to sneak them into my bag before Adam could see.

I had no intention of saving a horse this weekend. Especially not with a cowboy who was still hung up on his deceased ex-wife.

WE MADE IT AN EARLY NIGHT—ZACK, for all his bad boy vibes, took his rodeo work seriously and needed his sleep—and were back in our room by 9:30. I claimed the bathroom first to brush my teeth and change into my pajamas, which consisted of a flimsy tee shirt and tiny shorts. I kept my sports bra on, even though I was dying to shed it.

By the time I was ready for bed, Adam had put a

pillow and blanket on the floor. The second he headed into the bathroom, I returned them to the bed.

Predictably, he scowled when he saw what I had done. "James—"

"Hear me out." I held up a hand. "If waking up with a sore back is something you enjoy, fine. Sleep on the floor. I won't stop you. But if you're doing it to save my reputation or for whatever stupid notions of chivalry are in your brain, just don't. We're adults. I can sleep next to you the same way I would sleep next to Chloe if this happened. I trust you."

"I'm taking the floor," he ground out.

My eyes narrowed. Maybe this wasn't about whether I trusted him. Maybe *he* didn't trust *me*. "Is this about Emily?"

He stared at me like I was speaking gibberish. "What?"

"Because of what happened in your office. You think I can't keep my hands to myself? That's ridiculous. It doesn't matter that you look like *that*"—I gestured wildly at his stupidly muscular body— "and it doesn't matter that kissing you pretty much melted all my brain cells. I understand that no means no."

He kept right on staring at me while I babbled like an idiot.

"I'm not worried about you, James. I'm worried

about me. Because you're wearing those sexy fucking shorts and seventy percent of your body is wearing nothing at all. That's a lot of uncovered skin and at some point, that skin is going to come into contact with my skin."

"Oh," I said.

"That's not even the worst part."

"What's the worst part?" I asked.

"When that happens, I'm going to do the right thing. I'm going to keep my hands to myself. And fuck, that's going to hurt."

"Oh," I sighed.

"Yeah," he said. "*Oh.*" He looked at the floor and shook his head. "I guess I'd rather have an aching cock than an aching back. Get in bed, buttercup."

I scooted under the covers and he came in after me, flicking out the light of the bedside table lamp as we settled in.

"James," he said suddenly. "That kiss in my office, that wasn't about Emily, either."

I rolled on my side to face him, but I couldn't make out his expression in the dark. "It wasn't?"

"No. I kissed you because I was cold and you are the fucking sun."

I couldn't speak. Couldn't breathe.

But I could stretch my hand to find his in the darkness between us. Twine my fingers with his.

So that's what I did.

17

Adam

I WAS RIGHT. An aching dick was much better than an aching back.

But god *damn*.

I woke up with James's sweet body flush against my torso. Her face pressed against my chest and one of her legs was hitched over my hip like she was trying to climb me like a tree. My very hard, very achy dick was notched snuggly against her belly.

Morning wood with James was a very different thing than generic morning wood. This wood had *purpose*. Intent. And with the object of its desire plastered against me, I doubted it was going to dissipate on its own.

Still asleep, James made an adorable grumbly sound, like something annoyed her. She shifted slightly and I realized the thing that had disturbed her slumber was probably my very hard dick poking her in the stomach. Before I could rectify the situation, her hand slipped between our bodies and grabbed my dick. Full on *grabbed* it.

The sane part of me knew she had only meant to push me away, she wasn't really going to jack me off in her sleep, but the desperate, achy part of me hoped for the best.

She squeezed, her dainty fingers flexing around me, the thin cotton of my boxers doing nothing to shield me from the warmth of her hand. My hips bucked involuntarily and she came fully awake. Her eyes popped open.

I could feel every muscle in her entire body clench as she assessed the situation. She released my dick and gave it a friendly little pat, like it was a puppy she had accidentally stepped on. "Sorry about that. Sorry—oh, god." She lurched away from me and buried her face in her hands.

I blinked, trying to make sense of what had happened. Come to terms with what definitely *wasn't* going to happen. "Did you...did you just *pat* me?"

"Gahhh." She rolled, taking the sheets with her until she was a burrito, and slid off the bed. "Don't look at me."

I propped myself on one elbow and peered over the

side of the bed at the pathetic lump of sheet and woman on the floor. "James."

"Don't laugh."

"I'm not laughing."

"You are. I can hear it in your voice."

The lump moved as James inchwormed across the floor. I swallowed a chuckle. "I'm going to shower. When I come out, we are never to speak of this again."

When the bathroom door closed behind her, I gave into it. I rolled onto my back and laughed. Once I started, I couldn't stop. The floodgates opened. I laughed about her patting my dick and rolling to the floor. Somehow that segued into remembering our first meeting, when we fell into each other's arms and mashed our mouths together. Holy shit, my dad was right. Fucking *hilarious.*

The bathroom door flung open, revealing James, clutching a towel to her presumably naked body. Her dark hair lifted and swirled around her shoulders at the breeze from the door. She stared at me with wide brown eyes, her pink mouth comically gaping open.

"I didn't want to miss it," she said.

"What?" I asked, seriously confused.

"You. Mr. Resting Grump Face. *Laughing.*" With a smirk, she closed the door. "It looks good on you!" she hollered. A second later I heard the shower turn on.

Damn. My cock, which had gone to half mast during

the whole sheet-burrito thing, stood fully at attention. For a moment I let my imagination drift. If James weren't only my employee. If she were my girl. We would have booked the single room on purpose and gone to bed naked. She wouldn't have rolled away when she grabbed my dick. She would have kept going.

I touched myself, thinking about it. One stroke. Then another.

Maybe she would have laughed, that sound I loved so much, and pressed sleepy little kisses to my neck and chest. Her body would be so warm from being snuggled under the covers with me all night. I stroked faster as I imagined her taking over, rolling me to my back, gliding down on my cock. Smiling down at me, her dark eyes looking at me like they had when she caught me laughing. Happy, with a hint of mischief.

My chest squeezed tight. My balls drew up. My hand moved faster.

What would her eyes look like when I made her come? What sounds would she make? Would she collapse onto my chest and whisper in my ear words I'd never heard from a woman's lips? *Only you, I only want you—*

Hot ropes of cum spurted against my stomach as I thrust my hips up against her imaginary pussy. I came harder than I ever had with a *real* pussy, much less with my own hand. The shower cut off with a metallic squeak.

Fuuuck.

"You banged her, didn't you," Zack said.

My gaze shot to the back of James's head, searching for signs that she had heard my dumbass brother. "Keep your voice down," I hissed. "And no, I did not."

James and I had arrived at the makeshift staging area bright and early, to-go cups of coffee in our hands, to mingle with contestants and trainers. When I had spotted Zack's horse trailer, James had insisted we go say hi. *Sure*, I had agreed, thinking it might actually be nice to spend some extra time with my baby brother. A critical error on my part.

Zack studied me with narrowed eyes. "I don't believe you. Your face is...soft. No scowl."

"I'm having a good day." Or I had been, before this stupid conversation.

"Not to mention—"

"Then *don't*," I cut in. "Don't mention it."

Zack quirked an eyebrow. "*Not to mention*, you've

ELIZABETH BRIGHT

been avoiding eye contact with her this whole time, but the second she turns her back, you're eye-fucking her like a total perv."

Of course I couldn't make eye contact with James. Not after what I did this morning. If I had taken myself in hand, imagining her naked and wet in the shower? Fine. If I had thought about her plush pink mouth on my dick? Totally understandable and no one's business but my own. But I had jacked off to *feelings*.

What the actual fuck was that about?

It was embarrassing. No way in hell was I going to open up to Zack about it. He'd have Brax on the phone in ten seconds flat. I didn't need that shit in my day.

"All we did was sleep," I said. "And if you say one goddamn word to her about this that makes her uncomfortable, I swear to god—"

"Nah. Only brothers are fair game."

Zack glanced at James, who was conversing with Essie Price and another couple barrel racers, her hands moving with animated gestures. Networking like Brax wanted because she was a professional. Zack's gaze lingered on her ass—tactfully avoiding Essie's because both of us knew without being told that she was off limits. What Zack failed to realize was that James was, too. At least as far as he was concerned. I could literally feel my blood pressure spike.

"Can't blame you for the eye-fucking," Zack said. "Those jeans are doing mankind the highest service."

I shoved his shoulder. "Eyes off," I growled.

Zack smirked. "Ah, there's that scowl I know and love."

His phone buzzed and he tugged it out of his pocket. His smile was replaced with a frown as he looked at the screen. Then his thumbs flew as he texted a reply. "Shit," he muttered. "Shit, shit, shit."

"Problem?" I asked, though the answer was obvious.

"Yeah. Rex was supposed to partner with me for the roping event, but his little girl fell off a swing and broke her arm. He's with her at the hospital."

"Shit," I said. He looked at me and I knew exactly what he was going to say next. "No," I said preemptively.

"Come on, man. I need you. The ranch needs you. I'm riding one of ours today. When I win, it looks good for Lodestar."

James looked over her shoulder at us curiously. After a quick survey of our expressions, she ambled over. "What's going on?"

"My roping partner had to bail," Zack explained. "And Adam here won't do me a solid and step up." His expression was the picture of wounded brotherly love. I rolled my eyes.

"Oh." James bit her lip and peeked up at me from

under the dark sweep of her eyelashes. "Maybe he doesn't know how?"

Wow, way to slip a knife right in my gut.

"I know how," I said through my clenched teeth. "What is it you think I do all day? Those cows we have aren't for beef, you know."

James was great at training horses for show reining and rodeo events, but ranch horses were still a good portion of our income. Horses that were intended for actual work on cattle ranches. That was my specialty. Teaching them how to take a pull and track a cow. I was damn good at it, too.

"Well, sure," James said. "But that's not the same thing as doing it in front of thousands of people, is it? I mean, you don't even know the cow. It might not be so easy to rope as the ones you're used to at Lodestar."

Know the cow? I shot her a look that promised murder before I turned to my brother. "You got a horse for me to ride?" I asked him.

He whooped and slapped his thigh with his hat. "Hell yeah, I do."

When I looked back at James, she was grinning smugly. Like maybe she had never doubted me at all. My suspicions mounted when Zack winked at her.

Dammit. I had been all set to spend my afternoon watching events, not participating in them. That was where I was comfortable. Unlike Zack, I didn't crave attention. He could keep all the applause. I just wanted to do a job I was proud of.

But like a million men before me, I found myself agreeing to do something stupid to impress a girl. Suckered by a pretty face.

I could still back out, but I wasn't going to. Because I didn't want to let my brother down, but even more than that, I wanted to hear James scream my name.

In more ways than one, but this was the only way it was going to happen.

18

James

I MET up with Essie after her barrel race—which she won, no surprise—and together we took our seats in the stands to watch the team roping event.

"They're not on first," Essie said, scanning the list of names. She looked around, craning her neck. "Oh, there they are." She pointed to the area behind the metal gates, but it was unnecessary.

I had spotted him the moment we sat down.

And *damn*, my boss looked good. Faded blue jeans and a red plaid button down shirt. Black vest. Black chaps. Black cowboy hat. Hot as sin.

Oh, god, I had patted that man's penis.

It wasn't fair.

He deserved more than a dick pat, looking like that. He deserved a slow, thorough blow job. Too bad he would never let me be the one to give it to him. I wished he would. Just once, before we had returned to Lodestar Ranch and the real world. Seeing him sit there tall and proud in the saddle, I couldn't think of a single thing I would rather do.

But nooo. He had to be a decent human being. Responsible. Dutiful. A fantastic boss who owned his mistakes and actually cared about the people who worked for him.

"Adam looks nervous," Essie remarked.

That was true. There was a pinched look to his face. I chewed my lip, momentarily second-guessing myself. Maybe I shouldn't have goaded him into this. There was no doubt in my mind that he would do well, but there did seem to be a doubt in his.

"He's got this," I said firmly. But in case he didn't feel the same, I whipped out my phone and sent a quick text. I had no idea if he would get it before the event started. Maybe he didn't have his phone on him now, during his warm up.

But a second later he looked down at his hands and then up at the stands, searching. And then he found me. My heart kicked hard against my ribs as our gazes locked and held. His lips quirked and he touched the brim of his hat. I grinned.

Essie hummed. "Zack is looking good."

I arched my eyebrow. "Oh, is he?"

"Like you hadn't noticed!" she teased, nudging me with her elbow.

I laughed like that was true, even though I honestly hadn't noticed. I'd been too busy ogling his older brother. "You should come out with us tonight. We're going for drinks at a local bar. I can text you the address."

"Sounds fun. Brax isn't coming, is he?"

I side-eyed her, confused. "Brax? No, he's back in Aspen Springs. You know him?"

"Well, sure. We went to high school together. I've avoided him ever since. The man has a stick shoved up his ass. And not the fun kind."

I snorted. "He's not so bad."

"Trust me, he is." Essie gave a little smirk and tossed her bright blue hair over her shoulder. "Zack, on the other hand, seems like he could be fun. For a night, anyway. Although, I wouldn't say no to Adam, either."

Every cell in my body stiffened.

Essie burst into laughter. "Relax, James. I would absolutely say no to Adam, not that he'd ever put the offer on the table. I've seen the way he looks at you. Anyway, hos before beaus and all that."

"Adam is my boss. Nothing is going on."

Essie gave me a look of patent disbelief.

"There's not!" I said defensively.

"Okay, look. If we're going to be friends, then you can't lie to me. I hate that. No obfuscating the truth, either. Maybe nothing is technically *happening*"—she did air quotes around the word and rolled her eyes dramatically— "but that doesn't mean there aren't real feelings involved. Tell me the truth. You'd honestly be okay if I took Adam back to my hotel room?"

I glanced at Adam and my stomach twisted at the thought of him with Essie. Which was stupid. I had no right to lay claim to him when I knew I couldn't do anything about it. And Essie...well, it wouldn't hurt her career at all. It wasn't fair. But she had asked for my honesty, and I gave it to her. "No."

"Then don't pretend otherwise. What if I had believed you and banged his brains out? How would we be friends after that?" She shook her head, blue hair gleaming in the sunlight. "Just be honest. It's the only way to live."

"Okay," I said softly. Then, "Please don't bang my boss."

She grinned. "I won't. Definitely going to bang his brother, though."

"Go for it."

And then Adam and Zack entered the ring. I sat up straighter, moving to the edge of my seat. Adam didn't look nervous now. He looked focused. A competitor who was there to win.

Each cow in the small herd had a number. The judges called out the numbers, telling Adam and Zack which ones to separate from the herd. The buzzer went off, the clock ticked down, and the team surged to action.

It was incredible watching them work. Dimly, I knew Zack was doing...something...but I couldn't peel my eyes from Adam. He was just so *competent*. Entirely confident in every move he made, every decision.

I couldn't help but wonder if he would bring that same confidence to bed. Tell me what he wanted. Demand I take the same from him. I squeezed my thighs together, gripped the edge of my seat so tightly my knuckles whitened, and hoped Essie didn't notice. I was here for *work*. Not to ogle.

His plaid shirt was rolled up to his forearms, revealing flexing muscles and tendons as Adam gives his horse commands. Goddamn, I was such a slut for forearms. Pure cowboy porn, that's what this was. And I, for one, was soaking my panties in a very unprofessional way.

Adam tossed his lasso and I held my breath. When it caught the calf around the neck, I clapped my hands. Adam dismounted, Zack bound his feet, and just like that it was over. The buzzer sounded, calling time, and Essie and I leaped from our seats, whooping and hollering and stamping our feet.

"Adam!" I yelled. "Adam!"

Essie put two fingers to her mouth and let out a piercing whistle. Adam looked our way and lifted his hat high into the air before they both disappeared to the staging area.

For a moment I just stood there, hands still clasped together from clapping, beaming stupidly at the arena. That had been *amazing*.

Essie gave me a little nudge. "We should go down there. Congratulate them. That was a winning score."

"Sure," I said but I didn't move, even as she gave me a quizzical look.

Because the truth was, I still felt...heated. And the way I wanted to congratulate him wasn't professional. At all.

I counted to ten. Then I counted to twenty. It didn't fully cure me, but it was enough to stop me from humping Adam's leg. Hopefully.

"Okay," I said. "Let's go."

Fake it 'til you make it.

It was time to bring out the big guns. And by guns, I mean my tits.

In general, it wasn't my favorite weapon to deploy. Men were pigs and my breasts had a tendency to turn them into little boys. They gaped, they groped, they goggled. Basically, they treated me as a novelty instead of an actual person. I was just a pair of boobs to them.

Worse, they forgot about my clit.

But tonight I wanted attention, and if there was one thing my boobs were *great* at, it was getting attention.

Unfortunately, the only person I wanted attention from was the one person who refused to look directly at me.

Maybe I was being too subtle. I had kept it casual with a cutoff denim skirt that showed a little skin without risking accidental thong flashing. I paired that with a simple scoop-neck white tee shirt, because when it came to my tits, less was more. My turquoise pendant pointed straight to my cleavage. And of course, my pink boots.

I leaned against the bar, fiddling with the pendant as I ordered a vodka soda with lime. I angled my body to give Adam the perfect view, but his gaze stayed riveted to the beer taps. The bartender, on the other hand, about swallowed his damn tongue.

"On the house," he told my breasts as he placed my drink in front of me.

Before I could thank him, Adam's hand slammed a twenty on the bar. "For her drink," he said. There was a warning note in his voice that turned the simple words into a threat. "And her next one, too."

"Gotcha." The bartender slid the cash into his palm and headed for the other end of the bar where customers were signaling for his attention.

I side-eyed Adam, but he still refused to look at me. I sighed.

"So, James." Essie sounded like she was struggling not to laugh. "Tell me about your name. How did that happen?"

"You mean, how did a nice girl like me end up with a boy's name?" I laughed. "It's not all that interesting, really. There's an actor my mom likes and he named his daughter James. She was pregnant and hormonal and she thought it was the prettiest name she'd ever heard."

"What would they have named you if you were a boy?" Zack asked.

"Marcus."

Zack and Essie laughed. Adam took a swallow of

beer. I had never felt so invisible in my life. I dipped my head, pretending to sip my drink while I sneaked a peek at my chest to make sure I hadn't suddenly sprouted hair or deflated or something. Nope. Still hairless. Still perky double d's.

"What about you?" I asked. "Adam is the oldest and his name starts with A." He didn't look up from his beer as I said his name and I checked my sigh. "Then there's Brax. B. And finally, all the way to the end of the alphabet with Z. Is that a coincidence?"

"Nope." Zack grinned. He had taken a few glances at my chest, quick and subtle with no gross gawking. I appreciated that. "There's a story. See, Mom had the idea she wanted five kids. Didn't care if they were boys or girls, but she figured it would be nice to have some of each. Dad was on board because Dad was always on board with whatever Mom wanted."

I felt Adam shift next to me, so at least I knew he was listening.

"Mom thought it would be cute to go down the alphabet, A through E. The first was Adam—would have been Abigail if he were a girl—and she had hopes that the fifth baby would be a girl so she could name her Eve."

"Aww," Essie said. "That *is* cute."

"As you know, Brax was next. Another boy. But Mom still clung to hope that her brood would be mixed. She was so sure the next one would be a girl that she refused to let the doctor tell her the gender. She just went right on ahead and bought girl clothes."

"All Zack's baby pictures are of him in pink onesies," Adam said, finally joining the conversation. "With butterflies and flowers and shit."

Zack wasn't at all perturbed. "That's true. I was fucking adorable, too."

"I bet you were," I said, leaning into my laughter, pushing out my chest a bit, but all it earned me was another scowl from Adam.

"Well, it crushed my mom. She saw the writing on the wall and had no intention of being a mom of five rowdy boys. She put a stop to it right then and there. Skipped C and went straight to Z."

"I'm sure she loved you just as much, once she got over her disappointment." I patted his arm comfortingly.

Now I had Adam's attention. He glared at my hand like he could incinerate it with eye lasers. Slowly I dragged my hand away from Zack's arm, re-evaluating my strategy. Maybe Adam wasn't a boob man, but sibling rivalry definitely got a response.

I wasn't sure that was a game I wanted to play, though. I liked Zack. I didn't want to cause problems between him and Adam. All three of us had a stake in

Lodestar Ranch, but I was the only outsider. They were family. No matter who won, I would be the loser.

Anyway, flirting with one man to make another jealous? That wasn't me.

None of this was me.

"Ladies' room," I mumbled.

"Want me to come with?" Essie asked.

I shook my head. "I'll be right back."

A lie. The bar was fortunately right across the street from our hotel room. I elbowed my way through the crowd and pushed open the door. Crisp air slapped me in the face. I welcomed it, took it deep into my lungs, letting the sharp sting pull me back to my senses.

A group of women dressed for attention surrounded me, trying to get in. I was blocking the door like an idiot. I dodged out of the way and leaned against the brick wall as I watched them strut their way inside. No doubt they were going to succeed where I failed and get the attention they wanted. Maybe even *his* attention.

Ugh.

It was better this way. I had enough standing in my way between me and my goals without adding sleeping with my boss to the mix. I fished my phone out of my bag, intending to text Adam that I was going back to our room with a headache. By the time he came back—*if* he

came back, a thought that churned bile in my stomach—
I would be asleep. Or pretend to be, anyway.

I had gotten as far as *hey, sorry* when the door banged
open.

"What the hell do you think you're doing?" Adam
growled, catching sight of me.

"I was just about to text you," I said. I waved my
phone as evidence. "Headache."

The corners of his mouth turned down further.
"You're going back to the hotel?"

I nodded. "Go back inside. Have fun."

"I'll walk you back."

"No, no. It's fine. Really. The hotel is right there. I'm
going straight to bed. You stay here with Zack."

Two steps and he was towering over me. My head
tilted back, thumping softly against the brick wall
behind me, as I took in all his irate glory. The man was
downright livid. A thrill shot through my belly. Finally,
finally, I had pushed his buttons hard enough to get a
response.

"The fuck I will," he said. Furious enough to give me
delicious goosebumps up and down my arms. "You're
not going anywhere in the dark alone. It is my
responsibility—"

Oh, lord. This shit again. Duty. Responsibility. The
things that made him so goddamn attractive when it

came to Lodestar Ranch made me want to shake him when it came to me.

"We're not at Lodestar right now. It's after working hours and we're at a bar. You're not my boss here."

For a moment there was nothing but the heavy sound of his breathing. Not mine. I had lost the ability to take in oxygen. I squirmed inwardly, holding my breath, waiting.

"Is that a fact?" He leaned forward, crowding into my space, one forearm braced against the wall next to my head.

I swallowed and forced myself to breathe. "Yes. You're not my boss tonight." *Please, for the love of Dolly Parton, do something about it.*

His hand fluttered over my hair. Captured a lock and twirled it slowly around his finger. Gave it a sharp tug, making me gasp. "Are you drunk, buttercup?"

"Yes," I lied. I had barely touched my vodka soda. But I *wanted* to be drunk. Wanted somewhere to pin the blame, because I had a feeling I was about to be a very bad girl.

"Now, that's a shame." He released my hair. It pinwheeled off his finger, brushing against my cheek. His fingertips lingered on my jaw.

"Why?" I whispered the question, almost pleading.

He captured my chin, pressed his thumb to my

bottom lip. "This fucking mouth. Always smiling. I wonder what this mouth would look like moaning my name when I fuck you deep. What it would look like stretched around my cock."

It was practically a dare, and I never backed down from a dare.

Locking my gaze to his, I touched the tip of my tongue to his thumb, then closed my mouth around his thumb. Reveled in the flare of heat in his eyes when I sucked.

"Are you drunk, buttercup?" he asked again, rougher this time.

I gave him the truth. "No."

"And what do you want me to do about it?"

I was wet and slick when I pressed my thighs together. Anticipation shivered through me, silencing the voice in my head that warned I was in danger of damaging my career and my heart. "I want you to fuck me."

The words had barely left my lips when his hand found mine and tugged me close. "Let's go."

19

Adam

THE SECOND THE door clicked behind us, I hauled her against my body and kissed her with all the pent-up need and longing that had been building since...well, since the last time I kissed her. But this time was different. I wasn't cold, selfishly trying to absorb her sunshine inside me.

That kiss had woken me up. This kiss set me on fire.

It was all-consuming, this desire for her. This *need*.

She'd screamed my name in the rodeo arena. *Mine.* Not Zack's, even though he deserved as much—if not more—credit for our win. That meant something to me.

Because I meant something to *her*. Something beyond being her boss or even being her friend. It had been a long time since I had mattered to a woman. Hearing her cheer for me, seeing that lust-glazed look in her eyes when she told me to fuck her...it was a powerful drug, being wanted like that. I was almost lightheaded from it.

The kiss turned desperate and rushed as she dragged my shirt off over my head and immediately went for my belt buckle. We were up against the clock and we both knew it. Time was ticking down. Thirty-six hours until I was her boss again.

But as far as I was concerned, that was thirty-six hours to savor her. I didn't want fast. I wanted thorough. If thirty-six hours was all I could have of her, I was going to make every second count. Touch every inch of her skin. Leave no part of her undiscovered. Fuck her every way she'd let me.

I pulled back. She clung to me, her breath labored. "Easy, baby. We have time. All the time you want." I meant it, even if I hadn't worked out exactly how to make that happen. "I want to explore you. Taste every inch of you. Are you going to let me do that?"

She stared at me, eyes glassy. "Fuck," she whispered on a soft exhale.

"We'll do that, too," I promised.

I kissed her again, nice and slow this time. She took advantage of my shirtless state, running her hands over my bare chest and shoulders, dragging her nails down the rippled muscles of my abdomen. When she followed the sparse trail of hair that started at my belly button and disappeared into my jeans, anticipation licked down my spine.

I needed her naked. Now.

But still slowly.

Not leaving her mouth, I put a little space between us, enough to slide my hand up the curve of her body. My thumb flicked against her nipple when I reached her breast. She whimpered against my lips and her hands gripped the waistband of my jeans.

"Adam," she pleaded, but I was not to be rushed.

I cupped her breasts in my hands, feeling the heavy weight of them. My eyebrows snapped together. "How the hell you kept these hidden from me, I don't know."

"I have a few tricks," she said breathlessly.

"But not tonight. Tonight you damn near gave me a crick in the neck from keeping my eyes up like a gentleman."

"I wanted your attention." Her confession was soft. Shy.

Her words spread through me, soothing a wound that had laid open and bloody for longer than I cared to admit. My hands left her breasts so I could take her face and force her to look nowhere but me.

"You have my attention, James. You've had it since you walked into Jo's. You could wear a brown sack

ELIZABETH BRIGHT

covering every inch of your body and I'd still follow you around just hoping to hear you laugh."

Her dark eyes searched mine for the truth of that statement. I let her find it. I had spent the last month trying to keep this attraction locked down, but I was done hiding.

With a quick motion, she snatched the shirt over her head and tossed it aside. Before I could get my hands on her, she stepped back, unclasped her bra, and gave her shoulders a sweet little shimmy that sent the lacy blue bra falling to her feet.

Fuck.

I groaned. She was perfect. A pocket-sized pinup meant to drive me to my knees—a place I had every intention of going tonight. Her breasts were full and luscious, with soft pink nipples hard and pointed right at me.

"Skirt off," I ordered.

She flicked open the snap with a small, self-satisfied smirk hovering on her lips. My girl knew exactly what she was doing to me. I bit my knuckle as she shimmied it down her hips, leaving her in a midnight-blue thong and those pink fucking boots. She started to toe them off, but I stopped her.

"The boots stay on, buttercup. I want to feel your

heels digging into my back when I make you come on my tongue."

An audible breath whooshed out of her. She stared at me, wide-eyed.

That was fine. She could contemplate that while I feasted on those glorious tits of hers.

I boosted her into my arms and she instantly wrapped her legs around my waist, clasping them at the ankles. I lowered my head, dropping kisses to the adorable sprinkle of freckles along her collarbone and chest. Her head fell back, giving me better access, and I took it. I kissed down the curve of her breast. Relished in the soft fullness of it. Found her nipple and flicked it with my tongue. She gasped, her hands digging into my shoulders. I sucked her nipple into my mouth with a deep, languid pull.

Then I went for the other one, kissing and sucking as I took us to the bed and laid her down gently.

I greedily ate up the sight of her spread before me. Her breasts, the flare of her hips, that sexy blue thong wedged up and lewdly showing the shape of her pussy lips. Her shapely legs in those pink boots. A fucking wet dream come to life.

"Christ, baby, you should see yourself. So pretty."

She bit her lip, arching her chest, her cheeks flushing at my praise.

ELIZABETH BRIGHT

I went to my knees. Dragged my finger down that flimsy triangle of fabric. Found it soaked. I tsked at her softly. "So fucking wet, James. How long has this sweet little pussy been needing me?"

She moaned as I slid the fabric aside and pushed a finger in. Her hands went to her breasts and she rolled her nipples between her fingers. *Fuck*.

I pulled my finger free. "How long, James?"

"Since four-fifteen."

My start time.

My attention jerked to her face. "What?"

"Since the second you rode into the arena and bossed around a baby cow." She lifted up on her elbows and served me a disgruntled pout. "It's been *hours*, Adam."

My cock jerked as I stared at her. Then I sprang into action, frantically dragging her panties down her legs before I tossed her booted feet over my shoulders one at a time.

"Remember what I said, buttercup. I want to see bruises tomorrow."

I didn't wait for her response before I delved between her thighs. I slid my tongue right into her, tasting all that sweetness that was there for me. Got drunk from it. When she squirmed beneath me, I splayed a hand across her belly and pressed her into the mattress. Giving her nowhere to go except my mouth.

She responded, canting her hips toward my seeking tongue. I sucked her clit, gently at first, and then with more suction when she let me know she liked it. Her strong thighs clamped tightly around my head.

"Oh, god, oh, god, oh, god," she chanted.

I knew she was close. Too close. I slowed the rhythm of my tongue. Brought her away from the edge. Bought myself a few more moments of drinking her, delving my tongue through all that soft, warm flesh between her legs. I kissed her, teased her, until she whined my name.

I grinned against her pussy. And then I built her up again. Every little sound she made, every twitch of her body, made my dick throb desperately. Her thighs quivered and suddenly she was there. Her hips bucked upward, pushing against my mouth as her pussy clenched around my tongue in rhythmic spasms. Her boots dug into my trap muscles. Trapped me there in the vise of her thighs, my new favorite place on earth.

I licked until her tremors stopped and her thighs splayed limply.

I pushed to my feet, shucked my jeans and boots, took my aching cock in hand, and—

Shit.

"I don't have a condom," I said.

She waved a hand weakly and let it flop back on the bed. "My bag."

I found her purse and then glanced at her. "Can I?"

"Go for it."

Inside were five condoms. I felt some kind of way about that, but I wasn't going to decipher it now. I pulled one out, ripped open the package, and rolled it over my cock while she watched me, eyes half closed.

"You want this?" I asked, knowing I sounded needy and desperate but I didn't fucking care. I *was* needy and desperate.

She looked at me and it was like she saw straight into my soul and understood exactly what I needed to hear. Her hand stroked my cheek gently.

"I want *you*, Adam."

I swallowed hard. Her attention was on me, so warm it felt like standing in a sunbeam. Sweet and playful, that smile of hers lighting up her face. And I knew—I *knew*—that she had the power to wreck me. And fuck, I was going to let her.

I pushed into her slow and steady, a delicious glide into her tight heat. She sucked in a breath as I filled her.

"God," she whispered, her breath fanning against my cheek.

"Are you okay?" I asked through gritted teeth. My control was paper-thin.

Her lips curved. "Fuck me."

I pulled all the way out and shoved back in. *Bliss*. Her

gaze locked onto mine with an intensity that made me close my eyes, as if I could shield myself.

She pressed damp kisses to my neck, then bit gently on the tendon there. I fucked her hard. So deep. Lost myself in her body. If I was going to break apart, at least I would make it worth it first.

Then I felt it again, the sweet clench of her pussy around my cock. Her back bowed as she said my name like a prayer. I was right there with her, coming so hard I saw starbursts behind my eyelids.

I collapsed on her, entirely spent. For the moment, at least. I had plans to make this a long night. She trailed her hand along my arm. I kept my eyes closed until my breathing returned to normal.

And when I opened my eyes again, all I saw was her.

20

James

I woke up the same way I had yesterday morning: my body plastered to something deliciously warm and hard, a spicy, masculine scent surrounding me, and something poking insistently at my belly. Still half asleep, I reached down and grasped it. A low growl brought me fully awake and I giggled.

I was half tempted to give it a pat on the head to keep the joke going, but it was so thick in my hand that I couldn't resist an admiring stroke.

"Someone's happy to see me," I murmured against Adam's chest.

"I would be happier *in* you," he said, his voice thick and rough from sleep and arousal.

"That can be arranged." The voice was back, telling me this was a bad idea, but I pushed it aside. One weekend. That's all this was. How much damage could one weekend possibly do?

I pushed his shoulder and he rolled onto his back, taking me with him. My legs straddled his waist. We didn't bother with clothes last night, which meant my bare pussy was snuggled against the hard ridge of his cock. I rocked my hips against him until I was wet and slick.

"Fuck," he muttered. His fingers dug into my hips, his eyes glued to our connection between my splayed thighs.

Wanting to see what had him so riveted, I looked down. Saw his cock, ruddy and glistening, slide under my pussy. I rolled my lip under my teeth. Unable to resist, I slid off him and wiggled between his legs.

And licked his dick in one long glide, balls to tip. "Mmm."

"Fuck, James." His hips bucked.

I sucked him into my mouth, relishing the way his breath stuttered and his hands clenched into fists. I tasted myself on him and that only turned me on more. A few delicious pumps of my mouth and then I slid him from my lips with a loud pop.

"Condom," I said.

He reached for our stash on the bedside table. Two empty wrappers, leaving us three. After this round, that left us with only two to get us to tomorrow morning.

Funny how five had seemed like a ridiculous amount when I had opened Chloe's pastry bag. Now it didn't seem anywhere near enough.

He rolled the condom over his length. I lined him up to my entrance and sank down with a little moan. For a moment I didn't move. Waited for the feeling of fullness to dissipate enough to feel good.

"You okay?" he asked.

I nodded. Rose up and sank down again. It was easier this time. "I'm a little sore from last night. You're a big guy, you know that?" He shrugged a little and I laughed. "What? No one's ever told you that before?"

"I figured it was something women said to make men feel good about themselves."

"Well, in your case, it's true." I set a steady rhythm, easing into it. "Surely you know that. You can't tell me you've never seen another dick before."

"I guess size depends on comparison. It's an unfortunate fact that you can't escape adolescence without seeing your brothers' dicks. I figured I was slightly below average."

I froze. My brain whirled. If Adam thought he was below average in comparison to his brothers, then what the hell kind of fire hydrant dicks were *they* sporting? "Wait, are you saying—"

His eyes narrowed. "No. Absolutely fucking not. You

are not going to sit there on my fucking dick and think about other dicks. Especially not *their* dicks."

He grabbed my turquoise pendant with one hand and tugged me down so he could capture my nipple with his mouth. His other hand delved between my legs, found my clit, and applied the perfect pressure to send me flying. He bucked his hips, thrusting into me again and again.

The sudden onslaught of pleasure knocked me off balance. I whimpered, pleaded. "Adam—"

"That's right, baby. Tell me who makes this pussy feel good."

There was a bite to his command that made me blink. He couldn't really believe I was interested in either Brax or Zack, could he? He had to know that he was the only one I wanted.

But maybe he didn't know that. Maybe underneath all that masculine confidence was a shimmer of doubt. It wasn't hard to understand why. Hearing the love of your life say her heart belonged to another man was bound to leave a scar.

I turned my face so my lips brushed his temple. Pressed a kiss there. I thought it would be hard to make myself vulnerable, but the words came easily. "You're the one who makes my pussy feel good. So fucking good, Adam. Only you. I've never wanted anyone the way I want you. You feel so good inside me—"

He made a sound somewhere between pain and pleasure. I cried out as he worked his thumb faster against my clit. His hips surged up, setting a brutal pace. I ground down on his hand and his dick as we both came apart together, shaking and panting.

Sated and boneless, I collapsed on top of him and pressed my cheek against his damp chest. He kissed the top of my head tenderly and his arms banded around me, holding me tightly like he never wanted to let go.

"Bruises." I arched up from the bed and rolled onto my knees to examine the red halfmoon marks on his upper back. The exact shape of my boot heels. I lightly traced the marks with my fingertips, then pressed a kiss to each. "Does it hurt?"

Adam, fresh from the shower, sent a self-satisfied smirk over his shoulder. "No."

"I'll try harder next time," I teased.

He turned to face me. "That's my good girl." He gave my bare ass a slap, making me giggle.

My laugh turned to a gasp when he hooked me around the waist and brought me fully against him. He was half hard in his boxers already. "Don't," I pleaded. "We only have two condoms left. Save them for tonight."

"We can get more."

"It seems like a waste to buy a whole box for one more night. You'll be my boss again tomorrow." I worried my lip with my teeth. It was the truth. I knew that. This thing with us was a one-weekend deal, for very good reasons. But I still hoped he would refute it.

He pulled back, his gaze intent on mine. "Right."

He released me and I felt silly for thinking he might say anything else. Of course I was right.

We both got busy getting dressed for the day, but now everything felt awkward. Adam kept glancing at the remaining two condoms and every time he did, his scowl deepened. Something was on his mind, but he didn't seem interested in sharing that with me. Well, I wasn't going to drag it out of him. I disappeared into the bathroom to fix my hair. I had already showered and moisturized, but I hated blow drying my hair so it was still damp.

"You didn't know we would have to share a room." Adam's voice sounded far away and vaguely annoyed.

I made eye contact with my reflection and we shared a perplexed look. "That's true."

When he said nothing in return, I grabbed a hairband and exited the bathroom, braiding my hair as I faced him. "Something you want to say?" I asked.

He glowered. "No."

"Really?" I prodded. "Because you look like you have something on your mind."

"Nothing worth saying. You can have all the condoms, sleep with all the cowboys you want. It's not my business."

My eyebrows shot to my hairline. "You think I'm a buckle bunny?"

"I don't care if you are."

He crossed his arms, chin jutting like a stubborn child. Why was that adorable? I wasn't normally into man-children who hadn't learned how to use their words.

"Okay," I said slowly, "but if you did care and you told me why you cared, maybe I would say something you wanted to hear."

I watched him process that, the look of doubtful hope in his bright blue eyes doing awful, achy things to my insides. Most of the time, this man had confidence to spare. But when it came to how much I truly wanted him, he couldn't believe it.

He scrubbed a hand over his jaw and his gaze darted away from me. "I hate the thought of you taking some random rodeo guy back to your hotel room. I hate the thought of you planning for it. I know it's not my place to care. I have no claim on you. It sounds stupid to say all this out loud. But...I hate it." He shook his head. "Sometimes I come to these events and I bring condoms. I figure, maybe I'll meet someone. Maybe something will happen. But I didn't this time. You know why? Because I knew nothing could happen with you, and you were the only one I wanted."

Normally possessive, jealous men were a huge turnoff for me, but hearing him tell me that made my stomach whoosh happily. He wanted me. Only me. Not for forever, I knew that, but I wasn't asking for forever. Right now was enough, and right now he wanted me the way I wanted him.

"Well," I said. "Good news. The condoms are Chloe's. She slipped them into the pastry bag when we picked up your decaf. I had no intention of doing anything other than work this weekend because I didn't think there was a chance in hell of doing *you*."

He stared at me. "I didn't order decaf."

Whoops. I waved a hand dismissively. "My point is that you're the only one—"

"Why would she give me decaf? She wouldn't have unless—" His eyes narrowed as he worked it through. "You told her to. And then the Willy Nelson and the hoof oil and the windows—" He jabbed a finger in my direction. "You drugged me and made me take a nap!"

"You're welcome."

"Oh, you will pay for that, buttercup."

He lunged for me but I dodged, laughing. "Wait, wait! Let me explain—"

He lunged again, this time tackling me to the bed.

An hour later, we were down to one condom.

21

Adam

W<small>E CAUGHT</small> the sunrise at Garden of the Gods on our way out of Colorado Springs. Being a rancher meant bearing witness to countless sunrises and sunsets and it had been a long time since I had paused to appreciate the moment.

But now, seeing the pastel glow of the clouds and rocks reflected on James's skin, the sunrise felt new again. I paused. And I appreciated the hell out of it.

Good god, she was beautiful. Here, in the soft glow of the sunrise. In bed, fulfilling my fantasy with whispered words. On a horse, looking like she had been born in the saddle. There wasn't a place on this earth that wouldn't be improved by her presence.

Shit, I was turning into a sentimental fool. Dad would be so proud.

"Oh, my god," James whispered, awed and reverent, for the hundredth time. "Oh, my god."

I dropped a kiss on her upturned face. I couldn't help it. She blinked, surprised, then took a swift, guilty look around, like she was expecting people we knew to pop out yelling, *surprise!*

"I'm not your boss here," I reminded her. To prove my point, I kissed her again, longer this time and with a slide of my tongue against hers.

"I think we both know that logic only works as long as no one finds out," she said when we pulled apart, her lips damp from my kiss.

"And what happens if someone finds out?" I asked. "You think anyone is really going to care?"

She smacked my shoulder. "Of course people are going to care. It's hard enough getting anyone to take a woman seriously in this business. Have you seen the statistics? Women and girls dominate the amateur fields in every horse sport. But when it comes to making horses our careers, we get pushed down and out. Even my own dad—" She broke off, shook her head, pressed her lips into a flat line.

Like a girl. That was what he had said to her. Anger on her behalf simmered in my stomach. Carl Campos was one of the most respected trainers in the business. The man might be brilliant with horses, but I was beginning to suspect he was also downright stupid. If he'd had one lick of sense, James would still be at Blue Skies instead of here with me.

"I respect you, James. You're a damn good horse trainer. The progress you've made with Belle is nothing short of incredible."

"Thank you," she said softly, "but it's not your opinion I'm worried about."

Oh. Well.

Not gonna lie, that stung a little.

Something of that sting must have shown up on my face because she laughed and tucked her arm through mine like that was a totally natural thing to do.

"I meant that in a good way, Adam. Not like your opinion doesn't matter to me. It does." She sat down on a stone wall and pulled me down next to her. "I'm saying that you never made me feel anything less than respected. Not after we sorted the Ben stuff out."

"So what are you worried about, then?" I asked.

She heaved a sigh. "What everyone else will think. What my dad will think. In this industry, women drop like flies. If I'm banging the boss? I'm the one they'll think less of. *You*, they'll high five."

She wasn't wrong. I knew that.

"You know why my dad wouldn't promote me?" she asked. When I shook my head, she continued, "He thought investing in a woman was a bad business decision. Because someday, she'd want to pull back. She'd get married or pregnant and want to focus more on her family. Leave the money-making to her husband. And then he'd be left needing to replace her. All I ever wanted was to run Blue Skies Farm shoulder-to-shoulder with my dad. And all he ever wanted was to see me married and popping out grandbabies."

"Are you serious? Jesus, that's awful." I couldn't fathom it. Her own father thought promoting her was bad business? What an idiot. Hiring James was the best decision Lodestar Ranch had ever made.

"He would never say that a woman *couldn't* do the job, although he believes that the woman who could do it well is pretty rare. But he thinks a woman *shouldn't*. Better to leave it to a man. Because a man can't have babies, you see. That's what women are for. She should be home to raise kids and cook dinner." She wrinkled her nose. "I guarantee that if people find out about us, that's what they'll say. They'll ask when we're getting married. When we're having kids. They'll say I found myself a nice, cushy exit plan."

"You can do both," I said. That seemed important to clarify. "If you wanted to." I was out of my depth here, half panicked at the mere mention of marriage and babies. My chest felt too tight for my heart.

Her lips quirked. "With you?"

"What?" A drop of cold sweat ran down my spine.

She burst out laughing. "I'm kidding. Trust me, Adam, I am not asking you to have babies with me. Putting aside the fact that I don't even know if I want babies, your ex screwed you up. I don't think you've dealt with that yet."

Our arms were still linked. Her fingers idly sifted the hair on my forearm like we were discussing the weather instead of my ex's dying wish to be free of me. I didn't know why it felt like that mattered, but it did. It felt like that mattered a whole hell of a lot.

What would make her let go?

"Marriage, babies...I don't know if I can do that again," I said carefully. "I don't know if I want to."

Her fingers stopped playing with me. I braced. But her arm stayed tucked through mine as she asked, "What *do* you want?"

"I realize this is the wrong thing to say to the woman I spent all weekend in bed with, but I don't have a fucking clue, buttercup." I glanced down at her hand on my forearm. She didn't let go. We sat there, connected, while I cut myself open and showed her the mess inside. Somehow that made me keep going. "I want more than a weekend fling. I know that much. But I don't know what more means or what it looks like."

She hummed a little at that. Her fingers resumed their soft, fluttering strokes.

It struck me all of a sudden that this was something new. Sitting, touching, talking. The intimacy of it. Emily and I had never done this. We had never talked about our feelings, other than the standard *I love you* and *I miss you*. Our conversations had never gone deeper than that. We had never worked through a problem together. At the time, I had thought that was because we didn't have any problems. We were perfect together. What was there to discuss?

Obviously I had been wrong about that. So damn wrong. Maybe if we had spent time like this I would have realized that sooner. Maybe I would have been able to fix whatever it was she needed that I wasn't giving her.

"What if we just...keep doing this?" she asked.

"Doing what?"

"This. What we're doing right now. When we're at Lodestar, we keep everything professional. And when we're not..." She grinned. "That's no one's business but our own."

"You want to keep us a secret."

"For now. I've worked too hard and sacrificed too much to throw away my reputation now. My career is just getting started. There's so much I want to accomplish, but I can't do any of it if people don't respect me enough to give me a chance. You understand, right?"

I understood. I didn't like it, but I understood it.

I wasn't a forever guy. Why should she toss aside her reputation for a relationship that was going to end eventually anyway? That wasn't something I could ask her to do. *I* respected her and her career too much for that. If she wanted to keep us a secret, fine. I would take my time basking in her sunshine for as long as she would have me.

And when she decided it was time to let me go, I would take that, too.

22

James

I KEPT my promise to Ben.

On my way out of the barn Monday evening, I grabbed the box of Emily's stuff from the office and brought it with me to the big house. I took out the photos and artwork and then shoved the box—along with those damn journals—in the back of my closet.

After dinner, I ripped off the band-aid. "Let's clean up and then we can look through those photos of your mom Deacon gave us. Okay?"

Dishes clattered in the porcelain sink. I looked over to find my dad staring at me, slack-jawed. I shrugged.

"Okay," Ben said, the epitome of cool, like it didn't matter to him either way. But I didn't miss the way his eyes lit up and he hustled through the chores with a purpose he'd never once shown before.

James was right. He needed this.

And dammit all, if Ben needed something, I was going to provide it, come hell or hailstorm. I might flail my way through solo parenting, and lord knew I'd made a mess of things more than once, but there was nothing I wouldn't do for my son.

Even if it hurt.

But I wasn't above taking a deep swallow of the finger of bourbon Dad had wordlessly left for me next to the sofa.

We settled onto the couch, Ben and me, with the photo album and stack of artwork a pile on my lap. Dad made himself scarce, muttering something about catching up on his television show, and left us to it. I wasn't sure if I was grateful for the privacy or annoyed at the abandonment.

I hadn't so much as glanced at the photos when I grabbed them from the box, and I found myself reluctant to do so now. If I could have found a way to procrastinate another five minutes, another five years, I would have. But I could feel Ben's eyes on me, that expression on his face, the one that worried me the most because it said he felt responsible for things he had no business feeling responsible for. He was about to offer me an out, I could tell, and fuck that.

I opened the photo album to the first page. Emily,

looking tired but happy, smiling down at Ben in her arms. One of his chubby fists had grasped a lock of her blonde hair. By this point, cancer had ravaged her insides, but on the outside she was as beautiful as ever. For one breathless moment, I felt slapped. She looked so damn *alive*.

"She has her hair," Ben said. I glanced at him, surprised. Of all the things to say, I hadn't expected that. "Grandma lost her hair when she had cancer."

That was true. Emily had never lost her hair. The first infusion of chemo had slowed the cancer somewhat and bought her some time. The second infusion hadn't done anything at all. There had never been a third infusion. "Chemo affects people in different ways. Most people lose their hair, but some don't. I remember...I remember she was happy about that. Her hair was so pretty. She didn't want to lose it."

I flipped to the next photo. Ben in his crib, holding his feet, looking shocked that he even had feet. We both laughed and moved on. Most of the next photos were just Ben, in that adorable newborn stage I had missed so much of. I ached at that, but I couldn't be mad about it. I hadn't been there the first time he rolled over or crawled or sat up. I wished with all my heart that I'd had more than an hour every day. I'd missed his first year, but Emily had missed all the years after. It wasn't fair.

I did my best now to tell Ben little memories I had of her, to fill in the gaping hole she had left in his life. It was interesting to see the art she had continued to work on while she was sick. She had never shared much of that with me when we were together. But it was clear now how much it had been a part of her.

"Can I hang this in my room, Dad?" Ben asked, holding a small watercolor painting.

"Yeah, of course. I'll get it framed for you the next time I'm in town. We can also frame one of the photos of you and your mom. Maybe put it on your dresser where you can see it. If you want to," I added, because maybe he *didn't* want that. Maybe seeing her everyday would hurt more than help. Ben could be hard to read sometimes.

"Really?" he asked. Like he needed permission to have a photo of his mom displayed. That was a kick in the gut. A *deserved* kick in the gut. I shouldn't have waited this long.

"Really," I assured him.

The last photo was a sweet one. Ben, nestled on Emily's chest with his legs curled under him and his big diapered butt in the air, sound asleep. She looked directly at the camera, her eyes filled with love, a soft smile on her lips.

No, not at the camera.

At Deacon.

The person holding the camera was Deacon. The person she was looking at with all that love in her eyes was Deacon.

I waited for pain to replace shock, but it never came. I felt sadness. For Ben's loss, mostly, and a little bit for mine. I didn't feel like I was looking at my wife. It was like looking at an old friend, someone who should have been there for milestones and birthday parties and first days of school.

What would things have been like for us, if she had lived? We would have co-parented Ben. I would have been forced to make peace with the idea of her and Deacon, for Ben's sake. Maybe I would have gotten over myself and found someone to share my life with. I saw it play out like a movie in my mind's eye, the parallel life. But it wasn't some faceless woman I imagined.

It was James.

23

James

NOTHING about this was a good idea.

Sleeping with my boss was stupid. Deciding to sneak around so we could do it again was even stupider. But that didn't stop me from climbing in Adam's truck Tuesday afternoon on the pretense of having errands in town.

We never made it to town.

Instead, we parked in one of those Colorado fields that seemed to stretch forever. Afternoon clouds rolled in as we fumbled with each other's clothing, hot and desperate, taking off as little as possible to get the job done. It had been barely forty-eight hours since the last time we had touched each other like this, and still, when he finally slid inside me, the relief was so intense I nearly orgasmed on the spot. Hail pelted the truck, drowning out our sounds.

I collapsed against his chest, trying to catch my breath, while we waited out the storm. These things tended to pass quickly. Adam stroked his fingers through my hair while we cuddled against each other, my legs straddling his lap.

"Ben and I looked through the photos of his mom," he said.

I stopped breathing and craned my neck to look at him. "Yeah?"

"Yeah."

He was quiet, his fingers still sifting through my hair. I didn't push, giving him space to consider his words.

"It didn't feel like I thought it would," he said finally. "I'm not mad anymore. I'm sad. Sad that Ben doesn't have a mom around. Sad that Emily missed out on his life. But it doesn't feel like it used to."

It was on the tip of my tongue to ask whether he was sad for himself, too—sad because he missed the woman he loved. Pride choked the question down. Of all the stupid things I was doing, falling for a man still hung up on his dead ex-wife was probably the stupidest. But quite frankly, I didn't care.

But I also didn't need to hear him validate my fear. I didn't need to hear him say he missed her. Especially not right now, feeling sated from the orgasm, his dick still tucked against me.

"I'm sure that was hard, seeing photos of her. You're a good dad, Adam." I pressed a kiss to his neck.

His lips quirked. "I try."

We stayed like that for a long moment. Then suddenly his arms tightened around me and squeezed.

"Thank you," he said quietly.

Outside the storm kept raging.

TWO WEEKS after our return from Colorado Springs, my body was experiencing severe Adam-induced orgasm withdrawal. We hadn't found much time in the last week to sneak off the ranch. Vibrator-induced orgasms took some of the edge off, but Saturday morning I had witnessed Adam unload a feed delivery, his back and biceps bulging as he threw a fifty-pound bag over one shoulder like it was nothing. By the time I arrived at the library and claimed the steel folding chair between Chloe and Essie, who we had also recruited to Hannah's sewing circle, I was a grumbly, horny mess.

What I wanted to do was bend over the nearest

haybale and demand he put me out of my misery. Instead, I jabbed my needle into the linen fabric—stretched drum-tight in a bamboo hoop—with a satisfying little *ping*. Because I was a lady, dammit.

"Nice stitch." Hannah leaned over to check my work. "So tight and firm."

"That's what he said," Chloe murmured, making me snort.

Hannah smiled patiently. She didn't laugh much, although I suspected that had more to do with the ribald jokes we traded than her lack of humor. She was definitely a little odd. But, hey, a month into our sewing circle, she hadn't stabbed anyone yet.

Embroidery, it turned out, was actually pretty fun. I wouldn't call it relaxing, exactly, the way a bottomless mimosa brunch was, but somehow the repeated stabbing of the needle released a lot of frustration.

"So, James," Chloe said as she slowly and methodically worked her way through a cluster of French knots that would serve as the center of a daisy. "Did you save any horses with those condoms I gave you?"

My next stitch was impeccable. I gave it all my attention, focusing on the soft scrape of the thread pulled through the fabric rather than the ridiculous pounding of my heart. My cheeks burned. Why was I so embarrassed?

I hadn't done anything wrong. Banging the boss was stupid, but it wasn't illegal.

"You did!" Chloe shrieked. "Look how red your face is."

There weren't any mirrors for me to do that, thank heaven for small mercies or whatever, but I could feel the truth of it in the heat spreading from my cheeks down my throat.

"Ohhh." Essie drew out the two-letter word to five syllables. "I bet I know who the cowboy is. Otherwise that only-one-bed situation would have been pretty awkward. Unless he's into that."

Hannah looked up. "Only one bed? That's something that actually happens outside a Tessa Dare novel?"

"I don't know who Tessa Dare is, but it's definitely something that happens when you make last-minute reservations at a hotel during a big rodeo weekend. You know who else saved a horse?" I added in a blatant bid to shift the focus from me and more than willing to take my new friend down with me. "Essie."

"Nice try," she said. "Unfortunately, it won't work. I saved zero horses last weekend."

"Really? What happened with Zack? I thought you were hitting it off."

"I did, too." Essie stabbed the needle through the fabric with a little more force than necessary. "But Zack thought Brax would have a problem with it. Now, in my mind, pissing off Brax would be a bonus, but Zack apparently disagreed. Something about a stupid brother code, blah, blah, blah." She made an annoyed sound. "It's so ridiculous. Brax doesn't care what I do."

"Then I say we move the conversation back to James," Chloe said. "Exactly how many horses did you save? I'd like to know my ROI."

"ROI?" I repeated. Stalling.

"Return on investment." She looked up from her hoop to study me like I was a third-grade science experiment gone awry. "That's the second time you dodged. What gives? Are you uncomfortable talking about sex? Or was it...bad?"

"Definitely not bad." Best sex of my life, actually, though it was hard to say why. It was more than him knowing how to use his tongue and fingers. We had connected in a way that I hadn't experienced before. "I don't want everyone thinking I'm banging the boss."

"But you *are* banging the boss."

I cringed. "Ugh."

"This seems to be a problem for you. Tell me more about that."

Hannah looked up and I could see from the narrowing of her eyes that both of us remembered Chloe saying that exact phrase to her during the inaugural meeting of the sewing circle. "You sound like a therapist."

"I'm working on my doctorate in psychology at the University of Colorado. It's interesting, figuring out why people are the way they are." Chloe shrugged. "Especially when it comes to sex."

Essie blew out an exasperated sigh. "It's the patriarchy. That's why we are how we are when it comes to sex. And to that I say, fuck it. Right, Hannah?"

Hannah laughed and held up her work. "I'm literally embroidering it on a pillow."

"Exactly." Essie turned to me. "Listen, babe. Don't bang the boss is good advice if you work in corporate culture, or where there's a power difference, or your boss is a billionaire. That sort of thing. But Aspen Springs is a small town. If people can't bang their co-workers, who the hell *can* they bang? Anyway, I've known Adam forever. He's a good guy. Grouchy, yes. But a fundamentally good, decent human being. And hot as sin. Bang away, James. That's my advice."

I was horny enough that her logic was compelling. But the problem wasn't just public perception. He wasn't ready for a relationship. He had told me so himself.

Adam Hale was an Emotionally Unavailable Man. And like any overachieving girl with well-honed daddy issues, that happened to be my special brand of catnip. I could already hear the hopeful voice inside my head. *I can fix him. I can be what he needs.*

No matter how much I wished it were otherwise, I knew better. I had chased my dad's approval my whole life. Twisting myself like a pretzel to be the daughter he wanted me to be. It had never worked with my dad, and it wasn't going to work with Adam. He was never going to love me the way I wanted to be loved. Wholly and completely, with no regrets.

Emily was the love of his life. I remembered what he had said about his dad's theory. That it was a *relief* that a love like that only came around once in a lifetime. That once-in-a-lifetime love had broken his heart and his spirit. It wasn't only that he didn't believe he could have a great love twice. He didn't even want to try. Honestly, I didn't blame him.

And I sure as hell wasn't arrogant enough to think I was the woman to change his mind.

24

Adam

I FOUND lots of reasons to disappear with James off Lodestar property. Coffee runs, feed store, groceries, fuel for the backup generator...chores I had put off for months were now deemed urgent. So long as it meant I could put my hands on her, I didn't care what else I was doing. One day we took a couple horses right up to the furthest property line from the stables...and then we went a foot past it so I could have the pleasure of eating her pussy.

But every time we left, we had to come back. My hand on her thigh, tracing the inseam of her jeans, until the moment we passed under the Lodestar Ranch sign, when she would gently, firmly push me away. And I let her. Because keeping work and us separate was what she needed. I wouldn't stand in the way of her career.

But it felt like shit. And I had no clue what to do about it.

I felt like a horny teenager again. My thoughts were consumed with James and sex and sex with James. I didn't know how much longer I could keep pretending she was nothing more than my employee.

But she didn't seem bothered by it at all. Somehow in between all the errands I dragged her on, she found time to do her job and do it well.

Because what the hell was I looking at right now? A goddamn miracle.

Belle loped around the ring with James sitting tall in the saddle. Despite the lack of bridle, James was in complete control. She rested her hands on the saddle horn and used her legs and seat to guide Belle.

"Fuck me," Blaine muttered at my elbow. "Did you ever see the like?"

I couldn't tear my eyes away. "No, I never have."

James looked like a legend. The kind of woman people told stories about around the campfire. Her hair streamed in a wild, dark river under her helmet as they loped around the ring. James's body melded to Belle's, her commands so precise and perfect that it was hard to see them at all. But Belle felt them. And she obeyed. Willingly. They were completely in sync.

But the real surprise came when James took Belle

down the center of the ring on the diagonal. When they got to the center, Belle gave a small hop, changing her lead leg, and continued the lope in the other direction.

Blaine whipped off his ballcap and smacked it on the fence. "Did you see that? A perfect lead change. Holy shit, Belle the Bitch might have some real potential."

"She's been working on that all week," Ben piped up. "We wanted to surprise you. I promised not to say a word. Are you surprised, Dad?"

I glanced over at my kid, who was beaming with pride. Pride in himself for keeping a secret and pride in his friend for pulling it off. "Yeah, I'm surprised. I had no idea Belle had come so far."

Blaine rested one foot on the bottom rung of the rail. "She said she thinks Belle has a problem with the bridle. Considering she's doing more without it than any of us could do with it, I'd say there's a good chance she's right."

"She mentioned that."

I watched as James slowed Belle to a trot and then a walk. It wasn't as quick a transition without the bridle, but she got the job done. I shook my head, awed. Any decent rider understood the importance of an independent seat, but what James had just accomplished with Belle was nothing short of extraordinary.

"Can't enter a show without a bridle," Blaine said, stating the obvious.

"That's true." I scrubbed a hand over my smooth jaw. For once, I had remembered to shave. Yesterday I had left an rosy red burn between James's thighs. Considering the amount of time those thighs spent in the saddle, I figured I ought to do my part to keep them comfortable.

"Maybe Belle doesn't like people yanking at her face," Ben suggested. "I sure wouldn't."

That gave me pause. When was the last time someone had actually been gentle with Belle? Even Blaine, having seen plenty of other trainers hit the dirt first, had gone in with a strong hand right from the start. Not in a cruel way. Blaine would never be cruel. But for a sensitive animal already in pain? Maybe it had been too much.

"James will figure it out," I assured Ben. "Whatever Belle's issue is, James is a good trainer. She's patient. They'll work through it together."

Steven exited the barn and headed straight for James. "Hey, James, you forgot this." He shook the bridle, making the metal bit clang.

Everything happened at once. James had started to dismount, leaving her balanced on one leg in the stirrup when Belle leaped into the air and kicked her hind legs out behind her. James never stood a chance. She landed like a sack of potatoes against the rail. Her helmet made an ominous thump as it hit.

I crawled through the fence rails and sprinted to James, shouting orders as I went. "Stay back, Ben! Blaine, get Belle."

I sank to my knees in the dirt next to her. Still breathing, thank god. Her eyes were closed, her skin pale, her helmet dented. At least she had been wearing one. That would have been her skull. Muttering curses, I gently unbuckled the chin strap.

"Please wake up, buttercup. Please."

25

James

"I'm FINE," I said for the millionth time as Adam leaned across the center console to unbuckle me. "Stop babying me."

"You *will* be fine," Adam corrected. "Right now you have bruised ribs. The doctor said not to do anything strenuous for the next couple days."

I rolled my eyes. "Yeah, I was there. This isn't my first injury, and I'm pretty sure unbuckling a seatbelt does not count as strenuous activity." I did air quotes around the words and immediately regretted lifting my arms.

Shit, that hurt.

I breathed through the pain, turning my wince into a smile. From the look of Adam's furrowed brow and flat mouth, I wasn't fooling him one bit. "I'm fine. I just want to go inside, take a hot bath, and get into bed until tomorrow." Except I didn't have a bathtub. Dammit. "A hot shower, I mean."

Adam leaned across me to grab the seatbelt and buckled me back in with a click. He threw the gear shift in reverse.

"Where are we going?" I asked as we rolled away from my cabin.

"The big house. I have a bathtub." Then, like he knew I was about to protest, he sweetened the deal. "And Epsom salts. You aren't the first of us to get dusted and you won't be the last."

I chewed my bottom lip. Getting naked and wet at my boss's house didn't seem like the best plan for keeping things strictly professional here at Lodestar Ranch. Then again, I was injured. I could barely lift my arms. Anything that involved hot and heavy breathing fell into the category of things I would like very much to avoid for the time being.

I didn't bother arguing when we pulled up to the big house and he unbuckled my seatbelt again. I rolled my eyes but I sat obediently when he told me not to move, then waited until he opened the passenger door and held out his hand before I got out.

"I swear to god if you try to carry me inside the house I will go boneless and take us both down," I warned.

He smirked. "I know your legs work, buttercup. Good to know your mouth does, too."

His gaze lingered there on my lips. I sucked in a breath, making my ribs burn.

"Don't," I said. "Don't look at me like that."

"I can't seem to look at you any other way."

"Well, you have to. Because...you have to." *Because it hurts to breathe when you look at me like that.* The sharp feeling in my lungs was mostly the fault of my bruised ribs, but my bruised ribs had nothing to do with the ache in my chest.

"Are you sure?" His hand was so gentle as he brushed my hair back from my forehead. "It might be fun to make Brax's head spin around."

"I want to be respected as the head trainer at Lodestar Ranch. That's going to be hard if everyone knows I'm banging the boss," I said.

That wasn't my real reason. Yes, I wanted respect, but my work spoke for itself. I did a damn good job and I knew it. I hadn't slept my way into the job and there was no higher position to promote me to. People would gossip, no doubt, but eventually they would find something more interesting to talk about. I would hate it, of course. I had worked so hard to be taken seriously.

Love was worth fighting for. I believed that. But with Adam, I'd be fighting alone.

The second we got inside Ben came barreling into the foyer with Ted right behind him. He slid to a halt on his socked feet, grabbing the staircase banister for balance.

"James!" His blue eyes were wide and anxious as he looked me over. "You look okay."

"I'm good, bud," I assured him. "Banged up a bit, but no broken bones."

"I wasn't worried," he lied and I arched an eyebrow, amused. "Dad sure was, though. I thought he was going to cry."

"I was *not* going to cry," Adam said, exasperated. His hand went to my lower back, guiding me toward the staircase. "James is going to use my bathtub and then she's going to stay for dinner."

"Got it." Ted was already steering Ben into the kitchen. "Let's go figure out what we're going to make."

I stared up the staircase. That was a lot of steps. The normal amount, probably, but right then it was daunting. My ribs had taken the brunt of the fall, but there wasn't a single part of me that wasn't sore.

"Right," I muttered. "This is going to hurt."

It was the wrong thing to say. He had me off my feet and in his arms before I could take a single step.

"I told you not to carry me!" My outrage was feeble against the onslaught of squishy feelings from being held against his muscular chest.

"You told me not to carry you into the house. You said nothing about up the stairs. Totally different."

"You wouldn't carry Blaine up the stairs. Or Jesse."

"I would if they needed me to."

I actually believed him. But I also knew that need was a different standard. Both Blaine and Jesse would have to be on death's door before they let Adam haul them up the stairs. "*I* don't need you to."

"Again, that's different. Because in this case, *I* needed to carry you. I needed to not see you in pain." He set me down at the top of the stairs and gave me the gentlest nudge. "This way."

He led me into what was very obviously a bedroom. A queen-size bed was front and center, decked out in linens of a deep, masculine gray. The large window had matching gray drapes. A knotted pine dresser stood between what I assumed was the closet door and the bathroom door. Next to the left side of the bed was a pine table. The right side was empty, giving the room an unfinished look. That was the extent of the décor. No paintings, no framed photographs, no flowers or mementos.

"Your room?" I asked, even though I knew it was. Something about the lonely nightstand gave it away. A different man might have bought the matching pair on the hope that someday there would be a woman to use it.

Not Adam. Spending the rest of his life single was a foregone conclusion. He wanted it that way. No matter how the way he looked at me said otherwise.

"Yeah. I figured you'd be more comfortable here than Ted's bathroom or the hall bathroom. And this one has the best tub." He moved to the dresser, opened the bottom drawer, and removed a towel, which he tossed on the bed.

"You figured right."

He stared at me for a beat. "You don't have any clean clothes here," he said as realization dawned that I was about to be fully naked.

"Right again."

He stared at me for another second, assessing. "You can borrow a shirt and shorts from me. I'll leave them on the bed for you."

"Thank you."

"Bathroom's right there." He jerked his head toward the door to the right of the dresser. "Epsom salts are under the sink. Holler if you need anything. I won't be far."

He was halfway out the door before I finally pushed his name from my suddenly dry mouth. "Adam."

"Yeah?" He stopped and looked back at me.

I wet my lips nervously. "I need help."

"You want me to run the bath for you?" He started for the bathroom without waiting for a response.

"I need you to get me out of my bra."

He froze. "Come again?"

"Under normal circumstances, removing a sports bra is like wrestling an anaconda. It requires strength, endurance, and dexterity. Quite frankly, I'm lacking all three right now." I lifted my tee shirt over my head. Slowly, carefully, painfully. "Getting the rest of my clothes off is going to be bad enough. A sports bra is beyond me."

He frowned at my chest. "All right," he gritted out. He took me by the shoulders and turned me so my back was facing him. "There's no clasp."

"I know. That's what makes it hard. You're going to have to cut me out of it."

Silence.

His fingers flexed into my shoulders in a quick, involuntary spasm. I would have done anything to see his face right then...except show him mine. I kept my gaze glued to my pink boots, not daring to turn around.

"I'll get the scissors." His voice was polite. Distant.

I blew out a shallow breath as he disappeared down the hallway. A moment later he returned, shutting the door behind him.

"Let's get this over with," he said grimly. Like it was punishment to cut my sports bra off my body.

He hooked a finger under the thick band, right between my breasts. I gasped as the heat of his finger was replaced with the cold steel of the scissors. His eyes shot to my face.

"It's fine," I said. "I didn't expect it to be so cold. Keep going."

He nodded, his brows pushed together into a dark slash across his forehead. With each cut of the fabric, my breasts expanded and his brows contracted. It was almost funny. The kind of funny where you don't know whether to laugh or cry.

After the last snip, my mangled bra split open to reveal the inner curves of my breasts, he raised his gaze to my face. He kept it there as he gently slid the bra from my shoulders and let it fall to the ground.

"Thank you." Already it felt like I could breathe easier.

He plucked something from my hair and showed it to me. Hay. "You're filthy."

"Well, yeah. I was rolling around in the dirt." My lips tilted into a rueful smile. "My hair is probably going to be sandy for a few days. I don't think I can scrub it the way it needs right now."

For some reason, that seemed to annoy him. "You won't feel right until you're clean."

"I'll be fine. Now let me—"

"I'll do it. Come on, we'll get you cleaned off in the shower and then you can soak in the tub until you're ready for dinner."

I gaped at him. "What?"

"I've already seen you naked. Hell, I've touched every part of you naked. I can wash your hair. Anyway, if you get in the tub now, you're just going to be wallowing in your own filth."

He had a point. Still, I hesitated. "Are you sure?"

His lips tilted in a wry smirk. "Buttercup, if I can survive cutting a bra off you, I can survive anything. Now let's get you clean."

I followed him into the bathroom, which was roughly the size of the bedroom. There were his-and-hers sinks, a toilet closet, a large shower, and—best of all—a deep soaking tub. I couldn't hold back my gasp of delight.

His mouth quirked. "Yeah. My mom was a big fan of fancy bathrooms. And Dad was a fan of giving her everything she ever wanted."

"It's beautiful." Both the bathroom and the sentiment behind it.

Adam toed off his boots and shucked his clothes with

an unembarrassed efficiency that left me gaping at his naked body before I could gird myself. He squatted by my feet, his mouth inches from my pussy. I used his shoulders to keep my balance as he removed my boots and socks.

"This," he said conversationally, "is so much worse than cutting off your bra."

His breath tickled my belly and I squeezed my eyes shut. "I'm injured," I ground out.

"Baby, I know that. You could lie spread-eagle on the bed, begging me to take you, and I still wouldn't fuck you." He unclasped my jeans and wiggled them gently down my legs. "You're too precious for me to risk hurting you like that."

Goddammit, this man. What was he trying to do to me?

"I was reminding myself, not you," I groused. "Because certain body parts keep forgetting. And you... Don't say things like that to me. It makes everything too confusing."

He didn't say anything to that, just turned the faucet so water sprayed from the showerhead. He tested the temperature with his hand, made an adjustment, tested again, then nudged me through the glass door, stepping in behind me.

I tilted my head back, letting the water soak my hair.

"Turn around, baby."

"Don't call me that," I said, even as I obeyed, giving him my back.

"As long as pain is twisting your mouth like that and you're making those little whimpers, I'm calling you baby. You're hurt," he said quietly. "It feels inhuman to do anything else."

My insides melted. Adam hid it well, but beneath all the grunts and scowls was a man who felt deeply. He was a caretaker at heart, no matter how hard he fought against it.

He squeezed a dollop of shampoo into his palm, rubbed his hands together, then got to work on my hair. Good lord, the man had magic hands. His fingertips kneaded my scalp with perfect pressure as he scrubbed away the sand and stress of the day.

"Okay," I relented, barely biting back a moan as he gave my hair a gentle tug. "But not around other people."

I turned around to rinse my hair and found him scowling. "What?"

"You're covered in bruises."

"Yeah," I said drily. "I fell off a horse."

"I don't like it."

I laughed and rolled my eyes. "Calm down, daddy. Falling off is a part of riding. You said it yourself. I'm not the first to get thrown, and I won't be the last."

He turned me around again to apply conditioner.

When he tried to put me back under the water, I stopped him. "It needs to soak in a while first."

"Oh." He blinked. "I don't do that."

"It doesn't matter on short hair." I stretched my arm up and ruffled his hair. It hurt, but it was worth it.

Apparently Adam didn't agree. He captured my wrist with a low growl. "Dammit. Don't hurt yourself touching me."

Unperturbed, I blew a raspberry at him and rinsed out my hair. "Stop treating me like I'm fragile. I'm fine."

He grunted. I took that for agreement.

He rubbed the bar of soap between his palms until his hands were covered in a rich, scented lather. Hooking an arm around my waist, he pulled me against him, my ass nestled below his cock. He ran his soapy hands along my shoulders, breasts, and belly, cleaning me. My head fell back against his chest on a gasp.

One hand dipped between my legs and I widened my thighs for him helpfully. Hopefully. But he refused to give me what I really wanted. I groaned in frustration.

He chuckled in my ear. "Come on, buttercup. You know that's off limits."

"Right. You're my boss." I moaned as he cleaned me with nowhere near enough pressure to get me off.

"I only care about that because you care about that. I care a lot more that you shouldn't be doing any heavy breathing for the next few weeks." His hand was still moving between my legs with soft, leisurely circles, even though we both knew that by now my pussy was cleaner than it had ever been.

My nails dug into his thighs for support. "I hate you so much right now."

"No, you don't."

He pushed me forward by my shoulders. I took a step, putting space between our bodies, and felt something poke me in my lower back. I glanced over my shoulder to see his cock, fully hard and jutting forward.

"Ignore that," he murmured as he soaped my back. "I'll handle it later."

Handle? *Hand*-le? I snickered because I was a child.

"Liked that one, did you?" he asked, sounding pleased.

"Wait, you punned on purpose? *You*, Mr. Resting Grump Face." I shook my head in mock disbelief. "Wait until I tell everyone. No one will believe it."

"Yeah?" Amusement laced his voice. "You're gonna tell everyone how I made a pun about jacking off while we showered together?"

I reconsidered. Then I pouted. I couldn't tell anyone.

"James." The thick, rough way he said my name licked down my spine, following the same path he trailed with his finger. "When I handle it? I'm going to think about you. The way you are now. Soap running down your back. Down your ass. Imagine it's my cum."

I shivered. *Ached*. "You fucking better."

AFTER A NICE, hot soak in the most wonderful tub to ever exist, I came down the stairs wearing Adam's clothes and smelling like his shampoo. It was a weird feeling. I wanted to cuddle my arms around myself, a poor substitute for who I really wanted. Sounds of banging pots and laughter led me to the kitchen, where I found Ted manning the stove, Adam doing dishes at the sink, and Ben at the table, pouring over what looked like a pile of records.

I hesitated in the doorway, enjoying the scene. There was so much love in this room. Grief could have torn this family apart, but Adam had simply refused to allow it. He was the glue that held them together. I could have spent another hour there, soaking it in, admiring the way the muscles in Adam's back bunched and moved beneath his gray t-shirt as he scrubbed a pan, but Ben spotted me.

"James! Come see what I found."

"Sure," I said, but I stayed rooted to the spot as Adam

turned from the sink, his gaze heated as he took me in. He took two steps forward, hands soapy and reaching for me, then froze as my eyes widened. He blinked and scowled at his hands, like he had suddenly come to his senses.

Okay, *now* I felt awkward. Wearing his clothes, smelling like him, standing in his kitchen with bare feet and wet hair? Totally fine. Adam reaching for me like a quick kiss was how we always greeted each other? The most natural thing in the world. Pretending he was nothing more than my boss? Soooo awkward.

"What's all this?" I asked Ben as I joined him at the table.

"I found Dad's old record player." Ben held up a Def Leppard album with a red triangle and bright mouths screaming. "It's the music of his youth."

"Hey, now." Adam shot Ben a look of affectionate exasperation. "I wasn't even born yet when those albums came out."

I flipped through the stack. Most of them I had never heard of. Skid Row, Guns and Roses, Poison, White Snake. Definitely not the country music I had grown up with. Heavy on the hairspray and eyeliner. I quirked an eyebrow at Adam. "Pretty tough names for groups of boys rocking beach waves and shiny pants."

"They're performers," Adam defended.

Ben peered over my arm. "They look weird."

"There's no easy way to tell you this, kiddo," Ted said somberly as he ripped open a box of macaroni and cheese, removed the packet of cheese powder, and dumped the rest of the contents into the pot of boiling water. "Your dad had a phase—"

"Dad!" Adam protested.

Ted grinned. "Picture this. Adam was sixteen and had just discovered a Mötley Crüe record and fell down the rabbit hole of eighties hair bands. But it wasn't enough to listen to the music—always on vinyl, because he was a snob—he had to have the whole look, too. Leather pants, grew his hair long, begged us until we finally let him get a perm—"

My gaze shot to Adam. "Oh, I'm picturing it, all right."

He buried his face in his hands and groaned.

"Dad, no!" Ben laughed, his face flushed pink like he was suffering from second-hand embarrassment. Which he probably was. I, on the other hand, was enjoying first-hand glee.

"Yes, your dad was a huge dork," Ted said. "Probably would have gotten his ass kicked daily if he weren't the best tight end Aspen Springs High had ever seen."

I didn't know what a tight end was, but I was certainly a fan of Adam's tight end. My gaze lingered on him. "I don't suppose there's any photographic evidence of this phase?"

"I'll dig some up," Ted promised.

"Dad," Adam said. "You cannot show James those photos."

Ted was apparently too engrossed in chopping jalapeños to hear him. I smothered a smile.

"Can we listen to something, Dad?" Ben asked hopefully.

Adam shrugged. "Sure, why not. Pick something." He plugged in the record player, then took the album Ben held out and glanced at the cover. "Van Halen. This is a good one."

He dropped the record in place, fiddled with something, and a second later pulsing guitar and drum beats filled the room.

"Show us how you danced to this, Adam." Ted didn't look up from his task, but a sly smile hovered on his lips.

From the way Adam's eyes narrowed on his father, I fully expected him to say no. But Ben piped up, "Yeah, show us, Dad!" and Adam grabbed a dish towel and held the short edge to his head.

"Pretend this is hair," he said.

I was still trying to process that very weird command when the singer screamed "Panamaaaa!" and Adam leaned forward, whipping his dish towel hair in perfect time to the music. Ted put down the knife and stared slack jawed at his son like he couldn't believe what he was witnessing. Ben doubled over with laughter, clutching my shoulder for support.

I couldn't laugh. I couldn't do anything but sit there with a cheek-splitting grin on my face as I soaked in the sight of my grumpy cowboy who carried the weight of the world on his broad shoulders cutting loose like a complete goofball.

"And that's how it's done." Adam tossed the dish towel aside, his face completely neutral like the whole performance was totally normal. But his eyes glimmered at me as he grabbed a clean dish towel and resumed drying the dishes. "It's called headbanging."

Ben slid to the floor in a heap of giggles. "Headbanging. Do another one!"

"My turn to pick." Ted rinsed his hands and dried them on his jeans.

He flipped through the stack, made his selection, and placed it on the record player. I caught a glimpse of the cover. A band named Sheriff. I smirked. Tough name. Permed hair.

This song was different. Softer. Slower. Instead of driving drums, it began with a sweet melody tapped out on the piano. And then came the lyrics. *I never needed love like I need you.*

"You can't headbang to this," Ben complained.

"It's a power ballad," Adam said. "Every hair band needed a good power ballad. Guns N Roses had *November Rain*. Poison had *Every Rose Has Its Thorn*. And Sheriff had this. *When I'm with You*."

"It's a kissing song." Ben made a disgusted face. "You can't dance to it."

Maybe it's the way you touch me with the warmth of the sun.

Adam's gaze snagged mine. The heat there made my insides tremble. Did that lyric make him think of what he said to me in the hotel room before we fell asleep? *I kissed you because I was cold and you are the fucking sun.* Because suddenly that was all I could think about.

"You can dance to it," Adam said. "Come here, James. We'll show him."

I could feel my skin flush as I let him pull me gently into his arms. My ribs hurt too much to lift my hands to his shoulders, so instead I wrapped them around his waist. His arms circled me like a hug. As we swayed to the music, our bodies flush against each other, his hand swept up my back and under my hair, where he gently squeezed my neck. The first power chords burst through.

Baby, I get chills when I'm with you.

But it wasn't just the music coming from the record player I heard. It was Adam's rough whisper in my ear.

My skin erupted in gooseflesh. Everything around us faded as the intimacy of the moment wrapped us up like a warm blanket. A sweet, achy feeling bloomed in my chest.

Oh, hell.

I was in trouble.

I knew it as the last strains faded and Adam slowly released me. Sex with Adam had been mind-bogglingly good. But this? The way he had so gently washed my hair? And now, dancing in the kitchen? This was something else.

This was something that could break my heart.

26

Adam

"What do you think?" I asked after Blaine eased Belle from a lope to a trot and then slowed to a walk. Next to me James practically vibrated with excitement.

Blaine shook his head side to side, the movements slow and shocked. "I can't believe I'm sitting here on Belle the Bitch. Thought she'd dust me for sure."

"Hey!" James protested. "Don't call her that. She's a horse. She doesn't know you're joking."

I snorted and she flashed me a cheeky grin. I soaked up all that warmth like she was the last of my wood stores in a brutal winter and the groundhog had just predicted a late spring. My girl had blown hot and cold since the night we danced in my kitchen. Sometimes I could swear she was avoiding me. But other times I managed to get her off Lodestar Ranch property long enough to remind her how things were when I wasn't her boss.

In the week since her accident, James and Blaine had worked together to keep Belle's training moving forward. James had re-introduced Belle to the bit and bridle the same way she had with everything else—one slow step at a time. She had started her on the bridle without a rider. Just walking around, learning it didn't have to hurt. Yesterday Blaine had gotten on for one ride around the ring at a sedate walk.

Today marked her first real ride.

A fucking miracle.

"You did great, Blaine," James said. "Nice, quiet hands, just like we talked about."

He slid from the saddle and patted her on the neck before he handed the reins to Jesse for her cooldown and grooming. "You were right. She has a sensitive mouth."

For some reason that made him frown. Maybe he was remembering all the mistakes we had made that had led us here. All of us thinking what Belle needed was an attitude adjustment and a firm hand when really the opposite was true. Each new trainer more determined than the last to be the one to bring her in line. I rubbed my jaw. I didn't like being the cause of a horse's pain, and because Blaine wasn't an asshole, I was willing to bet he felt the same way.

I turned to James but her eyes were on the stable.

"I'm going to help Jesse," she said, pushing away from the rail.

Avoiding me again.

"She says her ribs barely hurt anymore," Blaine said. He tugged his hat off, swiped the sweat from his forehead with his shirt sleeve.

I nodded. "Another week or two and she'll be good to ride again." That was good news, so I was surprised when Blaine frowned again. "Something on your mind?"

"Been thinking about the bridle. She told you she suspected Belle's issues were in her mouth?"

"She did. We talked it over before we went to Colorado Springs for the rodeo."

"Right. She told me, too." He turned the brim of his hat in his hands. "Makes me wonder why Steven came out here that day, swinging the bridle around like a fucking fool. Knowing James was on Belle and Belle was afraid of the bridle."

I stilled. "He said he didn't know."

Blaine looked at me. "He knew."

He knew? Son of a bitch. White hot fury churned in my gut. "I think it's time I had a talk with him."

Blaine cocked his head and eyeballed me suspiciously. "Talk, huh? I'll come with you."

"Probably best if you don't."

Blaine snorted. "Best if you don't have a witness, you mean."

STEVEN WAS IN THE BREAKROOM, scrolling whatever-the-fuck on his phone, legs stretched out and crossed at the ankles, his boots on the table. It pissed me off. People had to eat there.

"What's up, boss?" he asked with that stupid little smirk that suggested everything was a joke.

"Get your shoes off the goddamn table."

Part of me hoped he would refuse, or at least take his sweet time about complying. Anything to give me a reason to put my hands on him. The saner part—the voice that unfortunately sounded a lot like Brax—warned me that if I touched him now with all this rage boiling my blood, I might not be able to stop.

His eyebrows shot up as he slowly lowered his legs to the ground. "Sure thing."

I crossed my arms over my chest, tucking my hands safely underneath my biceps. "Thought you might be interested in knowing that James seems to have worked out Belle's bridle issues."

Steven twitched his hand, like he was flinging something off. His gaze skated from mine. "That's good."

And I knew. I fucking *knew*.

"You want to explain?" It was a struggle to keep my voice even. To keep my hands tucked away where they couldn't wrap around his neck.

His eyes met mine only briefly before darting away again. His fingers flexed against his thigh. "Explain what?"

"Why you walked into the training ring, where you knew James was on Belle, shaking that bridle when you knew goddamn well Belle would react?"

"You think I got James hurt on purpose?" He pushed to his feet. "You think I would do that?"

I didn't move. Couldn't, or I would throttle the man where he stood. "Did you?"

"We've all been dusted by Belle. How the hell was I supposed to know your delicate princess would get her ribs cracked?"

That was as good as a confession that he had purposefully taunted Belle into throwing James without stopping to think through the consequences. He was right that we had all been tossed at one time or another, by Belle or another horse—I had personally lost count of how many times I had hit the ground doing dumb shit as a teenager—and most of the time, all we walked away with was bruised muscles and sore pride. Zack got a concussion once, terrifying my mom.

But some people didn't walk away at all.

And we all knew that, too. That was the risk that came with sitting on top of a thousand-pound prey animal. They were hardwired to lose their shit and take off.

This dumb fuck had put one of my people in harm's way, carelessly and without remorse. I didn't take that lightly.

I intended to say all that, but what came out was, "Watch your fucking mouth when you talk about her."

He stared at me while I silently dared him to say it again. To give me a reason to take out my hands.

But he shook his head and exhaled hard through his nose. "Right. Whatever you say."

"Pack your things. You're out of here by the end of the day."

From the way he reared back, I knew he hadn't been expecting that. That surprised me. This entitled dickweed actually believed he hadn't done anything wrong.

"You're firing me over a goddamn joke?" he demanded, disbelief dripping on every word.

"Your goddamn joke could have gotten someone killed. You're lucky all she got was a few bruised ribs."

Steven snorted. "She gets a little banged up and runs straight to you. Of course. Should have seen this coming. Fucking slut."

I moved. One hand grabbed him by the collar. I planted my other fist in his face. Once to teach him a lesson. The second punch was just for fun. Pure fury demanded a third blow, but before I could land it, Blaine was there, hauling me back.

"Enough," he said. "You made your point—"

Steven took the opportunity to get in a blow of his own, getting me right on my jaw. My head snapped back, knocking against Blaine, who fell back only a step before quickly recovering.

"Seriously, man? You can't take a swing at someone who's being held back." Blaine rubbed his forehead where we had knocked together and shot Steven a look of disgust. "I should kick your ass for that." He grabbed him by the shoulder. "Count yourself lucky that I'm gonna walk your pathetic ass out of here instead. Let's go."

Finally showing a lick of self-preservation, Steven didn't protest as Blaine marched him to the door.

Our eyes met on his way out. He touched his hand to his mouth, found the blood there, and wiped it on his jeans. "This isn't over."

"Stay away from James, or you'll be begging me to finish it before I'm done with you," I promised.

Blaine's quick head shake held a warning, but I was too furious to care. James was off limits and the sooner Steven made his peace with that, the better for everyone involved.

But I suspected he meant what he said. This wasn't over.

27

James

SOMETHING WAS UP. Steven hadn't shown up for work this morning. When I asked Blaine if he had heard from him, he directed me to Adam. Adam had been avoiding me since Blaine's ride on Belle yesterday, but I finally found him repairing a fence.

"Is Steven sick?" I asked. "Maybe someone should go check on him."

Adam didn't look up from his work. I couldn't see his face beneath his ball cap. "Gone," he grunted in a non-enlightening way.

"Gone?" I repeated. "Gone where? How long? For today? A week?"

"For good."

My forehead furrowed. What the heck did that mean? "Is he dead?"

I was mostly joking, but then Adam muttered, "Not yet," and that made me nervous.

"What's going on?" I asked.

"We'll talk about it later."

"But—"

"Later."

I knew Adam well enough to know I wasn't going to drag it from him until he was ready to talk. "Fine."

I stalked back to the barn. Now that Belle had proven rideable, it was time for her real training to begin. I set my sights on preparing her for a cow horse open reining class in Denver—an event big enough to get a feel for how she performed under pressure, but small enough that a bad showing wouldn't be much of a hit to the ranch. That gave us a month to teach her the basics of herd work, rein work, and fence work.

It also gave us a month to find a rider. For that, I turned to Essie Price.

Essie had shown up at Lodestar Ranch bright and early to take Magpie for a ride and check on his progress. Watching Essie take Magpie around the barrels, I knew she was the one I wanted on Belle for her first show. Her hands were soft, her seat independent. She exuded grace and confidence and I was sure she could convince Belle to do her best.

"What do you think?" I asked her after I had explained my plan for Belle.

She fingered the reins thoughtfully. "Maybe. I'm already one of the oldest on the barrel racing circuit, and I've been trying to figure out my next move. This could be a good opportunity to get a start in reining." She grinned at me. "With one of the top trainers in the country, no less."

I smiled back. "You and Belle would have my undivided attention for the next month."

"That sounds great." She chewed her lip. "But you can't pay me. I want to keep my non-pro status next year as I get my feet wet."

"Still bending rules, Essie?" Brax drawled, joining us at the rail. "People really don't change after high school, I guess."

Essie arched one perfectly shaped brow. "Well, you still have that stick up your ass, so I guess you're right."

It was hard to tell if this thing between them was true animosity or some bizarre mating ritual. The air practically crackled between them. I stepped back, not wanting to get electrocuted.

"You really think it's fair for a rider of your capabilities to compete as a non-pro?" Brax challenged.

"In the first place, we're not talking about a non-pro event. I'd be riding Belle in an open class against pros and non-pros. As I'm sure you know," Essie said, her words laced with sarcasm, "the difference between the two is whether you get paid to ride, not skill level."

Brax leaned into her space, bringing his hand to her cheek under the pretext of stroking Magpie's mane. Although from the way her eyes spit fire at him, maybe she didn't know it was a pretext.

"The other difference is ownership of the animal," Brax reminded her. "As I'm sure *you* know. Non-pros have to be the sole owner of the horse they ride."

"The class is actually a Limited Open, which means any non-pro who hasn't received more than twenty grand in prize earnings for the year can enter without owning the horse. Which you would know if you had bothered to ask before butting your nose into our conversation. I'm not breaking any of your precious rules."

There didn't seem an end in sight to their standoff, so I cleared my throat. They both looked up. Brax stopped fiddling with Magpie's mane. I was sure I saw his fingertips skim her throat as he stepped back. *Interesting.*

"Are you looking for Adam?" I asked. "He's out in the pasture grunting at fence posts."

Brax smirked at that. "Sounds like Adam, but since I told him I'd be here, he should be waiting for me in his office. I'm heading there now. Actually, you should come, too."

"Sure." I didn't know what this was about, but paperwork seemed like a fair assumption. As far as I could tell, paperwork was Brax's specialty at Lodestar. I glanced at Essie. "Jesse can help you get Magpie squared away, but you're welcome to hang out as long as you want."

"Thanks. I'll take care of Magpie myself. I like doing it."

A horsewoman after my own heart.

I nodded to Brax. "Let's go."

"YOU WANT to tell me why Steven McAllister thinks he has a case against Lonestar Ranch for assault?" Brax asked pleasantly, wasting no time.

I froze with my butt halfway to the chair, then fell the rest of the way with an audible thump. "What?" I turned to Adam with eyes wide. "What?"

Adam drummed his fingers against his thigh. My attention snagged on the ugly red welts along his knuckles.

"What happened to your hand?" I asked, forgetting Brax was still waiting for an answer. And then Adam turned to look at me and I got a clear shot of his face for the first time. I gasped. "What happened to your *face*?"

His expression was an inscrutable scowl. "Nothing."

I bristled. "It's *not* nothing—"

Brax cleared his throat. "According to Mr. McAllister, at approximately eleven-fifteen yesterday morning, you entered the breakroom. The two of you argued and then you attacked him."

Adam crossed his arms. He refused to look at me no matter how hard I stared at him. "I fired him. Then I punched him."

Brax looked to the ceiling as though praying for divine intervention. "That doesn't sound better."

"Well, then how does this sound? Steven put one of my employees in danger. When I confronted him about it, he admitted it. So I fired him. He didn't take kindly to that, and we scuffled a bit. The end."

"Not quite," Brax said mildly.

I split a look between them, trying to figure out what the hell they *weren't* saying. As far as I knew, the only person who had been in danger at Lodestar was me. But no one had put me in danger. Falling off horses was part of riding. "Is this about me? Because I fell off Belle?"

When Adam didn't answer I looked pleadingly at

Brax, but he just shook his head and sent me back to his irritating brother. "Adam, answer me. *Look* at me."

He turned to me, finally, and when he did his mouth softened. "He scared Belle on purpose, James. He wanted you to fall."

I reeled back. "But why? Why would he do something like that? It doesn't make sense."

"I don't think he actually wanted to see you hurt," Adam said gently. "He didn't think of the consequences, that's all. He was being a dumbass, but I can't let that kind of thing happen here. He had to go."

"Okay," I said slowly. "But you didn't have to punch him."

A muscle twitched in his cheek. "Oh, yes, I fucking did."

Brax's mouth flattened into a grim line. "He claims you hit him first after"—Brax paused and squeezed the bridge of his nose— "after he called your girlfriend a slut."

Girlfriend? Adam had a girlfriend?

What. The. Fuck.

I twisted in my chair to reach past the space between us and slap him across the stomach. "You have a girlfriend?" I shouted. "Who? Who is she?"

"Ah!" Adam grunted, lifting his arm to block my next hit. "Woman—"

"James," Brax said.

"What?" I snapped.

"You're the girlfriend in question."

"Me? What are you talking about? I'm not…" I looked from Brax to Adam and my voice died on the look of *Come on, seriously?* he served me. Oh, shit. I cleared my throat. "I don't know why Steven would think that." My voice pitched higher than normal.

Brax stared at me. Hard. I chewed my lip and tried to look like someone who hadn't had the best sex of her life with his brother.

Brax turned his stare to Adam. "He also says you threatened his life."

"It wasn't a death threat," Adam protested. "It was a boundary. So long as he stays away from James, he's got nothing to worry about."

"Fucking hell." Brax dragged his hands down his face like he couldn't believe what he was hearing. "All right. Here's what I need to know. Are you two together? Because that determines how I handle this."

"In what way?" Adam asked. Carefully. I took note of that.

"If you're together, he has a stronger case. He could paint you as a jealous boyfriend who went crazy on him. Maybe that would put wrongful termination on the table, seeing how you're his boss…and hers." Brax shrugged. "If you're not together, that weakens his case. I might be able to convince him to walk away with a small payment for his troubles. He seems more interested in money than pressing charges."

Tension rolled off Adam in waves. And I knew he was about to do something stupid. Like tell Brax the truth out of some misguided sense of duty toward me. But I couldn't let him do that.

Lodestar Ranch and his family were everything to Adam. And I was...Well, I wasn't the love of his life. That title had already been claimed. And I refused to be another duty to him. Another responsibility. Not when we could both walk away from this before either of us got hurt. Before the *ranch* got hurt.

"We're not together," I said firmly. I could feel Adam's eyes burning into me but I kept my gaze focused straight ahead on his brother. "I'm not his girlfriend."

For a long moment no one said a word. The room was so quiet I could hear the sounds of horses chewing their oats in the barn.

"You're sure?" Brax asked. "Because I can—"

"You heard the woman. We're not together," Adam bit out.

I blanched. I wanted to touch him. Soothe whatever sore spot I had rubbed open. But I couldn't do that here. Later. Later we would talk it through and everything would be okay. We would go back to a strictly professional relationship, on and off Lodestar property. He understood as well as I did that putting the ranch at risk wasn't acceptable.

Brax looked from Adam to me and back to Adam again. He shook his head.

"All right," he said finally. "I'll make this go away."

28

Adam

ZACK

> Swinging through Aspen Springs on my way to Texas. Anyone up for the Painted Cat?

BRAX

> Hell yeah

ADAM

> On dad duty. Next time.

ZACK

> Let Ben have some granddad time. When was the last time all three of us went out together?

ADAM

> Not long ago enough to miss it.

ZACK

> Ouch. Wtf, man.

BRAX

Ignore him. He's in a bad mood because his girlfriend dumped him.

ADAM

She wasn't my girlfriend, jackass.

ZACK

Just texted Dad. He's on board with watching Ben. You're coming out with us.

ADAM

You can't make me.

BRAX

Ballsy thing to say to a steer wrestler, bro.

THERE WERE a million things I would rather be doing right now. Playing a cutthroat game of Sorry with Ben and Dad teaming up to take me down. Reading a chapter of the domestic thriller that had been on my nightstand for the past week now. Having my balls waxed by a sadistic Russian with a score to settle.

Literally anything would be better than sharing a booth with my two asshole brothers, a mere twenty feet away from the bar where I had the perfect view of James having drinks with Essie, Chloe, and some blonde woman I didn't recognize.

She was smiling. Laughing. Having a good time. Living her life like she didn't care if I wasn't part of it.

I took an aggressive slug of a whiskey that was meant to be sipped and let it burn through me. It hurt a hell of a lot less than James pretending I wasn't sharing the same bar as her.

"Do you ever wonder," Zack said in a way that had me steeling my nerves for hearing something I knew beyond a shadow of a doubt I didn't want to wonder about at all, "if we're sitting in the exact spot where great-great granddaddy Thomas met great-great grandma Celine and bought an hour in her pussy?"

I slammed my glass down on the worn pine table. "No, I fucking do *not*."

"Jesus fucking Christ, Zack." Brax curled his top lip in disgust. "Why do you say shit like that?"

Zack shrugged, unrepentant. "Pops into my head. No reason not to share. That's how conversation works."

"Conversation shouldn't involve thinking about how and where our grandparents had sex," Brax said.

"Why not? We never met them and they're long dead. Granddaddy Thomas had access to all the whores he wanted. What sort of sex tricks did Grandma Celine know to convince him to make an honest woman out of her? You can't tell me you aren't curious."

Brax scrubbed a hand over his face and groaned. "Make him stop."

Maybe I would have, but my eyes were already easing past them to James at the bar. She was twisted sideways on her barstool, an elbow propped on the bar, facing Chloe and Essie and the blonde woman. One pink-booted leg swung idly as she listened to Essie recount some story with wild hand gestures. Her hair was up, exposing the elegant length of her neck. Beautiful. So goddamn touchable.

If I were her man, that's where I'd be right now. Standing behind her, my thumb tracing circles along the side of her throat, letting her use my body as a backrest while she listened to her friends, knowing later tonight she'd be all mine.

And that was something else I would much rather be doing than brooding in a corner while my idiot brothers discussed the sex life of our great-great grandparents.

Snapping fingers flashed in front of my eyes, blocking my view of James.

"Stop staring at her, man," Zack said. "It's getting creepy."

I blinked and refocused on my brothers. "It can't be creepy if she doesn't know I'm doing it." Which she didn't. Because to know I'd spent the last hour staring at her, she would have had to look in my direction at least once. Which she hadn't.

And god *damn*, that stung.

"Said every stalker ever," Brax said. "What the hell is going on? You said you weren't together. So why are you staring at her like...like..."

I glowered. "Like what?"

He shook his head. "Like you're about to go caveman and throw her over your shoulder."

"I'm not going to do that." Although the idea was not without appeal.

But she didn't want that. Didn't want me. Or maybe she did...but not enough. She had sat right there in my office, faced down my brother, and told him as much. And I couldn't blame her. We had so much to lose, and for what? She'd made the right call. I knew that.

The terrifying thing was that it wasn't the call I would have made.

If she hadn't spoken up, I would have told my brother the truth. Brought our relationship into the light and figured out how to deal with the aftermath later. Taken that risk.

But I would never force her to do the same. Who was I to tell her being with me was more important than her reputation? If that risk was too much for her, I had to accept it. Her career meant everything to her. And she meant enough to me that I didn't want to screw that up for her.

The blonde touched her shoulder. James nodded and slid off her stool. Together they headed in the direction of the ladies' room with Chloe right behind them. More than one pair of male eyes watched her ass in those skin-tight jeans as they went.

I took another violent gulp of my whiskey and then glared down at my glass, resolving not to look at James for the rest of the night. No point in torturing myself with something I couldn't have.

"Hello, boys," Essie's husky voice greeted us. "And prig."

"Hellion," Brax returned.

The smile on her cherry-red lips widened. I had the feeling she wasn't mad about the nickname. But she turned away from him and leaned into me. "Come on, sunshine. Buy me a drink."

That confused me. She wasn't into me, I knew that much. I wasn't into her either, although I had eyes and therefore understood that, objectively, the woman was a smoke show. We had never been anything more than friendly acquaintances.

And then there was her whole weird history with Brax. Way back in high school, they used to be friends. Until one day they suddenly weren't. He never talked about why, and as far as anyone could tell, they were now mortal enemies. But instinctively I knew that if I hooked up with Essie and Brax ever found out about it, there wasn't a lawman alive who would find my body.

I shrugged and got to my feet. The woman wanted a drink, and I was still gentleman enough to oblige her. I followed her to the bar.

"What are you having?" I asked.

"Vodka martini with extra olives."

I nodded and took care of it, throwing some cash on the bar. "So what's this about? You trying to get Brax to commit fratricide?"

Her forehead scrunched and for a moment she looked honestly baffled. Then she burst out laughing. "You think Brax gives a damn who I talk to? Please. He hates me."

"Essie, I can feel his eyes trying to incinerate me from behind. He might hate you, but that doesn't mean he's okay with you and me having drinks."

She snorted. "Boys. Still fifty percent Neanderthal. Zack had the same stupid concerns. Trust me, Brax doesn't care what I do or who I'm with. If he's mad, it's because he thinks I'm not good enough for you." She scraped an olive off the toothpick with her teeth, then took a lingering sip of her martini. "Anyway, this has nothing to do with him."

"Yeah?" My curiosity was piqued. "What are we doing, then?"

Her gaze slipped over my shoulder and her lips tilted in a smirk. "I'm going to do you a big favor, Adam."

And with that, she grabbed my hat off my head and placed it on her own, laughing.

Wear the hat, ride the cowboy.

Goddamn it, was Essie trying to get me killed?

"Essie—"

But I didn't get another word out because suddenly my face was full of water. I blindly reached for a napkin and wiped my eyes clear.

Right in time to see James's fine ass storming out of the bar.

"What the hell just happened?" I demanded.

Essie calmly sipped her martini, the picture of innocence. "Go get your girl, big guy."

When I stared at her dumbly, she rolled her eyes. "Go," she prodded. "You're not really going to let her think I'm taking you home with me, are you?"

My gaze shot to where the door banged shut behind James. Hell no, I didn't want her thinking that.

"Tomorrow we're going to have a serious conversation about minding your own damn business."

But I was settling my tab even as I spoke. Of course I was going after her.

"Adam," she called after me, her voice husky with laughter. "Don't forget your hat."

29

James

I COULDN'T BELIEVE I did that.

Literally threw a glass of water in Adam's face. It might not even have been his water. Or Essie's. Maybe it was a stranger's water and now he had a faceful of a stranger's germs. Gross.

What the hell was wrong with me?

I never did things like that. Never. Dad had deemed any show of female emotion to be too much, so I had learned to siphon big feelings into palatable, carefully chosen words. The more I felt, the more cautious and deliberate I became. It served me well with horses, even if I resented the hell out of it when it came to people. Because I wasn't hotheaded and brash, no matter what Dad said.

Until tonight. Until Adam.

Essie had told me she wouldn't do anything with Adam, and I believed her. But that hadn't stopped me from losing my shit when she plopped his hat on her head. If I had stopped to think for even a second, I would have known it meant nothing. Emotion had pushed out every rational thought in my brain.

I stormed into my cabin and kicked the door shut behind me, buried my face in my hands, and screamed into them.

A heavy fist pounded on the door. "James, open up."

Adam. My heart kicked pitifully, like it wanted to burst through my chest and run to him. Stupid, stupid heart. "No," I said.

There was a pause.

"Open this door or I will break it down."

The words sounded like a promise. I rolled my eyes. "It's unlocked. Maybe try opening it yourself instead of moving straight into property damage."

He opened it, strode inside, and then stopped. Scowling. Dangerous and delicious all rolled into one grumpy cowboy package. I crossed my arms over my torso in a futile attempt to shield myself from wanting him.

"What the hell, James?" he demanded.

"What?" I asked, like throwing water in his face had been perfectly reasonable.

"First you tell my brother we're not together, then you ignore me all night, and *then* you throw water in my face without saying a fucking word. I don't get it. What are you so pissed about?"

My anger had eased into embarrassment somewhere between the Painted Cat and my front door, but now it came roaring back.

"There is a *code*," I snapped. "You can't hook up with my friends for at least ten years. Or never. Never is probably better." Because even though she had assured me she had no interest in him, *he* didn't know that. He had been perfectly happy to hit on my friend.

He squinted at me like he was trying to figure me out. "Are you *jealous*, buttercup?"

Seriously? *Seriously.* This man.

"Obviously I'm jealous," I huffed. "She's Essie Price. And you...you let her put your hat on her head like your hers now and you're not. You don't belong to her, Adam. You can't be hers because you're—" I clamped my mouth shut, trapping the word inside where it couldn't ruin me.

He moved so fast I didn't see it coming. One second he was by the door, the next he had me backed up against the wall.

"What am I, James?" His face was inches from mine, his heated gaze boring into me. "Tell me."

My heart pounded hard. I lifted my chin defiantly. "Mine."

"Prove it."

My gaze didn't leave his as I dragged my nails down the thin cotton of his t-shirt. When I reached his waist, he swallowed hard. For a moment I paused there, my fingertips hooked slightly over the edge of his jeans, my thumb rubbing the hefty silver buckle. We stared at each other and breathed. His cock twitched against my palm.

And then I couldn't wait any longer. I tugged frantically at his belt, fumbled with the button, yanked down his zipper. With one hand on his chest, I pushed him back, reclaiming my space. He gave it, but he made me work for it. Fight for it. Leaned against my touch, his mouth hovering so close to mine that I could feel the warmth of his lips. The heady rush of having this big, strong man obey my command made me feel more powerful than I ever had. I could feel the control he kept tightly tethered start to fray. I wanted to make it snap.

I dropped to my knees.

He inhaled audibly. His hands clenched into fists. I was eye-level with his thick cock that tented his boxer briefs. I freed him with both hands, then rocked back on my heels to admire the view. Big and beautiful and glistening with a bead of pre-cum on the tip.

"James," he said, sounding tortured.

My eyes flicked upward to meet his gaze. I leaned forward, licked up the pre-cum with a swipe of my tongue, and pressed a kiss to the silky tip like I was staking my claim. Which I was.

"Mine," I said.

"Yes. *Fuck.* Take what belongs to you."

His head tipped back on a groan, exposing the dark stubble of his jaw and neck. I think he needed to hear it as much as I needed to say it. Maybe that was the curse of being alive. Of being *human.* All we wanted, underneath the layers of bullshit and scars, was to belong to someone.

I slid him into my mouth, torturously slow, letting my tongue glide down his shaft as I took him as far back as I could go. My mouth was so full of him I could barely breathe. I paused there, inhaling and exhaling to steady myself, swallowed, and took him a little bit farther.

"God*damn*, baby."

I would have smiled at the breathless pleasure in his voice, but I wasn't willing to risk loss of suction for even an instant. I was on my knees, but I had him right where I wanted him. On the brink. And I couldn't wait to push him right over the edge.

As slowly as I took him in, I slid him out again. My hand worked his shaft while my mouth toyed with his tip, stroking it with my tongue and gently sucking, never taking him further than an inch. His hands dove to my head, one hand molding to the shape of my skull while his other hand wrapped my ponytail into his fist. Trying to take control.

But I wouldn't let him.

I licked him balls to tip and was rewarded with the squeeze of his fingers on my scalp and the tug of my hair. My tongue swirled against his tip, tasting more pre-cum, one hand sliding along his shaft while my other reached back to cup his balls, everything working in tandem to drive him completely insane.

"Please—goddamn it, James—suck me—"

The need in his voice made me squeeze my thighs together. I purred as I rubbed my thumb over the slick crown. "All you had to do was ask. I take care of what's mine."

And with that I sucked him in again, but this time I didn't stop.

I relinquished control and let him guide me into the rhythm he liked best. His thrusts turned longer, harder.

"Fuck, James. I'm going to..." He gave a frantic tug on my ponytail, trying to pull away from me.

But I held on, refusing to surrender. And then he

couldn't stop himself. His hips bucked against my mouth as the last thread of his control finally snapped. He came apart in my mouth and my hands. His cock jerked and pulsed in my mouth and I swallowed, never taking my eyes from his face, even when he closed his.

His hands loosened, his body went slack. He fell back against the wall with a soft thud and I grinned as I swiped the back of my hand over my mouth. I had literally made the man's knees buckle. Damn right, I was proud of myself.

He stared down at me with eyes at half-mast, gently stroked his thumb over my swollen lips. For a moment, neither of us said anything and the only sound was our heavy breaths.

And then he pushed from the wall, grabbed me under my arms, and hauled me up to his mouth so he could plant a searing kiss on my lips. My feet dangled somewhere around his knees. His lips were soft against mine. Sweet and gentle, like I was something delicate. I twined my arms around his neck and gave in to the tenderness of the moment.

"Tell me what you need," he whispered.

I laughed, still breathless. "You just gave me what I needed."

"No, I mean—" He huffed. "And we're not done with

that, either, just to be clear. That pussy of yours is going to get exactly what it deserves."

"All right." I shivered happily.

He shifted so his arms were supporting my butt. I wrapped my legs around his waist. "But before we do that, tell me how to make this work."

"This works just fine." I wiggled against him to demonstrate.

"That's sex. I'm talking about you and me, buttercup. I want *us* to work. Out in the open, no hiding. I want to be yours everywhere, all the time. What do you need to make us real?"

Wait, what? I clasped my hands behind his neck and searched his face. His blue eyes were focused on me, open and warm. "It's not only about me. What about Lodestar? What about Steven—"

"Let Brax worry about that. He's good at what he does. He'll figure something out."

"What if he can't?" I asked softly.

"We'll cross that bridge if we come to it," Adam said.

I swallowed hard. Right. A solid plan, except I knew what was waiting for me on the other side of that bridge. Heartache. I knew that. I knew his history. Whatever bridge there was to cross, I would have to walk it alone, leaving him safely on the other side.

"I don't know what this is between us. I don't know

where it will go," he said, completely oblivious to the way my heart sank a little further with each word. "I don't even know if I have anything to offer you worth having. Maybe I'm too used up to have anything good left to give."

I shook my head wordlessly. How could he believe that? Banged up and bruised, sure. But used up? This man? Absolutely not.

"What I do know is that tomorrow night, I want to pick you up in my truck and take you on a date. A real date. Not coffee or errands or something we can hide behind. I want to kiss you good night. And then the next night, I want you to come over for dinner. And most of all, I want you to be around so much that Ben doesn't even blink when I make you both pancakes in the morning."

"That sounds like something worth having to me," I said. It sounded like everything. But no way in hell was I going to say that to the man who didn't *want* to be my everything.

A smile ghosted his lips. "You need to set the bar higher, buttercup. You deserve more."

"Oh, yeah? What is it you think I deserve, Adam?" I trailed my fingertips down his neck. "Tell me."

"Everything," he growled. "You deserve everything, James. So much more than fucking pancakes."

"Then give it to me." It was half demand, half plea.

He shook his head. "What I have to give isn't anywhere near good enough. I don't believe in happily-ever-after anymore. But I'll do everything I can to make you happy today. No more sneaking around. No more hiding. I'm yours, James. I don't care who the hell knows it."

"I'll take it." My heart jackhammered in my chest.

He stared at me like he couldn't quite believe it. "I'm serious, James. You and me, out in the open. You really want to do this with me?"

I narrowed my eyes. "Are you trying to talk me out of it? You just talked me *into* it, for heaven's sake. You can't run scared already."

"Baby, I'm fucking *terrified*." He rested his forehead against mine. His breath shook on the exhale. "What if I wake up one day and you're gone? You realize I'm not enough and someone out there is better. I'm terrified that I won't see it coming and I won't be able to stop it. But I'm not running from this."

I nuzzled my nose against his. "Adam, I promise you this. If I leave, it won't be for another man. And you will know exactly why because I'll tell you every damn day. I won't leave you with a question mark. Suffering in silence is not my style."

He chuckled softly. "That's oddly comforting."

I love you, I wanted to say. The words lodged in my throat. He wasn't there yet. Maybe he never would be. He cared for me. He wanted me to be a part of his life. That had to be enough. I wasn't going to ask for more. I had learned that lesson already.

Asking for more was exactly how you ended up with nothing.

30

Adam

ADAM

I'm gonna need you to be calm about something

BRAX

What did you do?

ADAM

You already know what I did. The only difference is that James and I are together.

BRAX

Yeah, I already knew that. Everyone knew that. You are absolute shit at hiding how gone you are for her.

ADAM

Steven?

BRAX

Don't worry. It's handled.

I WASN'T GOING to ask Brax for particulars. Some things were better off unsaid. Brax was a stickler for rules and law, but he also had a way of making people feel it was time they updated their last will and testament. There was no law against staring a person down until they took it upon themselves to get right with Jesus.

Blaine and Jesse took the news about the same as Brax. I had told them because, while PDA was not my thing, I was done pretending James meant nothing to me, and I didn't want either of them to say or do anything that would make her skedaddle back to the friend zone.

"Should I pretend to be surprised?" Blaine had asked, proving Brax right. We were shit at hiding.

Jesse had more to say on the matter, however.

"She makes cookies and tamed Belle. Don't screw this up."

Coming from a toothpick-thin kid like Jesse, the

warning didn't mean much. But I swallowed my smile. "I'll do my best."

And hoped to every deity that my best was good enough.

Ben was the only one who hadn't already known. And since he was the one who mattered most, at his response of *that's cool, I guess,* my sigh of relief could have powered a sailboat to China.

James invited us for dinner Saturday night. Something low key and casual to ease Ben into the idea of his dad dating his favorite person. We opted to walk from the big house to James's cabin rather than take the four-wheeler. I took the opportunity to pick some wildflowers as we went so I wouldn't arrive emptyhanded. It had been more than a few years since I'd actually dated anyone, but I was pretty sure flowers were still a popular choice.

"The blue ones." Ben pointed. "Those are her favorites."

He knew something about her I didn't. Their relationship existed outside of what James and I had together. That was something I needed to be mindful of. If things didn't work out with us, James wouldn't disappear from Ben's life—or worse, if she did, it would break his heart. I wasn't the only one with skin in the game.

I squatted to retrieve a couple of the star-shaped blooms and added it to the buttercups and some white flowers that neither of us knew the name of. "Columbine. It's the state flower of Colorado."

"Okay." He plucked one carefully and studied it for a moment. "Do you think that means she likes Colorado better than California?"

I doubted James's flower choice meant any such thing, but that wasn't what Ben wanted to hear. What was I supposed to say? If James had her way, she would still be at Blue Skies right now, not here with us. I knew that. But dreams and reality were two different things. The reality was, James was here. And she liked it here, I was certain of that much.

I was still considering my response when Ben handed me the flower.

"People don't seem to stay here very long," he said. "Trainers, I mean."

"James isn't going anywhere," I said firmly.

"What if Belle doesn't win at the show next week? Does James have to leave?"

"Ben, listen to me, bud. You don't need to worry about that. Belle is still in the early stages of her training. James is doing a good job, okay? I know that. Everyone knows that. If Belle doesn't win, we try again next season. Okay?"

"Okay." Ben seemed appeased by my reassurance. He grinned. "Gramps says you can't fire her until December and it doesn't matter if you do because he'll just hire her back anyway."

My eyes went heavenward. Of course he would. "Good to know," I muttered.

"Come on. I don't want to be late." Ben was already two steps ahead of me.

We found the pine door when we arrived. The scent of pizza wafted through the screen door. Ben didn't bother to knock, a sign that he had been here before without me. He yanked open the door and ran inside, hollering, "James, we're here!"

Shaking my head, I grinned and followed him inside. James was at the kitchen counter, preparing a salad, while Ben filled the vase with water for the flowers.

I leaned over her shoulder with the pretense of watching her peel carrots into long orange strips, but really I just wanted to be close to her.

"Hey," she said, a little more breathlessly than peeling carrots warranted.

"Hey," I returned. "We brought you flowers." I held them up so she could see.

"They're beautiful." She lifted her face, her lips a mere inch away from mine.

"Columbines," Ben said proudly.

James pulled back slightly at the reminder that we weren't alone and my eleven-year-old son was watching our every move with keen interest. "And buttercups." Her cheeks flushed as she snuck another peek at me.

It was too much for me to resist. I reached over the counter to hand the flowers off to Ben to deal with and dropped a kiss on her upturned mouth, lingering just long enough to make a point.

Begin as you mean to go on, as my mom always said. I meant to go on kissing her every chance I could get.

Ben made a gagging face at me, but he didn't look mad about it. I smirked. He was going to have to get used to that.

"I hope pizza is okay," James said, her voice cheerful despite the deepening blush spreading down her throat. "I picked it up from that take-and-bake place in town. I don't really cook."

She said this last part apologetically and I squinted down at her. "You cook all the time."

"I bake," she corrected. "Totally different thing."

"Seems the same."

"Trust me, it's not."

The oven timer beeped and I stepped away. After a quick glance around the small kitchen, I located the oven mitts hanging on a nail. The pizza was cooked to a perfect golden brown when I pulled it from the oven.

"Pizza is great," I said truthfully as I slid it onto the cutting board. "We love pizza."

The sweet, hopeful smile she flashed me over her shoulder told me this dinner with us meant as much to her as it did to me. She was nervous. And it hit me then.

That old clichéd fantasy was fucking dumb. Coming home from a long day of work to a woman with dinner waiting for me. I'd had that before, actually. Emily had been a great cook and she'd enjoyed it. More often than not, she'd had food ready to eat when I walked in the door.

Back then, Emily and I had rented a little ramshackle house in town. I'd leave for Lodestar before dawn and return home just before sundown. I'd had big plans to build an addition on one of the Lodestar cabins so we could move in after the baby was born, but that never happened. Most evenings we'd plop down on the couch to watch dinner in front of the TV, balancing our plates on our knees, and stay there until it was time for bed.

And I had been grateful. Grateful to be living the exact life I had pictured for myself. It was a rare day I didn't think to myself, *I have everything I always wanted.* Maybe I told myself that to convince myself it was true. To stop myself from looking below the surface of that fantasy and discovering that underneath it all, I had nothing.

Because even back then, when I'd thought I had everything? It had never felt like this. Not even a little bit.

This wasn't my cabin. I had never spent a night here. My favorite beer wouldn't be stocked in James's fridge for me. Hell, I didn't even have a toothbrush here. But somehow, it felt like coming home.

I suspected it had nothing at all to do with the hot pizza ready to eat after a long day of work and everything to do with the woman who had popped it into the oven. It had to do with the way her smile lit up the dark places inside me. I wouldn't care if she never cooked anything ever again, so long as she kept looking at me like that. Like she saw me, all the way down to my soul, and she liked what she saw.

"Grab the salad dressing from the fridge, will you?" James asked over her shoulder as she brought the salad bowl to the table.

"Sure."

I located a bottle of ranch and a bottle of Italian on the fridge door and then my gaze snagged on the other items. I closed the fridge with a smile.

My favorite beer was here, after all.

WHEN I VOLUNTEERED to clean up after dinner, James and Ben headed to the barn to bed down the horses. I took my time washing the dishes, wanting to give them a moment together, aware that James and me being together necessarily shifted something in their relationship as well. Twenty minutes later, I followed them out.

I found them in the pasture behind the barn, bringing in the horses for the night. They had paused, lead ropes in hand, to take in the sunset over the paddock. James stood at the fence, one pink-booted foot on the lowest rung, her back to me. Ben mimicked her position, which made me smile. They were almost the same height.

My boy, my woman, my ranch. All lined up against the pretty backdrop like a postcard. Colorado was really showing off tonight, painting the sky with deep plums, pinks, and golds. My throat clogged with some emotion I was too scared to look directly at, but it felt suspiciously like happiness. Happiness and gratitude.

I came closer, my footsteps muffled by the whinnies of horses, but stopped when Ben turned and said, "Do you like watermelon, James?"

"Sure," she said. "Watermelon is great. Do you like watermelon?"

"I think so. It's been a while since I've had it. Grandma used to make us fruit salad in summer and she always threw in some watermelon. She said it was dad's favorite. I'm growing some in her old garden now. They're almost big enough to eat."

I sucked in a breath at the memory of my mom. How had I forgotten that?

James shifted so she was fully facing Ben, her knee pointed at him, her elbow leaning on the top rung. "You want to make fruit salad?"

"Maybe." He paused. "Do you know who Kurt Vonnegut is?"

"He's a writer, I think?"

"Yeah. I haven't read any of his books. He was our fifth-grade graduation speaker. I mean, not really. He was the graduation speaker at another school and they played the video for us at ours. Anyway, he said it often feels like everything sucks, but when things don't suck, we should remember to look around and say, *if this isn't nice, what is.*"

"I like that," James said, her voice so soft that I had to strain to hear it.

"I think Dad is grouchy because he misses Grandma. He doesn't have anyone to put watermelon in his salad anymore. I bet he'd think it was nice to have some watermelon. Don't you?"

The quiet stretched long enough for me to wonder if James had answered too softly for me to hear. Her face when she looked at him...warm as a hug, that look. And then she finally spoke.

"I can't think of anything in this world nicer than having watermelon with you, Ben, and I bet your dad feels the same way."

Something sweet and achy bloomed in my chest. Fuck it all, I *did* miss my mom. It was something I had never let myself sit with because what grown man had time for that? My dad had fallen apart. The ranch had damn near crumbled after him. Grief had been shoved into a deep, dark recess of my heart so I could focus on the work that needed to be done.

My boy had seen all that. He had seen me struggling when I barely understood what I was struggling with. He was a good kid. Compassionate. I didn't hate that he cared so much, even if I wished death hadn't touched his life so much, so young. I didn't hate that he had grown watermelon in his grandma's garden for me. He was special, that kid.

His bond with James...that was special, too. He had turned to her and she had known exactly what to say. She wasn't his babysitter or his nanny. She wasn't his mom. But somehow she had become a person he needed.

And just like with his mom, I was in a position where I could ruin everything for him without even knowing I was doing it. Emily's journals probably had something to say about that. But the thought of reading them, of seeing all the ways I had failed her and therefore Ben laid bare, made me physically nauseous. I couldn't face it. Still, after all these years, I couldn't face it.

I stood there, rooted to the spot, my hand held protectively over my aching chest, while they ducked through the fence into the field.

The crunch of a twig underfoot alerted me to my dad's presence. He cleared his throat. "They bringing in the horses?"

"Yeah," I said, my voice hoarse.

He looked at me, then out to the field where James was bribing a chestnut with a carrot. He put a hand on my shoulder and shook his head. "You've got it bad, son. Can't say I didn't see this coming."

Funny. Because I hadn't seen James coming at all.

31

James

I was a nervous wreck.

Belle didn't seem nervous at all as Essie urged her into a trot, letting her stretch her legs in the warm-up ring before their event. She was curious and energetic as she took in her strange surroundings and—to my great relief—not fighting the bit. Essie, too, was totally calm and collected, even when another rider in the ring cut her off, causing her horse to kick dust in Belle's face.

"You got wipes, James?" Adam asked. Calmly, because he was another person who apparently had nerves of steel.

"Of course." I was about to puke up my breakfast—pancakes, courtesy of Adam, with a side of chocolate chips, courtesy of Ben—but I was still a professional. I had a full grooming kit in the trailer, plus emergency supplies in my bag.

"Let's go make her pretty again."

"Why aren't you nervous?" I demanded. "I'm literally sweating right now."

"Everyone's sweating. It's almost August. And I'm not nervous because there's nothing to be nervous about. Honestly, I never truly believed we'd be here. But we are. Because of *you*. You got Belle here. Of course I hope she'll do well, but you know as well as I do that we can't control that outcome. Doing well requires both training and luck. You did the training. Now we have to wait and see if our luck holds. If not, there will be other shows. Your training made sure of that."

"Oh." I blinked. I had worked myself to the bone, hoping to hear those words from my dad. They never came. And here was Adam, spouting them off, easy as pie.

He was a step ahead of me, scanning the crowd for a way through, and his hand bumped against mine as he reached for me behind him. A voice inside my head told me to push it away. It wasn't professional to hold hands. I had to prove I was good enough to be here all on my own, without anyone else helping me. No one would take me seriously. I wasn't enough. That voice sounded a lot like my dad.

But there was another voice that whispered to put my hand in his. I did my job well. My proof was in the horses I had trained. Holding hands couldn't diminish that. I was enough, right now.

And *that* voice sounded like mine. So I listened.

I watched as my hand, so much smaller than his but just as calloused, was engulfed by his. He glanced over his shoulder at me like he was seeking reassurance. *You okay with this?* I smiled and nudged him forward with the toe of my boot. *I'm okay.* Like we had our own private language that consisted of eyebrow twitches and lip tilts.

It was the right choice, I realized, as he led me through the crowd. Wherever this man went, I wanted to follow. And when I was in the lead, I one hundred percent knew he had my back. That was how it worked with us.

And *that* was why I was ready to puke pancakes while he was cool as a cucumber.

I wasn't nervous for myself. I wasn't nervous for Essie. I wasn't even nervous for Belle. I was nervous for *Adam*. More than anything—even more than proving myself to my dad—I wanted it to go well for *him*. I wanted Belle to be so awesome today that it lifted some of the weight he carried on his shoulders. I wanted her performance to launch Lodestar Ranch back into the spotlight where it belonged.

Adam wasn't worried about any of that. Because he trusted me to get it done. If not with this show, then the next one. He believed in me.

Damn.

It felt *good*.

"How does she feel?" Adam asked Essie as I produced a packet of wipes from my bag and gently cleaned the dust from Belle's white star.

"Good." Essie leaned forward and gave Belle a firm pat on her neck, right below her cream-colored mane. "Ready."

"How do *you* feel?" I asked.

She tilted her head. "You know how sometimes before a show, a string of little things go wrong, one right after the other, and it's a sign? Like, this isn't your day. You should have slept in instead."

I nodded slowly. Off days. Nothing you could do except laugh and try again next time.

"Today is the opposite of that. Everything is easy. Belle has the right amount of energy and focus to do the job and *look* how beautiful she is today." Essie grinned. "I have a feeling this is going to be a good ride. A really good ride."

"Don't say that!" I twisted frantically, searching for wood.

Adam snickered. He squatted low, snagged a

woodchip off the floor, and handed it to me. I rapped the knuckle of my index finger against it and he tucked it into his pocket.

We left Essie to finish her warmup, making it back to our seats right when her number was called.

I held my breath as Belle pranced into the ring. If there was a ribbon for prettiest pair, Belle and Essie would have claimed the blue. They were gorgeous together. More importantly, they *worked* beautifully together. Essie cued Belle with nearly imperceptible commands. Belle complied eagerly, as though she had been waiting her whole life for the opportunity to do just that.

When it was time for the circles and spins, some of the flashiest and hardest moves, Belle made it look effortless. Both horse and rider were having fun out there and it showed.

Adam squeezed my hand. "My mom would have loved to see this. God, she loved this horse."

I squeezed back.

When the score lit up the board, I jumped to my feet. First place! With a score that would be damn hard to beat. There were only two riders after Essie and Belle, which meant that at the very worst, we were looking at a third place ribbon.

Over the applause, I heard a familiar voice call my name. "James!"

I looked up, stunned to see the last person I expected. "Dad."

MY PARENTS HAD PLANNED to stay at a hotel in Aspen Springs, but Adam, probably thinking he was doing me a favor, insisted they take Blaine's cabin at Lodestar Ranch. No matter how much I glared, sending telepathic words with my eyeballs, he refused to read my mind.

He dropped a kiss on my furrowed forehead. "Go get them settled in. We're all going to the big house to celebrate. You can meet us there."

It only took a minute to get them situated for what I dearly hoped would be a brief stay. But then Mom wanted to see my cabin, and of course I agreed. *She* wasn't the one I was mad at.

"It's beautiful." She was as smitten with the view of mountains and horses as I was. She wrapped her arm around my waist and squeezed me against her side. "You must love it here."

There was a question in her voice, one I didn't hesitate to answer. "Yeah, Mom. I love it here. I wake up every day and I honestly can't believe this is my life. I get to do what I love in the most beautiful place on earth. I know I'm lucky."

Dad huffed. "You used to say Blue Skies was the most beautiful place on earth."

"They're both beautiful, in different ways." Mom laid a pacifying hand on his forearm. "You look happy, James."

"I *am* happy."

"Hm." Her expression turned coy. "And does a certain handsome rancher have anything to do with that?"

I had known she would ask sooner than later. That forehead kiss wasn't subtle. I shrugged, like it was no big deal, even though I couldn't stop the warmth from spreading through me at the thought of him. "Maybe."

I glanced at Dad and found him frowning. Unsurprising. Well, that was his problem. I wasn't going to let him cloud my sunshine today.

But then he decided to *make* it my problem.

"I expected more from you, James." Parental disapproval laced every word.

I sighed heavily. Apparently we were really going to do this. There had been a sliver of hope that maybe he had come here because he loved me and missed me. But no. Of course not. He had driven the thousand miles from Blue Skies to Lodestar for the joy of lecturing me on all the ways I had failed, both as a daughter and as a horse trainer.

"Expected more than what, Dad? More than taking on a horse that everyone else had given up on and turning her into a success? More than earning the respect of the trainers and riders I work with every day? More than falling in love with a good man?"

"In love?" Mom squeaked. She clasped her hands like a prayer. Visions of grandchildren danced in her head, no doubt.

"*Hypothetically*," I said, because no way was I going to tell my parents I was in love with Adam before I told him. "My point is that he is a good man, the kind of man I could see myself building a life with someday." If he let me.

The divot between Dad's brows deepened. "Blue Skies is your life, James. You were born there. Raised there. It's in your blood. Blue Skies is where you belong. It's time to come home."

Like I was a child who had run away from home, rather than a grown-ass woman who had taken a job. "You're not making sense, Dad. I can't just leave. My job is here at Lodestar." A direct result of choices *he* had made, but I wasn't going to point that out.

"That was a mistake," he said to my utter shock. "And I mean to rectify that now. You've proved your point. Everyone is talking about Belle's performance today, saying she's one to watch for next year. You've done what you came here to do. Now it's time to come home."

What the heck was happening right now? I couldn't wrap my mind around it. "And do what? I already told you, I'm not going to run the woman's program for Blue Skies. I'm the head trainer at Lodestar. That would be a step down for me."

"I'm not asking you to take a step down, James. I'm asking you to take the position that should have been yours already. Come back to Blue Skies where you belong."

I sucked in air. Was this really happening? Was my dad seriously offering the one thing I had wanted my whole life on a silver platter?

My eyes narrowed. Carl Campos had never once offered me anything on a silver platter. I'd had to work twice as hard only to be constantly told I still wasn't good enough. In high school I had skipped parties and hangouts for barn chores. I had chosen a university close to home so I could continue working and my major—farm management—was chosen with Blue Skies in mind. When he told me I needed a wider experience, I went out and got it, even though it broke my heart to leave. Everything he asked me to do, I did it. It was never enough.

And now suddenly it was enough? Yeah, I was a little suspicious.

"What about Eli Stanford?" I asked. I had left California for Colorado the day before he had arrived at Blue Skies to start his new position as head trainer. Mom hadn't said much about him in our weekly phone calls, but I assumed he had settled in fine.

Dad rocked back on his heels and pondered the mountains. "Eli is a little greener than I had reckoned. He doesn't have your way. Not with horses. Not with people. He could use your guidance."

"So...you're demoting him? Firing him?" My forehead crinkled.

"He'll stay on. As I said, he could use your guidance."

"That's not an answer."

"You're my daughter." He crossed his arms over his chest. "That's all the title you need."

I stared at him. That had never been true. He had never *allowed* it to be true. Which would have been fine, if I had sucked at my job or acted like an entitled brat. But I was good. One of the best, even. And I worked damn hard. The only thing that had stood in my way of being accepted as a boss and trainer had been *him*.

"Dad—"

"Don't answer me now," he cut me off. "Think on it some. Your mom and I will be here through the weekend."

32

Adam

Lisa Campos reminded me a lot of her daughter. Her smile came easy and she had the same big, bawdy laugh. I liked her immediately.

There were differences, of course. Where James had dark hair, her mom had blonde curls. I suspected the color wasn't God-given, but it suited her. James was a little more assessing, a little more thoughtful, behind that ever-present smile. But her mom had the same innate kindness—and was just as quick to say what was on her mind.

"What's going on between you and my daughter?" she asked as I poured her a glass of white wine.

We were at the big house, celebrating Belle's first-place win. Most everyone was out back on the patio, enjoying the warm summer evening, but James's parents had followed me into the kitchen for drinks. And, I suspected, to grill me about James without her overhearing.

"That sounds like something you should ask James," I said.

"What makes you think I didn't?" Lisa's laughter rumbled like her daughter's. Big and delighted. "I'd like to hear why *you* think dating your employee is appropriate. Is this something you do often?"

I looked up. Her voice was sugary sweet, her smile bland, but I wasn't fooled. If I gave her an answer she didn't like, the rodeo queen would become mama bear in the blink of an eye.

"We're two consenting adults who respect each other. There's nothing inappropriate about it." I handed her the glass of chilled wine. "And no, dating my employee isn't something I do often. It's not something I did at all."

"Before James." She sipped her wine, her gaze locked on mine above the rim of her glass.

"Now don't go making this into something it isn't," Carl Campos warned his wife. "They've had a few dates, that's all. I'll take a glass of that wine, too. Thank you."

A few dates? Is that what James told them? Technically, it was true. We spent more time fucking or lying in the bed of my truck, our fingers intertwined, talking about nothing and everything, than on actual dates. Still, it felt all kinds of wrong, hearing us defined like that. *A few dates* made it seem like this was nothing more than a casual summer fling. James meant a hell of a lot more than that to me.

She meant *everything*. I loved her.

Shit.

I had thought I was done with this. More than that, I had *hoped* I was done with this. Humans have an infinite capacity for love, she had said, and dammit all, she was right. Of all the things to be right about, why did it have to be this? It *sucked*. An infinite capacity for love meant an infinite capacity for pain. I didn't want more pain. I'd had enough of that, thank you very much.

It was different with Ben. He was my everything, too, and I loved him fiercely. But it wasn't a choice. Being a parent meant accepting that a piece of your heart lived outside your body, unprotected. If something happened to Ben, it would destroy me. I knew that. I accepted that.

I didn't have to accept that from James. I didn't have to choose this. I could walk away.

The thought of walking away from James, of being cold again after spending these last few months in her sunshine, was like a knife in the gut. It was too late. I was already in it. In so deep I couldn't extricate myself without pain any more than I could cut off my hand.

It was a miracle my hand held steady as I poured the wine while the epiphany rearranged my insides like an earthquake.

"You have a nice operation here," Carl said, in a clear attempt to steer the conversation away from his daughter's love life. "Not as big as Blue Skies, but you have a reputation for quality."

"That reputation is growing stronger by the day." I tipped my bottle of beer before taking a sip. "I have your daughter to thank for that." Whatever else was happening inside me, I still felt like I had a score to settle on James's behalf. This man—her own father—couldn't see her worth, but other men could. He needed to be made aware of this fact.

"Hm. Well, enjoy it while it lasts."

I froze with the beer halfway back to my mouth. "What's that supposed to mean?"

"Come on, now. You couldn't believe James was here for the long haul." Carl scoffed. "Blue Skies is her home. Eventually, she'll want to raise a family there. Be the next generation of Blue Skies. You understand that. Lodestar is family-run, too, isn't it?"

I didn't answer. I couldn't. I was too stunned by the thought of James leaving.

"She told me about the contract. You don't need to worry about her leaving you in the lurch. She'll stick it out until Christmas, I figure, before she comes home. But she's not getting any younger. It's time for her to be serious about this."

"She's the head trainer for a reputable ranch," I pointed out. "How much more serious could she be?"

Carl raised his gray brows. "As I said, Blue Skies is a family operation. That comes with certain responsibilities. She understands that. Anyway, it's all she's ever wanted since she was five years old."

I couldn't argue with that. Did Carl deserve her? No. Was it a little weird that he seemed more focused on her settling down and having a family than actually being a trainer at Blue Skies? Absolutely. But was Blue Skies what she wanted? One hundred percent.

She had told me so herself.

The truth of it nearly knocked me down. I gripped the bottle so tightly my fingertips turned white.

James was going to leave Lodestar Ranch. Leave everything we were building together. Leave *me*. And there wasn't a damn thing I could do about it.

"You disappeared."

James gave a guilty start and peered at me over Belle's creamy mane. "I wanted to bring Belle a treat. She deserves to celebrate, too."

"Right." I slid open the stall door and waited for her to come out. She moved toward me then paused to rub her cheek against Belle's velvety nose. I watched them and felt something I didn't want to feel. I crossed my arms over my chest and held it down. "Saying goodbye?"

Her gaze shot to my face. She eyed me warily as she closed Belle's door behind her. "You talked to my dad?"

She stood there in the yellow barn light, her big brown eyes dark and fathomless. Her fingers played with the hem of her dress—a soft blue thing with white daisies—like she didn't know what else to do with them. So beautiful I ached from it.

I couldn't stop my hands from grabbing her. Couldn't stop my arms from trapping her body to mine. "I fucking need you, James."

And then I slammed my mouth down on hers so she would think I meant her body. Her pussy. Anything but her heart.

She rose up on her toes and threw her arms around my neck, her body plastered to mine, meeting my need with demands of her own. When she opened to me, when her lips parted and I felt the soft slide of her tongue against mine...*fuck*. I went up in flames. I thrust against her so hard her back hit the stall door, making the wood reverberate loudly. Belle lifted her head and looked at us, nonplussed.

James laughed. "Maybe we should—"

"Here. Now." I was not waiting for whatever was at the end of that sentence. Some other place. Some other time. I couldn't wait for later. There might not *be* a later for us.

And I didn't care. I didn't care that James was going to go back to her real life and leave me wrecked. These last two months had been full of her laughs, her smiles, *her*. It was all worth it. So fucking worth it.

I grabbed her bare thigh and lifted it to my waist so I could more easily fit against her. Rocked my hips into her, letting her feel how hard I was already for her. How badly I wanted her. Our tongues tangled, hands groped, hips grinded. She whimpered in my mouth, a sexy little sound that made me lose my damn mind.

I bent and lifted her so both of her legs wrapped around my waist and carried her into the storage room. She tucked her face to my throat. Bit me gently. I could barely think with her mouth on me like that, but I managed to grab a freshly laundered saddle blanket from the basket and spread it over a stack of hay bales while balancing James with one arm, her strong thighs clenched tight around my hips.

"Thoughtful of you," she murmured when I set her down on the soft wool blanket.

"Can't have that sweet ass of yours chafing on the hay. You need something soft because things are about to get rough." My hands settled in the flare of her waist, my fingertips flexing. "I can't be gentle, James. Not tonight."

A lie. I was heated, desperate, every cell in my body roaring with the need to take her. But if she asked me to, I would hold all that in check. There wasn't a damn thing she could ask from me that I wouldn't move heaven and earth to make happen.

But holy hell, I was glad she didn't ask me to.

"Good." She grabbed me by the belt buckle and yanked me forward so that I stepped between her legs with sudden force. Her dark eyes flared with heat as we made contact. "I don't want gentle."

My hands slid up the smooth skin of her thighs, pushing her dress up as I went. She wiggled to free it from underneath her and I clutched her ass, bringing her even closer, desperate to get more of her. I wanted everything she could give me. Her mouth trailed down my neck, nipping and kissing, as she unbuttoned my shirt and spread it wide. With an impish grin, her tongue flicked over my nipple. And then she bit that, too.

"Fuck, baby." My hips bucked. I didn't even know I *liked* that.

Unzipping her dress, I pulled down the delicate straps so her dress circled her waist like a tire, and tossed her bra aside. The heavy weight of her breasts spilled into my waiting palms. I squeezed, rubbing her peaked nipples with my thumbs, and the lowered my head to suck.

"*God*." The word ripped from her throat as she arched her back, giving me better access, her pelvis rubbing against me. Every bit as desperate as I was.

Our mouths found their way back to each other, kissing, kissing, kissing, like it was oxygen. Her hands fumbled with my belt buckle and then she moved onto the button but she couldn't get traction. We were too frantic, our hips rocking too hard.

But my dick ached with need and I couldn't take it anymore. I wrenched away from her on a growl. Yanked open my jeans so hard the button popped off. Jerked my jeans and shorts down my hips. Immediately, her warm hand closed around me. My hips bucked hard but she held on with a low laugh. Her thumb traced the vein underneath, then circled the head where a bead of pre-cum gathered. She swiped her thumb across it, then sucked it off, her dark eyes on mine.

"Fuck, buttercup—I can't—" And then I came to a stuttered stop as I realized I didn't have protection. "Condom?"

She bit her lip. Shook her head. "I have an IUD."

I knew that. She had told me a couple weeks ago, when we both received a clean bill of health for our STD check. But even with that, we had kept using condoms.

She reached under her bunched dress and wiggled her underwear down her legs. "I want you. Just you. I want to feel y—"

I shoved into her so hard the haybales moved. Slick heat gloved me, gripped me, pulled me in deeper. Sensation rippled through my body, drawing my balls tight in a way that did not bode well for my stamina. I exhaled hard and held motionless as I tried to pull myself together.

And then she started moving, hips rocking, heels digging into my ass to urge me forward. Hard enough to leave fresh marks, I hoped.

She was moaning, sighing, making the sexiest noises I had ever heard in my life. I couldn't take it. I surged into her, meeting her hips with hard, vicious thrusts. I pushed her forward so she was on her back and ground down on her, circling my hips, rocking against her at an angle that, judging from her cries, hit her sweet spot.

Fuck, she was so slick, so hot, so tight. I was so close to coming, I couldn't breathe. I leaned forward and my mouth closed over her nipple in a hard, hungry suck.

"Adam!" With my name on her lips, fingers digging into my forearms, she found her release.

It sent me out of my mind. My thrusts turned desperate, relentless. Pleasure wound tighter and tighter and then roared through me as I emptied myself inside her.

"Mine." Her breath tickled my ear.

The truth of that settled into me, spreading through my blood like aspen roots. I was hers. But I had never claimed her in return. Maybe I had always known she couldn't belong to me. Not for keeps. I wasn't enough. I never had been.

And how stupid was I, giving myself so easily to someone who couldn't give herself in return? Hell, I hadn't even put up a fight. My walls had crumbled so quickly, so silently, that it was over and done with before I knew what happened.

I looked down at her, flushed and damp from sex. Sleepy and sated, unlike me. My legs were shaky from exertion, and I was spent...but not sated. I was a bottomless pit of need when it came to James. Nothing could ever sate me. Forever...maybe forever would be enough. But I wasn't going to find out.

All we had was now.

I ran a finger from the indent of her throat, down

between her breasts, the perfect dip of her belly button, to her pussy. She slapped her knees closed and shivered.

"Too much," she said.

Not enough. Never enough.

"I'm hungry. You said you take care of what's yours." I pushed at her knees. "You gonna let me starve, buttercup?"

Her eyes widened and her white teeth sank into her puffy bottom lip. She stopped fighting me. Her thighs fell open, revealing her pink, glistening pussy. Beautiful. I couldn't tear my eyes away.

Mine, I thought. For now.

I leaned in and feasted.

Her clit was swollen and sensitive, so after a few gentle licks I slid my tongue inside her, thrusting and licking. She gasped, shuddered, her fingers threaded into my hair. I tasted myself in her, remnants of what we had done together, my salt mixing with her sweet. And *fuck*, I couldn't get enough.

When her hips canted to my mouth, I rubbed my thumb over her clit. She came on my mouth with long, hard squeezes, her internal muscles pulling me deeper, coating my tongue in her flavor.

I was hard again, drunk on her pussy. I pushed up, slid my cock into her with a rough thrust that made her gasp. I went slower this time and came harder.

She lay there limply, arms and legs spread at awkward angles, panting. "Fuck, Adam. I mean...*fuck*."

There was nothing I wanted more than to stay just like this. Wrapped up in her. But putting off the inevitable had never been my style.

I hiked up my jeans as best I could without the button and buckled my belt. "You don't have to wait until December."

She blinked at me like she was having trouble following the conversation. "What?"

"Our contract says you get paid through December no matter what. I don't want you to worry about that. You don't need to feel guilty."

Her post orgasm glow dimmed slightly and her eyes narrowed. "I don't feel guilty."

"I mean you can go whenever you want." The words felt like razors in my throat. But I had to say it. As badly as I wanted her here with me and Ben, there was something I needed even more. I needed her to be happy.

So I shut down the part of me that wanted to tie her to my bed and forced out the words.

"You should go to California with your family."

33

James

You should go.

The words echoed in my head as I put my dress to rights and shook the straw out of my hair. Adam was quiet as we walked back to the big house to enjoy the rest of the celebration, but he held my hand the whole way, not letting go until we needed our hands to eat the burgers Ted had grilled for us. Even then he kept me close to his side, never letting me get very far without following me. Every time I looked up, his eyes were on me.

Strange behavior for a man hell bent on pushing me away.

You should go.

After everyone had cleared out, he didn't ask me to spend the night. He walked me home, kissed me good night like he hadn't told me to go back to California, but didn't ask to stay—not that I expected him to, because of course he couldn't leave Ben overnight. Despite the way his tongue lingered against mine and the very hard dick he pressed against my belly as we kissed, he felt distant. Aloof.

I went to sleep confused. I woke up mad.

I wasn't going to let him throw a grenade like that and then pretend the explosion had left everything the same. I had told him I wouldn't suffer in silence, and I meant that. We were going to talk this out.

Mom and I had brunch plans, but I swung by the barn before I picked her up from her cabin, knowing that's where Adam would be. I found him mucking out a stall, his back to me. His muscles bunched and shifted as he worked, which did nothing to improve my mood. I glared at his firm, round ass. Only Adam could look this good shoveling shit.

"Why don't you want me to stay?" I demanded.

He froze, pitchfork loaded with manure, not turning around. "Of course I want you to stay." And then he tossed the shit into the wheelbarrow. "You're the best trainer Lodestar has ever had."

If I had been wearing gloves, I would have scooped up a handful of manure and thrown it at him. "Oh. You want me to stay because I'm good at my job. Got it."

Finally he turned to look at me. "You know that's not it, James. But Blue Skies has always been your dream. I understand. I won't stand in the way of that."

He sounded so damn reasonable. But I didn't want him to be reasonable. I didn't want him to *understand* and nobly step aside so I could pursue my childhood dream of working with my father. I wanted him to beg me to stay. Tell me he couldn't live a day without me.

I wanted him to fight for me. For *us*.

Was that too much to ask?

Stupid me, asking a question when I already knew the answer. And god*damn*, I was so tired of men letting me walk away.

"This was good. You and me," he said, and I flinched at the way he had already put us in past tense. He leaned on the pitchfork, his blue eyes searching my face beneath his furrowed brow, like he needed me to reassure him that he wasn't being the bad guy here. "It was good, wasn't it?"

And there it was. Adam didn't want can't-live-without-you love. And I...I did want that. I wanted that with him.

But I wasn't going to chase him to get it.

Love wasn't the sort of thing you could force someone into feeling.

"Yeah," I croaked, forcing the words out of my dry throat. "It was good."

"This place is *adorable*," Mom, quite possibly the most adorable person on earth, said as we slid into a booth at Shenanigans, a restaurant in downtown Aspen Springs recommended to me by Chloe.

I glanced around, taking in the black-and-white tiled floor, the hanging plants, and the rattan furniture. If a tropical garden and a French bistro had a baby, it would be this restaurant. "Yeah, Mom. It's cute."

Mom gave me a sharp look at my flat tone, but before she could question me, a server—also cute—popped by to take our order. Mom asked for a bloody Mary, I went with a blood orange mimosa, and we both ordered French toast and a carafe of coffee to share.

"All right," she said when our drinks had arrived. "What's wrong, honey?"

"Nothing's wrong," I lied.

She arched an immaculate brow. "Please. You *love* brunch. Why are you sitting there all glum? It can't be the company."

I tried to smile but succeeded only in lifting the corners of my mouth a fraction. It didn't fool my mother at all.

"Oh," she said sagely. "Boy troubles."

I snorted. One thing Adam Hale wasn't was a boy. No, that grumpy cowboy was all man. I kept myself busy pouring coffee for both of us and adding cream, her eyes on me the whole time.

"Have you given any thought to coming back to Blue Skies?" Mom added sugar to her mug and gave it a brisk stir.

I blinked and then blinked again. I had spent a lot of time last night staring at my ceiling, wide awake when I should have been dead asleep, turning Adam's reaction over and over in my mind. *You should go.*

I had spent precisely zero minutes contemplating how *I* felt about returning to Blue Skies. Did I want to go back?

It should have been a no-brainer. Working at Blue Skies with my father had always been my dream. So why did it feel like a big question mark now when Dad was offering me everything I ever wanted?

Maybe it wasn't what I wanted anymore.

Maybe what he was offering was only a pale substitute for what I had wanted anyway.

"Why do you look like you're having an epiphany?" Mom asked.

I looked up. "Nothing has changed. He still isn't sure about me."

Her gaze sharpened. "Do you mean your dad or Adam?"

"Dad. Of course." *Both*. I swallowed hard. Why did I do this to myself?

"Oh, honey." Mom leaned back with a sigh. To her credit, she didn't try to pretend Dad was anything but himself. "Your dad loves you so much. If he had his way, you never would have left Blue Skies. You'd marry someone who would take over the business someday and raise our grandbabies there. It's all he ever wanted."

"And all I ever wanted was to be enough. No husband or grandkids. Just me, doing the job I'm great at." Our conversation paused as our food arrived. After the server disappeared again, I stabbed into my French toast. "Why am I not enough for him?"

"He loves you, James, but he's not going to change. Maybe it's time for you to stop asking him to be something he's not."

"Mom," I said, exasperated. "It's not like I'm asking him to go vegan. I'm asking him to be a little less sexist, that's all. I don't know how you put up with it."

She shrugged. "It's not like he thinks women are

stupid or incompetent. He is well aware that I run his life for him and he'd be lost without me. The difference is that what I want aligns with what he wants. It's a partnership. He wants the same for you, for you to be happy like he is. He can't wrap his mind around the idea that you might want something else for yourself." She reached across the table to squeeze my hand. "He loves you, James. So much."

"I know he loves me." I paused, frowning, and considered my words. "But I'm never going to be good enough for him. I'm not the daughter he wants me to be and it doesn't matter how good I am at my job, I'm never going to be the trainer he wants me to be, either. And you know what? I'm done trying. Because these last few months have taught me that I *am* good enough. For myself, for Lodestar, for Belle. I'm enough."

"For Adam?" Mom asked, her voice soft, her gaze sharp.

"Well." I sawed off a bite of French toast. Mom winced as the knife scraped against the porcelain plate. "I thought I was."

Mom tilted her head, studying me, and took a ladylike sip of her bloody Mary. "What makes you think you're not?"

You should go.

"You know, I spent years trying to convince Dad I'm

right for the job. *Years* trying to get him to see me as more than the deliverer of grandbabies. And he always told me I wasn't what he wanted for Blue Skies. He never hid that. So I left. I went to college where he wanted me to go, I went to other stables for experience. But the second he crooked his finger at me, I'd run straight home again."

"What does any of that have to do with Adam?" Mom asked.

"Everything." I blew out an exasperated breath. "What I learned from Dad after futilely chasing his approval is that when a man tells you what he wants, you should take him at his word. And Adam...he told me to go."

"So you're going to come back to Blue Skies after all?" she asked, sounding more confused than actually hopeful.

I growled. I didn't want to go to Blue Skies. I wanted to stay at Lodestar. I was happy here. Even taking Adam out of the equation, I didn't feel done yet. There was so much more I could accomplish with Belle and the ranch.

"I'll take that as a no." Mom delicately dabbed her mouth with a napkin, somehow managing to avoid smearing her lipstick even a smidge. "What did Adam say, exactly? I can't imagine he's disappointed with your job performance. Why did he tell you to go?"

"He knows how much I love Blue Skies and you and

Dad. He said he couldn't stand in the way of my happiness."

"Of all the nerve," Mom said dryly. She shook her head. "I love your father, but that doesn't sound like anything he would say. Adam must care for you a lot to put your needs before his."

I sighed. "You don't understand. Adam won't *let* himself care for me that much. He's been in love before, it was a disaster, and he doesn't want to go through that again. It doesn't matter if I stay at Lodestar or go somewhere else. Adam won't ever love me like that, and I'm not going to tie myself in knots trying to convince him to."

"Like you did with your dad," Mom said. "Hmm."

"Right," I said.

Except it didn't *feel* right.

Dad had always loved me, but I was never enough. Adam wouldn't let himself love me, because—my knife clattered on the plate as the epiphany hit—because he didn't believe *he* was enough.

Well, shit.

34

Adam

"You're in a foul mood," Brax remarked.

I didn't disagree with him. What would be the point in refuting what we both knew to be true? I *was* in a foul mood. The reason being that any hour now, James was going to come tell me what I already knew, that being she had decided to part ways with Lodestar Ranch and return to California with her family. And I was going to be a goddamn gentleman about it and wish her well.

Brax pushed his hat off his forehead, mopped up the sweat there with a towel, and pulled the brim down again. "You want to talk about it?"

I sure as fuck did *not*.

"Talking isn't going to get these heifers rounded up any faster," I said. "We've got a job to do."

Lodestar Ranch kept a small herd of cattle—about

twenty head, most years—to train ranch horses with and every August we rounded them up for their annual vaccines. We didn't sell them for beef, but we did breed them enough to sustain the herd, so this was also an opportunity to see how the younger calves were faring. It was a two-person job that usually fell to me and Dad, but for reasons he seemed inclined to keep to himself, Brax had shown up this morning ready to ride. I suspected it might have something to do with the fact that Essie was coming by later to take Magpie home.

I nudged Crackerjack into action. The chestnut gelding was coming up on four now and had taken to cow work like a pig to mud. Already I had interest from buyers around Colorado. Together, we worked to separate the calves from the mamas, always a harrowing experience.

The sun was high in the cloudless sky by the time we were done. We took a breather by the fence to give our horses a rest before we headed back to the barn. The cows congregated under a tree, occasionally eyeing us like they suspected we weren't done with our shenanigans.

"You staying for lunch?" I asked Brax.

He took a long gulp from his water bottle before answering. "Figured I would. Dad's sandwiches are better than anything I'd find in town." He nodded at my horse. "Cracker looked good out there."

"He's coming along real nice." I gave him an affectionate pat on the neck. It would be rough to turn him over to someone else, but that was the nature of the business. If I kept every horse I liked, we'd never make a single sale.

"Belle is, too. She's going to put Lodestar Ranch back on the map. You and James got big plans for her next year?"

I scowled at the mention of the woman who, any second now, was going to break my heart. "I have big plans. James won't be here to see them. Blaine will take over Belle's training."

Brax stared at me like I was speaking in tongues. "Come again?"

"You met her parents last night. They want her to go back to California with them."

"California?" Brax spat the word with disgust. "You've got to be kidding me. She's going to leave us in the lurch like that?"

"Working with her dad is her dream. I'm not going to stand in the way of that. Anyway, she did what we needed her to do. She got Belle to take a rider. Blaine can take it from here." I said it like I didn't care, but Cracker knew better. He felt the tension roll through me and tossed his head, demanding I ease my grip on the reins. I flexed my fingers and let the leather slide through a bit.

I fooled Brax about as well as I fooled Cracker. "What about you, Adam? Is Blaine going to take care of you, too?"

I narrowed my eyes at him. "Very funny. This might come as a shock to you, but I'm a full-grown man. I don't need someone to take care of me. I'll be just fine without her."

Brax tipped his hat back and leveled me with a hard look that saw straight through my bullshit. "Of course you'll be fine. You're not Dad. When your world falls apart, you don't fall apart with it. You muscle your way through like a damn robot. So, yeah. You'll be fine without James. But who the hell wants to spend their life being just *fine*? Don't you want to be happy?"

"I'm happy enough." Or I would be, anyway. At some point, this ache in my chest had to ease, right? "I have Ben. I have the ranch."

"Happy *enough*." Brax snorted.

Now I was pissed. "What do you want from me, man? James has wanted this her whole life. You want me to put myself between her and her dream? I can't do that."

"So that's it? You just give up?" Brax shook his head. "Some things never change, I guess."

"What the hell is that supposed to mean?" I

demanded. "You're the one who gave up on Lodestar and Dad, not me."

"First of all, fuck you. I never gave up on Lodestar and I sure as hell never gave up on Dad. I'm here, aren't I? You think because I didn't dedicate my whole life to the ranch, that means I gave up on it? No. Lodestar was Dad's dream. I don't owe *his* dream *my* life. And you don't, either. So don't throw that martyr bullshit at me. You *want* this life. That's the difference."

I glared, but he wasn't wrong. Hadn't James said pretty much the same thing? She had barely been here a week at that point, but she still had me figured out. Was that really two months ago? It felt like a lifetime. It felt like yesterday.

"If you need more help here, ask for it. I'll do what I can," Brax continued. He paused, then added somewhat reluctantly, "Do you need more help?"

I considered. James had lifted my burdens considerably since she'd arrived two months ago, in more ways than just training. Honestly, I had no idea how we would replace her. "Not so much lately. Six months ago, I would have had a different answer."

"Then six months ago, you should have come to me and asked for help. We would have figured something out. I'm not a mind-reader."

"Yeah. Okay."

"You're not a mind-reader, either. Neither is James."

Oh, there it was. I should have known he wasn't done with this shit. "You got something to say?" I challenged.

"I thought I just said it."

I shook my head. "We're done here. Let's head back."

"Sure."

Brax nudged Orion into an easy walk. The horses had earned an easy ride home. I squeezed my calves around Cracker's belly, urging him forward next to Orion.

"So, are you going to drive James to California?" Brax asked.

My brow furrowed. "Why would I do that? She drove here. She'll drive herself back again."

Brax shrugged. "That's what you do, isn't it? Your woman decides to go and you give her a lift to her next destination without stopping to ask why she's going or what it would take to make her stay."

"What the hell does that—" I drew up short with the sudden realization that he wasn't talking about James anymore. At least, not only James. He was talking about Emily. "Fuck you," I choked out, fury clogging my throat. "You have no idea what you're talking about."

"I know exactly what I'm talking about. From the time we were babies, our parents spoon fed us this soulmate bullshit. It only happens once. When you know, you know. It's not work when it's love." His voice pitched as he mimicked the words Mom and Dad had ingrained in us. "They were wrong. It *is* work. It's so much fucking work, Adam. And most of that work comes down to simply using your goddamn words."

"How would you know?" It was a fair question. Brax had always had girlfriends, but he'd never come close to marriage before, to my knowledge.

"I'm the only attorney in Aspen Springs. Half my caseload is divorce. And I'm here to tell you I would have a lot fewer clients if they had bothered to talk to each other from the start. By the time they see me, they're too far gone. Relationships take work, no matter what Dad told us."

"And...what? You think if I use my words, if I ask James to stay here with me, she's going to give up her dream?" I shook my head. "Life doesn't work that way."

"I think you're scared to find out. I think you're scared to lay it all out there and hear her say it's not enough. I hate to tell you this, but that's what everyone is scared of. No one likes rejection."

"It doesn't matter what I say. She's going back to California."

"All right, then. Let her go." Brax smirked over his shoulder like it was all the same to him. "Who cares if James is the best thing to happen to you since Ben? You'll be *fine*."

I was not fine. But I also was not like my dad, broken of both heart and spirit, half-drowned in bourbon. So. I would take that as a win. Even if it felt a whole hell of a lot like I was still losing.

Bourbon would feel pretty damn good right about now.

"Stop right there," Dad ordered as I strode past the kitchen. "You haven't eaten lunch."

"I don't have time." I had time. Probably. But I also knew Brax had taken his sandwich to the back deck, and I'd already had more than enough of his brotherly wisdom for one day. I'd eat when he was good and gone.

"You have time for a sandwich. I picked up a loaf of sourdough." Dad slapped two thick slices on the wood cutting board.

I loved sourdough. I lingered in the doorway, not fully committing one way or the other. "What are you making?"

"Roast beef. From the good deli, not the prepackaged shit from the grocery store." Dad reached for a small bowl and slathered the contents on both slices. From the pale-yellow color, I knew it was his signature mix of mayonnaise and mustard. He always premixed the condiments, swearing it tasted much better than adding each straight to the bread one at a time.

I sidled up to the counter. "What else?"

"Cheddar, of course. I figured that would go real nice with some arugula. And some radish slices for crunch."

It sounded odd, but I knew it would be good. Even the radishes—or maybe especially the radishes? Dad loved a good crunch on a sandwich.

My stomach rumbled as I watched him layer on the ingredients. Not being a heathen, he cut the sandwich in half on the diagonal, then slid it onto a plate for me along with a pickle wedge.

"Here you go." He nudged the plate closer to me. "I call it the Get Your Head Out of Your Ass on Sourdough."

I should have known Blaine would spill everything while I was washing up. Defiantly, I lifted one triangle to my mouth and bit off a large chunk. Delicious. I chewed while glaring at him. Swallowed while glaring some more. "Really? Because it tastes like Mind Your Own Business to me."

Dad gave me a look only a parent could give, full of exasperated fondness. "You *are* my business. You're my son."

"I'm a grown ass man."

"Then stop acting like a scared little boy."

Scared. The word was an echo of what Brax had said earlier. It chafed around the edges of some too tender place in my chest. And lord, didn't that piss me right off. The only thing that scared me was mountain lions. Or something bad happening to Ben. I wasn't scared of fucking *feelings.*

"All right, Dad. Since you and Brax think you have all the answers, how about you share them with me. You think I'm running scared? Fine. Tell me what I'm supposed to do, then. Because James—" My voice did something I wasn't proud of. Fury pushed me past it. "James deserves everything. Whatever she wants, she should have. She's loyal and strong and kind, and my god, the mouth on that woman. She deserves *everything,* you hear me? And I'm not going to let anything stand in the way of that, not even me."

Dad blew out a sigh and shook his head. "I hear you, Adam. I hear you and I understand. Hell, I even agree with you. James deserves to have everything she wants. I won't fight you on that. What I don't understand is why you seem to think that everything doesn't include you."

It was a direct hit to my solar plexus. "Because—" I floundered.

Because it couldn't possibly.

I stilled, feeling it. Where had that come from? Not James, I knew that.

"The thing is," Dad said carefully, "James didn't make the decision to go. You did. It seems to me you make an awful lot of decisions no one asked you to make."

"I didn't decide to end my marriage," I reminded him, because people seemed to be forgetting that lately. "Emily made that decision all on her own. With no input from me whatsoever."

"So now you figure it's your turn to make the decisions? That might be fine except, hell, son, you're making yourself miserable. But maybe that's the point. Maybe you *want* to be miserable."

"Dad," I said, not bothering to hide my exasperation, "no one wants to be miserable."

"I did." His gaze held mine, relentless. "After your mom died. It seemed a whole hell of a lot easier to be miserable than to be happy, so I settled in deep. I let everything go. Everything I loved. Horses, Lodestar, family. You know that and we're paying the price for that now. I'm sorry. Shit, I'm so sorry."

I swallowed hard. He had never spoken those words out loud. Never apologized. Dad had never hit rock bottom the way a true addict does. He hadn't bet the ranch to pay for booze or driven drunk or anything like that. Time seemed to be the biggest factor in his slow emergence from grief. That, and Ben. I had laid down the law that he couldn't be around Ben unless he was sober and he never once broke it.

"I get it, Dad. Really. I understand."

His lips twisted wryly as he fiddled with the knife, wiping the blade clean of condiments. "Do you? Because you had your own tragedy to face, but you handled it somewhat different, as I recall. You white-knuckled your way through Emily leaving and dying the same way you did with your mom. You didn't drink, but you pushed away anything that made you happy, same as me. Huh, how about that." He straightened and tapped the knife's blade against the cutting board. "Maybe underneath it all, our ways of handling grief aren't so different after all."

"Dad, I'm not—" I closed my eyes as the truth washed through me like a cold wind. "I'm not scared of James dying. And I'm not exactly scared of her leaving, either. I'm scared because I don't know how to keep her. I don't know how to make her happy. I'm scared I don't know how to make *anyone* happy. Because I tried, Dad. I thought I was doing everything right but it turned out I was all wrong. And I still don't know why."

Dad stared at me long and hard. "Well, shit, son. I knew that. I know you're scared, but I never took you for a coward. So the question is, what are you going to do about it?"

THE BOX of journals was right where I had left them, in the back of my bedroom closet, after I had dug out the photos of Emily and Ben. Out of sight, but never truly out of mind.

That fucking box had haunted me.

There was no doubt in my mind that I would rather have the devil himself rake my body with a molten pitchfork.

But there was also no doubt in my mind that I would rather read every damning word Emily wrote about me, about us, than lose James. I would do anything to make her happy.

Even this.

35

James

ALL I WANTED to do after brunch was find Adam, but Adam was nowhere to be found. He wasn't in his office. He wasn't in the big house, although Ben told me he had stopped by for lunch. I interrupted Brax's heated conversation with Essie long enough for him to tell me he hadn't seen his brother since they had dewormed the calves this morning.

My man was definitely avoiding me and I was *not* having it.

Frustrated, I headed back to my cabin to regroup. And that's where I finally found him. Sitting on the front step, back propped against the door, his long legs stretched out in front of him. He pushed to his feet when he saw me.

"There you are." He said it like he had been looking for me, too.

I moved toward him like a horse to sweet feed. I couldn't help it. He looked so damn good. All I wanted was to be as close to him as I could get. "Here I am. Want to come inside?" I asked. One hand fisted his shirt at the waist while I used my other to unlock the door. I wasn't really giving him a choice.

"Yes." He dropped a kiss on my mouth as I turned to look up at him, like it was the most natural thing in the world. Like he hadn't told me to go to California. "How was brunch with your mom?"

"It was interesting." I moved deeper into the cabin. Dropped my bag, keys, and phone on the table. Turned to face him and found him right behind me, so close I had to back up a step to look him in the eyes.

I took a deep breath, but when I let it out again, the words didn't come with it. They stayed clogged in my throat, choking me. I wanted to be brave. To say how I felt even though I knew he wasn't there yet. That maybe he would never let himself get there. That awful little voice in my head told me not to be a fool. *Don't let him hurt you like your Dad hurt you.* But the other voice, the one that had grown stronger and louder here at Lodestar, reminded me that Adam wasn't my dad, and he was every bit as scared as I was.

This man was worth chasing.

I had to try.

"James," he started. "I—"

"I love you," I blurted. The words came out strangled and shaking. I cleared my throat and tried again. "I love you, Adam." Better.

He said nothing, which, to be fair, I expected as much. Just stared at me blankly with those bright blue eyes of his while his brows slowly pushed together in a frown.

"Did you know the flight from Denver to Sacramento is under three hours?" he asked. "Cheap, too."

Okay, *that* I wasn't expecting.

Goddammit, he was still trying to make me leave.

"Stop," I said. "Don't—"

"James." He reached for me, pulled me close, dropped his forehead to mine. "Hear me out. Please?"

I swallowed hard, then nodded. "Okay," I whispered.

"The flight is less than three hours. It's cheap. I could come visit you a couple weekends a month. Maybe bring Ben sometimes, too, especially when he's on break from school. You could come to Lodestar whenever you want, for as long as you want. We could make it work, James. I know we could."

It took me a minute to puzzle through what he was suggesting. "You want to try long distance?"

"For now. I know it's not a long-term solution, you in California and me in Colorado. But it could work for a few months. Maybe even a couple years. It will give us time for me to get Lodestar running the way it needs to be so I can join you at Blue Skies. I'll need to—"

I jerked back, stunned. "What?"

"I think it will take me about a year to get everything in order so I'm not leaving Dad with more than he can handle. Eventually Zack will step back from the rodeo. He's getting older. And then—"

"Shut up." I clapped my palm over his mouth, stemming whatever fool thing he had planned to say next. "Shut up and let me choose you. I'm not going to Blue Skies. I'm staying here at Lodestar. With you."

He tried to speak, but it came out muffled against my hand. That was fine. Judging from the glower he was serving me, he planned to argue.

Also fine.

He could argue all he wanted. I planned to win.

Gently, he pried my fingers from his face. "James," he said, clearly exasperated. "We talked about this. Blue Skies is your dream. I won't stand in the way of you being happy."

"You're not in my way, dumbass," I said, every bit as exasperated as he was. "*You* are what makes me happy. Lodestar and Belle make me happy. Ben makes me happy. I want all of it. Yes, Blue Skies was my dream. But working with my dad...the reality was never going to live up to that. I want to work with people who respect and love me, people I love and respect in turn. That's my true dream. And I found that here at Lodestar. But Lodestar is just the very delicious icing on the cake. You, Adam Hale, are the cake."

His throat worked as he swallowed hard. "I read Emily's journals."

Now, *that* I wasn't expecting. "You did?"

"I needed to know." He heaved an audible breath. "I needed to know how it all went wrong. It's haunted me, not knowing."

"It wasn't all your fault." Even though I hadn't read a single word, I knew that. Because I knew him. "Whatever ended your marriage, it was on both of you."

He smiled a little. "I know. Logically, maybe I always knew. But it never felt like anything less than one hundred percent my fault. I was so damn blindsided. And now I understand why."

"Tell me."

"I didn't fight for Emily. When she told me she wanted out, I let her go. Hell, I literally drove her to her new man. But even before that, I didn't put in the work for our marriage. I had this idea of what I wanted for my life. The ranch, a wife, some kids. I pushed her into that box and ignored all the signs that she didn't really fit. That she didn't *want* to fit. She didn't want to be a rancher's wife. She wanted to be an artist and live in town. She didn't even like horses, but I thought it didn't matter, because she loved me enough to be where I was. I look back, and I see it. But we never talked about it. We never really talked about anything."

"You have to let go of that," I said. "It was just as much her fault as yours. More, even, because she was in love with someone else and she didn't talk about that, either."

"I loved her, James. I really did. But I loved her like a boy because that's what I was. That was all I had to give." His fingertips traced my jaw before he tilted my chin, forcing my gaze to his. "But you were right. I'm not the same person I was then. I'm a man now and that's how I love you. I'll fight for you, for us, for as long as I'm on this earth breathing. You got that?"

"Got it," I breathed.

"So if you want another minute to think about your dad's offer, that's fine. Nothing has to be decided today. You're mine, James. I'm yours. Everything else is negotiable."

I shook my head. I didn't need a minute. But the fact that he gave it to me anyway? Damn. I was falling more in love with him by the second. "Yesterday, I wished my parents had never shown up here, because it hurt so much when you told me to go. But right now, I'm glad I have a choice. Because it's an opportunity to choose you. Over and over again, every day, I will always choose you. I'm glad you were a footnote in someone else's happily-ever-after, because that's what made you who you are today."

"Yeah? And who is that?" he teased, but there was a pleading note in his tone that I would never ignore.

I rose up on my toes and pressed a soft kiss to his lips. "My fairy tale."

36

Adam

IT TURNED out there were lots of ways to eat watermelon, most of them good. There was my mom's watermelon salad, served cold with chunks of crisp, ripe watermelon, fat blueberries, feta cheese, and mint. Grilled watermelon was unexpectedly tasty, especially after a bite of burger. Watermelon margaritas were a big hit. And, of course, there was always the old standby: eaten straight off the vine, sliced in thick, red triangles, the sweet juice running down your chin with every bite.

We tried them all one bluebird Sunday in early August.

Ben's garden had supplied a bumper crop of watermelons. We celebrated by inviting all of our friends and family for a summer barbecue. My brothers both showed up—Zack swinging in from Texas, on his way to Idaho—and James's friends Chloe and Hannah joined us as well. Essie was here, her smile a nuclear reaction to Brax's scowls in her direction. One day maybe someone would explain to me how they had gone from being high school buddies to...whatever this was.

But today wasn't for airing grievances. Today was for family, friends, and fun.

I had given the ranch hands the day off to enjoy the barbecue. James and Ben had given me a hand with the early morning barn chores that came regardless of holidays or weekends. There were a thousand other chores I could have done, as well, but James put a stop to that right quick. For the first time in only god knew how long, I took a full Sunday off.

I tried not to be personally offended when the world did not collapse around me.

Two strong, slim arms wrapped around my middle from behind. "Is this everything you dreamed it would be?" James teased.

I lifted my arm so I could pull her against my side. She came willingly, snuggling in beneath the crook of my shoulder. "No. I never let myself dream of this."

She tipped her head back to stare at me. "You never let yourself dream of a family barbecue?"

She sounded more than a little surprised. I couldn't

blame her. My family ate together all the time—every Sunday, a fact she was well aware of. But not like this.

No, it hadn't been like this in a long, long time.

Never. It had never actually been like this, back when Emily had been the one at our family events. What I'd had with Emily was a shallow spring. Pretty and sweet, but barely shallow enough to even get your boots wet. What I had with James was ocean deep. And shit, I was glad Emily had found the same thing, had been able to experience that kind of love, before she died.

The miracle of that damn near knocked me on my ass. How had I gotten here, to a place where I was literally happy my ex-wife had found true love with another man? I looked down at the woman who had pushed me here, in spite all of my kicking and screaming.

"I didn't know how to dream of this. Of *you*. I thought I'd already had my shot at forever and didn't deserve a second one."

Her eyes looked like warm melted chocolate as she took that in. "Well, joke's on you," she teased, her voice suspiciously thick. "Because you're *exactly* what I deserve. And I'm keeping you."

It never ceased to amaze me that she said things like that. That we actually talked like this. Like sharing our vulnerable inner thoughts and feelings was completely normal. "You damn well better," I growled against her mouth. She giggled and her hand came up to touch my cheek.

I took that as permission to stretch the kiss a moment longer. Ben's laughter floated above the cacophony of friendly chatter. Maybe that should have distracted me from James's delectable mouth, but instead it made everything better. My kid was happy. James was happy. I was happy.

"I can feel you smiling," James breathed between kisses.

I dropped a kiss on her forehead. "How could I not smile? I'm kissing *you*, buttercup."

"Ugh." She cringed, laughing. "That's too sweet even for me. Give me back the grumpy cowboy who makes my panties melt."

A feminine throat cleared behind us and James froze, bugging her eyes out at me. I turned to see Essie smirking at us.

"Let's keep it PG, James. This is a family function. Here, try a watermelon margarita."

James buried her face into my side and moaned.

I roared with laughter. Across the yard, my dad lifted his head from the burgers he was grilling. His gaze met mine. There was something about his expression that seemed to echo the feeling I'd had only moments before. Gratitude.

"Give it to me. I'll help her drink it," I said, taking the cup from Essie.

James's head jerked up. "Like hell you will. I need every last drop to alleviate my mortification."

"Burgers are ready!" Dad announced.

We joined the small throng around the picnic tables we had set up for the occasion. Watermelon was the star of the day, but we also had piles of grilled corn on the cob, potato salad, and mac and cheese. We loaded our plates like it was our last meal.

"Try some watermelon salad, Dad," Ben suggested. I didn't miss the eagerness in his voice.

He had made that salad—my mom's salad—with James this morning, a couple hours before the event. Mom had always insisted the watermelon be ice-cold and Ben took that seriously. He took everything seriously, but I worried slightly less about it these days. He was surrounded by love and he cared deeply about people. That was a *good* thing.

Even if it sometimes hurt.

I couldn't protect him from that. I couldn't shield him from pain. Hell, I couldn't even shield him from *my* pain.

But I could show him joy. Because life was both, and it was important to recognize the good when we had it. To not be afraid of it.

I speared a bite of watermelon, feta, mint, and blueberry onto my fork. Ben watched me, his eyes wide.

"Did I get it right?" he asked. "Like Grandma?"

I swallowed the watermelon along with the sudden lump in my throat. "You got it perfect. Just like Grandma."

He grinned, first at me and then, triumphantly, at James. And shit. Shit. I wasn't going to cry over watermelon.

I grinned back. At Ben. At James. Feeling so damn *full*. "If this isn't nice, what is."

EPILOGUE

James

One Year Later

I STARED up at my cabin—now nearly twice its original size—and squealed with delight. "Can I go inside?"

"Sure. We didn't change the locks, so your key still works," Adam said.

It had been one month since I had arrived home after a weekend camping trip with Adam and Ben to find my darling cabin flooded. A pipe had burst while we were gone, leaving several inches of water soaking the wood-beamed floors. Ted had taken the opportunity to update the cabin with an additional bedroom and modernize the kitchen and bathroom a bit. Over the past month, Adam, Ted, and Brax built the addition—with occasional help from Zack—and I moved temporarily into the big house.

Finally, it was done. I could move back home.

Thank god. As much as I loved curling into Adam's warm body every night, I was one hundred percent done with living out of a suitcase.

I gasped as I stepped through the doorway. The cabin still had that rustic vibe I loved so much, but with modern finishes and conveniences. I squealed again and threw my arms around his neck, peppering his cheek with kisses.

"You haven't seen the rest of it yet," he said gruffly. "You might hate it."

I laughed. "I'll love it," I promised.

For some reason that seemed to irritate him. "Yeah. Probably."

"You made me pick out paint colors, cabinets, and the tile in the bathroom. Everything is exactly my taste. You made sure of that. How could I not love it?"

I peeked into the bathroom and shrieked with joy. "A bathtub! You didn't tell me you were putting in a tub. I can't believe you did that."

"You wanted a tub." He shoved his hands in the front pockets of his jeans, his lips twitching in a quick smile. "You can still use mine whenever you want, though."

I smirked over my shoulder. Sharing a tub soak after Ben went to sleep, talking over our day as we soaped each other's bodies, had become a nightly ritual for us this past month. I was going to miss it when I returned to my cabin. A *lot*.

Among other things.

And it wasn't just Adam I would miss. I loved eating breakfast with Ben and then driving him to school every morning. With summer vacation over, I didn't get to see as much of him. The three of us had settled into a routine that felt easy and right.

But I did hate digging through my suitcase every time I needed to find a clean pair of underwear or a hairband.

I sighed and took a look at the second bedroom. It had been furnished simply with a bed and a small dresser. If my parents ever visited when another cabin wasn't available, they could stay here with me. A blessing and a curse.

"I'll take a couple hours this afternoon to pack my stuff and move back in," I said.

"It won't take you more than ten minutes, considering you never unpacked to begin with."

I turned around to find him scowling at me. "How would I have unpacked?" I asked. "You didn't have space for me."

His glower deepened.

I laughed. My cowboy was grumpy today. "Someone needs a cookie. Come on, let's go home."

"Home." He pulled me against him and kissed me hard on the mouth. "I like the sound of that."

AFTER SATISFYING Adam's sweet tooth—and hopefully improving his mood—I headed upstairs to his room to pack.

Then I halted there in the doorway, staring inside. What the heck? His furniture was missing. Everything except the bed was gone. The lonely nightstand, the small pine dresser? Gone.

"Adam—" I called. I took a step back and found him right behind me. "What's going on?"

"Dad and Brax should be here with the new stuff in an hour."

He scraped a hand over his jaw, the way he did when he was anxious. I stared at him. Was Adam nervous?

"You bought new furniture?"

"Just two nightstands and a dresser big enough to share."

Just. I swallowed past the sudden lump in my throat as my stomach tumbled. There was nothing *just* about it. He was making space for me. That was everything.

"You have a choice." He crossed his arms over his chest and scowled at me. My heart flipped over in my chest. A year into our relationship, his scowl was still the sexiest thing I had ever seen. "You can either move back into the cabin built exactly to your specifications, or you can stay here. With me. Either way, this is your home now, as much as it is mine. It's *our* bedroom. You can—"

I jumped into his arms, wrapping my legs around his waist, and smashed my mouth against his. "You. I choose you."

His smile bloomed beneath my lips and he laughed. "I was hoping you'd say that. Dad already called dibs on your cabin if you agreed."

"There is nowhere else I would rather be."

This was my home. Here, at Lodestar Ranch, with the love of my life. He tumbled me backward onto the bed, laughing again as I squealed in surprise. Adam was still my grumpy cowboy, but these days he gave me as many smiles and laughs as scowls.

He gave me everything.

ABOUT THE AUTHOR

Elizabeth Bright is a USA Today bestselling author of smart, passionate romance with heart, humor, and heat. When she's not writing stubborn heroines and the men who adore them, Elizabeth can be found hiking and rock climbing. She lives in Washington, D.C. with her two daughters, who are every bit as stubborn and wonderful as the characters she writes.

Elizabeth loves to hear from readers! Please sign up for her newsletter at www.elizabethbrightauthor.com (link on website) so you can stay up to date on her latest releases.

Website: elizabethbrightauthor.com
Instagram: @elizabethbrightauthor
Facebook: facebook.com/ElizabethBrightBooks

ALSO BY ELIZABETH BRIGHT

HART'S RIDGE

Make Me Love You

Don't Call Me Sweetheart

Trust Me

Christmas at Hart's Ridge

WICKED SECRETS

Twice as Wicked

Lady Gone Wicked

Wicked with the Scoundrel

The Duke's Wicked Wife

Made in United States
North Haven, CT
23 August 2024